Revelation Crossfire

"The fun never stops"
-Mark Connelly, The Crossfire Team

Stephen L. Thompson

Revelation Crossfire

Books by Stephen L. Thompson

The Crossfire Series

Colorado Crossfire
Believer's Crossfire
International Crossfire
Israeli Crossfire
Spirit Crossfire
Faith Crossfire
Chinese Crossfire
Texas Crossfire
Dark Crossfire
Island Crossfire
Jagged Crossfire
Violent Crossfire
Russian Crossfire
Nuclear Crossfire
End Times Crossfire
Revelation Crossfire
Gates of Hell Crossfire
Assassin's Crossfire
Albatross Crossfire
Global Crossfire
Far East Crossfire

The SFO Series

Station Force One - Onset

Revelation Crossfire

The Crossfire team has been trained by Yahveh to stand against the enemy of mankind and their human tools over the last three years. Now they must stand against the RHONE's military and assassin corps of the New World Order as the anti-Christ tightens his grip on the world. Satan has told Yahveh that he will stop trying to destroy the Crossfire Team and instead he will get the Revived Highest Order Nazi Empire to do that in the human dimension. But then, the devil's truth is always a lie.

- Stephen L. Thompson

Revelation Crossfire

Published by
Stephen L. Thompson
Facebook.com/CrossfireNovelSeries

ISBN- 978-1-943879-19-9

Published in the United States of America

Foreword

To my Christian readers –

The Crossfire series of action/adventure stories include depictions of violence which are unusual in Christian literature. It would be nice if there were no conflict or violence in our world. But we live in a time when evil is increasing instead of diminishing, when some men seem to be controlled by selfishness, madness, or evil forces. When the enemies of decent mankind are bent on subjugation of other men and women, righteous men and women must stand against evil. Please remember that the yoke of oppression is not lifted by prayer alone. Yahveh is our Shepherd and we are his sheep. As long as there are wolves about, Yahveh will use some of us as sheep dogs to defend the rest of us. These stories are about people like that and the forces they fight against. The stories describe violence because it occurs in the real world and it is active in the lives of all people whether they recognize it or not.

To my non-Christian readers –

The Crossfire series include depictions of spiritual warfare and spiritual activity with which the non-Christian may not be familiar. These stories describe the realms and activities of both Yahveh and Satan because they are real and active in the lives of all people whether they recognize it or not.

Steve Thompson

CHAPTER ONE

The absolute silence in the darkness of the hard and cold backstreets of Tel Aviv, Israel simply heightened Jack Malone's sense of hearing and his spiritual sensitivity. He had spotted the tail eight minutes ago. He had immediately pressed the button on the Wide Area Network System (WANS) alarm. This sent an alarm signal to the COMSEC group in their underwater Sea Base with the information that there was an emergency and where he was. That was all that was needed.

He had tried to lose the tail but the driver in the car behind him was good. So Jack decided to stop being the hunted and become one of the hunters. He took three quick corners, pulled over to the curb, and quickly parked the car. He exited the vehicle and ran north through the crowd. He swerved left and ducked down an alley in the area of Allendale and Punster Streets. This was a notorious section of Tel Aviv. There were lots of people on the street this evening, many of them youth, some drunk, some looking for a fight. The alley he had selected had several homeless people and one prostitute in it. Jack had raced by them without a word.

At six foot four inches and 185 pounds, the sheer size of Jack and the intensity of his travel quieted the other inhabitants of the alley. The mere fact that this big man was obviously running from something made the others scatter or hide. If this guy was trying to get away from somebody or something, they didn't want to be involved.

Jack looked for some combat stretch where innocent bystanders wouldn't be hurt or killed in the battle to come. He found what he was looking for in a side alley to his right. The alley was wide, had little to hide behind as one came down the alley, and was fairly well lit. He raced down the alley and stepped into the darkness of a doorway near the dead-end. Then he waited. He knew that there were at least two men in the car behind him and they would be seeking him now.

There was some furtive movement at the mouth of the alley. Then one by one silenced pistol rounds shot out the street lights over the alley. The entire alley was plunged into a deep darkness. Then Jack could hear slow, measured steps coming toward him. He was pretty sure they were using the latest version infrared night sights. In the coolness of this alley they were probably tracking him by the heat of his foot prints. That would be why they decided he was in this alley. He also realized that the meeting he'd just come from was a setup. The man he met probably didn't know he was targeted and was also probably dead by now. These guys didn't play nice.

Jack was irritated with his choices. Instead of becoming one of the hunters he had simply boxed himself in with no way out. He thought that he would be able to hold the trackers off by sniping at them as they turned into the brightly lit alley. The people following him weren't stupid and they had returned the balance of the battle in their favor by shooting out the street lights.

He realized that he had under-estimated his enemy and decided not to let this become a habit. That was if he lived through the coming battle this time.

The people following him would see him as soon as they got near enough or he exposed himself to shoot at them. But, he couldn't see them. Jack continued to pray that Yahshua would protect him.

Just then a heavy rumbling sounded in the alley and it seemed the darkness got darker. Most likely a large truck running without lights with more RHONE troops.

Jack turned around and attempted to pick the lock on the door behind him. He couldn't bend over because his backside would be visible and probably get shot off. The lock resisted his efforts and he felt anxious about the outcome of this battle. He knew he fought for Yahveh's Kingdom but was fully aware that occupation did not rule out his being killed.

Deciding that he needed to make them worry about his capabilities instead of panicking and giving into fear. He took out his .40 caliber XD handgun from the paddle holster at his back and prepared to fire some random shots down the alley near the walls to make them back off. He might just possibly take out one or two of his followers.

He fired three rounds and used the strobe effect of the muzzle blasts to pinpoint four guys on the far side of the alley. He rapid fired two rounds at each of them at a low level in the event they ducked. Jack was rewarded by a scream and cursing. Then the return fire started chipping away at his little piece of safety. He changed the magazine in his pistol to a new, full one. He had to worry about ricochets, also. They knew where he was now. They would home in on it and obliterate him and his little niche.

The truck started to rumble toward him and then all hell broke loose. The heavy sound of helicopter rotors suddenly filled the alley and a missile streaked downward and the truck blew up with a mighty explosion. The concussion slammed Jack against the door hard enough to crack the door down the middle and cause dots to float through Jack's vision.

As his eyesight returned he peeked into the alley. The burning truck gave everyone an equal footing as far as visibility went and Jack looked to see if he could pick off any of the RHONE team that had survived the missile strike. But the sheer volume of mini-gun fire coming down from the helicopter above them quickly chewed up everything in the alley that wasn't Jack.

There were more explosions back along the alley he had come down at first. Then there was a lot of shouting and some more gunfire. Then the sounds of the helicopter faded out and the crackling and roar of the flames devouring the truck were the only sounds Jack could hear. Five minutes later a voice called into his alley. "Jack, don't shoot, it's me, Su Li."

Su Li and three of the Crossfire Team Sensitive Operations Group or CTSOG carefully skirted the burning truck and moved down the alley with lights and M-8s probing everything in the alley.

CHAPTER TWO

Jack holstered his pistol, walked out from the door frame, and put his arm around Su Li's shoulders. The shorter woman patted Jack's back and smiled at him. Jack shook his head, "I can't tell you how glad I am that you got here when you did. I was about twenty seconds from being dead."

Su Li had the black visor on her helicopter pilot's helmet raised. She eyed Jack and chuckled, "I'm glad we were able to get here before you were seriously wounded." She turned and whistled at the Corpsman with their group. It was a young man named Sean Murphy who jogged over, slung his rifle over his back, and set his kit down on the ground. He opened it up and started taking instruments and gauze out of it. Jack watched him somewhat puzzled.

Sean stood up and told Jack to strip to the waist. Jack asked, "Why?"

Sean pointed at the two places where blood was soaking through Jack's flight jacket and Jack realized his blood was running down his right arm and dripping from his hand.

Jack said, "Oh."

Murphy surveyed Jack's injuries and then spread out a blanket on the ground. He asked Jack to lay face down on the blanket. Jack did as he was asked without comment. He realized he had been hit more than once, probably by ricochets or during the missile strike. The adrenaline in his system and possibly the shock of the explosion had prevented him from realizing the damage. Now that he was aware of the injuries he felt the pain. It wasn't too bad and he could shut it off in his mind while Sean worked on him. Su Li kept her Nightfighter LED light on him illuminating the wounds. Jack prayed for Yahveh's mercy and favor to keep the wounds less than serious.

While he lay there he distracted his mind by recalling the file he had read on Sean Murphy when the young U.S. Marine had applied to join the Crossfire Team Sensitive Operations Group. Sean had been in some of the worst fighting in Iraq and then in Afghanistan. He had been wounded but stayed in the battlefield working on the American wounded until unit reinforcements arrived. He then passed out from a loss of blood. Three weeks later he was back at work with a Purple Heart awarded to him. He had been medically trained to be a doctor and had the college degrees and internship to prove it. He knew what he was doing and could have served in any hospital ER in the world but had opted out to serve in the Marine Corp Force Recon before he became one of the Crossfire Team SOG personnel.

Sean carefully irrigated a wound and told Jack he was going to give him a shot of local anesthetic so he could dig out a bullet in his back. He grinned after giving him the shot. "It's a ricochet and it was so mangled it only went in about a half of an inch, but it's going to hurt like fire getting it out and it's also going to leave a nasty scar on your back."

Jack mumbled something along the lines of "Okay" and continued to pray his thanks to his loving, Heavenly Father Yahveh that had protected him during the fire fight.

Sean got the bullet out and finished sterilizing the wound. He packed it with antibiotics and bandaged it carefully. The other two bullet wounds went all the way through. One that had creased Jack's side and only needed cleaning and bandaging, not surgery, and one that had nicked his right bicep. As he worked on Jack, Sean saw the tracks of multiple scars and pucker wounds of past gunshots and shook his head as he thought "This was an honorable leader that leads from the front of his troops, not the rear."

Sean said, "All right, you can get up, but, let me have another look at them tomorrow, or if any of them start bleeding again."

Jack got up and his wounds hurt as he moved. He thanked Sean for his ministrations and then proceeded to put his bloody shirt and jacket back on.

As he finished dressing, three drunken Israeli youths ran into the alley and saw the truck burning. "Wow! Look at that. It looks like World War III has . . ."

He stopped talking when he saw a laser dot moving around on his chest. He sobered up a lot when he looked up at the three SOG warriors in full combat gear and weapons walking toward he and his friends with their assault rifles locked on them.

One of the SOG warriors asked them what they were doing here. The Israeli police had closed off the alley to prevent enemy reinforcements and curious sightseers. Su LI went over and said, "You guys! Leave, now."

One of the young men smiled at her. His grin was crooked and his voice slurred. "Aren't you the pretty little Rambette?"

Su Li stepped quickly forward and punched one stiffened finger on her left hand into the youth's neck. He froze and couldn't move except to drop his beer bottle which shattered on the ground. Su Li eyed the other two, "You two to take him back to the street and if he is fortunate he might recover in an hour or two."

The two boys started to back up with the paralyzed youth between them when three big Israeli policemen grabbed all three of them and herded them back toward the street. One of the cops carried the stiff youth out under one arm like a cord of wood.

Jack sighed and realized he was tired as the adrenaline faded out of his system, "Let's get out of here and let the police and the Mossad clean up this mess." He looked at Sean. "Could you get one of the SOG to get my car and bring it back to the base?" He gave Sean the keys. "I think I want to ride back in the chopper."

Jack, Su Li, and Sean walked back to the chopper with the three SOG team members walking alert guard and met two more of them guarding the Blackhawk helicopter. The entire crew boarded the bird and Su Li wound it up and lifted straight up out of the parking spaces in which she had landed in. As they climbed, Jack voiced a worried thought. "Su Li, RHONE could be tracking us to see where we go. You need to shake any observation or tracking."

Su Li nodded and said, "Already taken care of boss." She rotated the helicopter toward Ben Grunion Airport. She flew relatively smoothly and slower than normal for her. As they reached the airport she descended and flared out near a special hanger. She shut down the chopper and gave it over to a Mossad team that was waiting for them. Then she, Jack, and the SOG warriors walked into the hanger.

There were a dozen SUVs, all identical, sitting in the hanger. One by one they left the hanger at one minute intervals. The team was in the seventh SUV. The SUVs crossed paths and went to different locations. As their SUV went under an underpass it stopped and everyone but the driver jumped out. The driver then drove on with a heater running that produced a thermal signal that looked like he still had eight people on board, just like the other vehicles. The team members got into a truck that was shielded to prevent heat signatures and ended up in the large Mossad garage next to the entry to the underwater Sea Base.

Jack smiled, "That should confuse their trackers and leave them with some real headaches. Did you think that up yourself?"

Su Li shook her head. "Talk to Charlie Wu. He's the one that likes to mess with people's heads."

CHAPTER THREE

Laura quickly evaluated Jack when he walked into their apartment. She could see that he was tired and the dried blood around the bullet holes in his jacket gave him reasonable cause. He was somewhat subdued but he let the pain he must been feeling show in his eyes. She raised one eyebrow in a wordless question and Jack shrugged and grinned at her. His attitude made her feel much better because he wasn't seriously hurt or discouraged.

She walked over and helped him carefully take off his jacket. She could see the gauze underneath the holes in his shirt and on his arm also. "Pick up a couple of new scars to impress the ladies?"

Jack stared at her for a minute, "Well? Did they impress you?"

"Don't know, they're still in the wrappings at this point." She looked intently into his eyes. "Are you really all right?"

Jack nodded and tossed the jacket into the laundry bag. "I liked that jacket; we'll have to see if it can be salvaged. Combat is sure hard on nice clothes." He hugged his wife who restrained herself from hugging that part of his back and only used her right arm to hug him back. "Yeah, I'm all right honey, but, until this group is eliminated I think body armor will be the mandatory dress code outside of the base."

Jack described the events and how close the RHONE assassins got to making him the late Mr. Malone. He also confided in her about his feelings of inadequacy by trapping himself.

She shook her head. "Yahveh was on your side and you did the right thing to get the combat away from the citizens. Now the question is, what are we going to do to prevent this type of constant attack?"

Jack nodded his head, "I'm getting very tired of the team and myself personally, being their targets. Let me get a shower and we'll get the core group together and brainstorm the right way to do this. What I've got in mind will take a lot of prayer on my part so I don't set out on my own without checking with Yahveh."

Jack was referring to a recent battle in Tel Aviv when he had decided to stop the demons from opening a bunch of rifts in the inter-dimensional wall between the supernatural dimension of the demons to the human dimension, to overwhelm the Crossfire Team. He had even gotten the IDF to use drone missiles with nuclear warheads. He hadn't asked the Father for advice or permission. This mistake on his part had made the team more of a target for Satan.

Laura clicked her combat link and rounded up the Core Team for a strategy meeting while Jack took a long, hot shower. He was glad that Sean had covered his bandages with a waterproof cover. It would still let air in but not water. He was still careful when he patted the new wounds down with the towel rather than rubbing them dry. Still, the pain was manageable and he prayed, "Thank you, Yahshua."

The other eight people of the abbreviated Core Team concentrated on Jack. Everyone had read Jack's detailed after-action report, which he had created when he had been debriefed by Charlie over the comm link, on the way back in the helicopter.

Jack smiled and realized he missed having David and Alexis there to consider the possibilities and their response to the murderous attacks by the RHONE.

He looked at the members there and realized they still had a wealth of talent and brains to handle this situation.

"Anyone got a special idea or two about how we should resolve this problem?" Jack watched the other people as he asked this. Mark was obviously already set with an idea as he just waited and watched Jack. Sarah was still running things through her mind. Charlie and Linda Wu sat there stoic and unreadable. Su Li and Mark White had obviously been discussing methods as they also waited. Laura was praying as she normally did during times of stress and decisions. Carol was smiling, almost grinning.

Jack looked at Carol. "Okay, you obviously have something that you think is good. Share it with us."

Carol stood up to address the group. "After I read your after-action report; I started praying for solutions to this

9

type of attack and I had a visitor. Rose appeared in my room and told me several amazing things. First, while Satan has technically backed off and given us to the RHONE, he is running true to form. He's lying. His demons are so much a part of RHONE that there is no way Satan isn't in on everything RHONE is doing, especially when it comes to the Crossfire Team."

Carol cocked her head to one side. "While I'm deeply involved in the Matrix of events, I certainly don't understand how Yahveh's rules apply in the millions of different circumstances we are involved in. But, and I think you'll like this, Yahveh has granted each of the members of the Team the right to use the Force Generators for the duration of our conflict with the RHONE!" The last was almost shouted.

Jack had to sit down when he heard that.

Carol added, "The reason seems to be that Satan affirmed to Yahveh and also in the Matrix that the demonic would not be involved in destroying the team, but he would turn it over to the RHONE. Since he is again transgressing against Yahveh with duplicity, and because the RHONE has over 100,000 warriors, his lying and the gross imbalance of the RHONE against our 35 members provide the need for the Generators."

Carol smiled at everyone and sat down.

Jack thought for several minutes and then stood up again. "Well, that changes everything I was planning to do. I've got to rethink this whole thing in light of our being able to use the Force Generators but we still have to keep them secret.

Mark spoke up. "The way I see it is that Yahveh knows a lot we don't and he sees where we will need to have that kind of protection in the near future. What bothers me is how can we use them without letting the whole world know that they exist?"

Jack agreed, "This could be a game changer. We only have five of the generators and I don't know how long it will take Dr. Clashire to create more Force Generators and get them to us without Washington knowing about them."

Su Li had been conferring with Mike White and she held up her hand to get Jack's attention. Jack nodded.

Su Li stood up which didn't make that big of a difference in her total height. Mike asked "Would you like me to speak for you? I mean, just because I am tall enough to be seen."

Su Li glared at him and it caused Mike to remember that she was extremely dangerous, even unarmed.

Su Li stepped up on her seat and addressed everyone. "There, does that make me tall enough for everyone to see me?"

When the giggles and the comments died out Su Li said, "If Doctor Clashire can make the Generators why don't we just make a quick, unannounced visit and pick them up ourselves and keep the Government out of the thing completely?"

Jack smiled, "I like the idea but remember we barely got away last time. How do you plan to get us permission to fly in and fly out?"

Su Li asked him, "Why don't we use the X76?"

Mark stood up and bowed to Su Li. "That's an incredible idea on several levels. First, it is very stealthy. Second, it's so fast most other aircraft wouldn't have a chance to catch it. And lastly, it would be extremely ironic to use an asset the U.S. paid to build, to circumvent their new dislike of us."

Jack shook his head. "Okay, I need to talk to Yahveh about this before my ego jumps up and causes me to sin again."

CHAPTER FOUR

Jack and Laura went back to their apartment and got on their knees and started praising and worshiping Yahveh in song. Jack registered contentment and joy as he felt the heaviness that seemed to always accompany the closeness of the Holy Spirit during his prayers. After singing two simple songs of praise they let the Father know how great they knew He was and how much they loved Him. Then they asked simply how Yahveh would like them to proceed getting the Force Generators and should they make the trip to get them from Colorado in the United States.

Jack felt an awesome wave of Yahveh's Glory that was so strong it made him humble and weak at the same time. He turned away from the bed where he'd been kneeling and fell to his face on the carpet. Yahveh's glory was more than his body could resist. He felt a love and an incredible joy that was so great that he couldn't describe it later. There were no tears, and no doubts that the Father's Spirit was there in the room.

Yahveh's voice had so many different timbres and shadings that Jack could understand the ancient writers that said His voice was like thunder, or rushing waters. *"My children, be at peace. I have ordained many things to come in this battle between Satan's servants and your team. Your team must stand and destroy the forces of Satan to show the world My power. Especially to those who seek to rule the Earth in Satan's name. Their pride in their evil power will shatter on the rock that is you, my children. No longer will they believe that they are in control of the world or that Satan will save them. In the last few moments of their lives they will come to realize, too late, that I am Yahveh Almighty. Due to Satan's repeated duplicity in his dealings with Me concerning your team, I have decreed that your Core Team may use the energy devices to protect yourselves. Beware; DO NOT allow the rest of the world to know about them. I will not allow others to use them, not even believers in Yahshua, other than you and your people and the other teams like yours. I will prevent the*

Government forces, now controlled by the anti-Christ, from seeing or understanding your voyage to your plant and your return. But, beware of traitors that want to hurt you. Go to battle in My Name and with My blessings. I will give your enemies into your hands."

The peace, the glory, and the heaviness all slowly lifted from the room. Jack pushed himself up and pulled his legs under himself and sat on the floor facing Laura. She simply rolled over onto her back and took a big breath. Letting it out slowly she opened her beautiful eyes and looked at her husband. "My mind is still listening to God, over and over again. I miss being in His Presence so much already."

Jack agreed. "I know." Jack stood up and offered a hand to Laura who took it and with Jack's help stood unsteadily to her feet. They held each other as they rested for a while and then freshened up and went back downstairs to the War Room. This time they were the first ones there. Jack sat at his terminal and entered everything Yahveh had told them. He then called Charlie. "Can you get me a secure line to Dr. Clashire in Denver?" It should be around 7 A.M. in Denver right now. As I remember it, Dr. Clashire was always there between 5 and 6 A.M."

Three minutes later Jack heard the doctor's precise tones. After catching each other up on their separate doings for the last eight months, Jack asked the primary question. "Doctor, would it be possible for you to create thirty-three more of the Force Generators?"

Dr. Clashire was quiet for a few moments. "How soon do you need them?"

"In three days if you possibly can do that." Jack knew that Yahveh wanted them to use them very soon and therefore He would have prepared the way for them to be available.

Dr. Clashire sighed, "No problem, which will only leave me one model after this order."

Jack laughed. "You built thirty-four more models? Why?

Dr. Clashire chuckled, "A beautiful angel named Rose visited me three months ago and told me that Yahveh would need more of the generators for the team, soon. It took me and a small but intense team, working over the last three months and we just finished the last of them five or six days ago. How do you want me to ship them?"

"Just have them packed up in a couple off duffel bags and we will drop by on Friday morning around 2 A.M. It will have to be a quick stop; so please be ready." Jack had figured the time required and felt sure that Yahveh would let them use the X76 too.

The Doctor said, "I'll be here to make sure they are ready and to shake your hand. I miss the excitement when you are around."

Jack laughed, "Don't worry, if the U.S. Military has any hint that we're coming over there, it might get very exciting. I think we can slide by their radar though. I will see you early Friday morning Doctor. Could you patch me over to Bob Wexler's office, please?"

Bob had just come into his office when he got the call from Jack. They had an abbreviated version of catching up because Jack already knew their end of things. "Bob, is the large open area in front of manufacturing still a large open area?"

Bob said that it had been shortened somewhat by new buildings but was still big enough to land ten helicopters in it. Jack explained that they would be dropping by to pick up some Force Generators from Dr. Clashire at 2 A.M. on Friday morning. "Listen Bob, I want as few people near that area as possible with the exception of you, Allen Dunhill, and the good doctor. The way we're coming in and leaving is classified way above Top Secret. Okay?"

President Allen Dunhill was a bright young SOG warrior who Jack appointed to run "Technology Alternatives" after the Crossfire Team had defeated the leadership of the Omicron Cartel. Allen had been wounded, ending his combat days and was a good match as Jack's replacement. He had advanced the company sales considerably and really improved the security around the plant site. He and Jack had talked every now and then to keep Jack in the management loop and for instruction, although, it had actually been a while since they had talked.

Bob said, "Jack, Allen went in the Rapture. I would have gone also, but an angel asked me to stay for the first three and one-half years. Obviously, you agreed to stay, also. Anyway, I've been filling in for Allen since then. I know you'll want to replace him with another person when you can and I'll help with that. I will be looking forward to seeing you again young man."

Jack hung up and wondered just how much of a young man he was anymore.

Jack called the Research and Development group housed at the end of the runway, between the Crossfire Team's base and the Mossad Base. He got in touch with a Commander of the group and asked if they could use the X76 for a Friday flight of several thousand miles.

The Commander, John Harrison, didn't hesitate. "I will make sure it's ready for you by Thursday night. What destination this time, more ICBMs or nuclear bombs?"

Jack laughed about their last flights in the X76 to the Arctic Circle. "No such drama this time John, but we need the best stealth in the world and I think the X76 is just the ticket. We're going to do an invisible mission to a suburb of Denver, Colorado, USA. I've got us scheduled for touchdown at roughly 0200hours, their time. Time on the ground will be less than ten minutes and then we need to get back here without detection, if possible."

Harrison ran a computer flight plan and looked for obstacles. "The only possibility of detection is from a new and very secret USAF satellite that will be crossing that part of the world just after you leave Colorado. The satellite's name is "Megalith' and it has some very new and powerful radar capabilities. I'm fairly certain that it would find and identify the X76. You have a ten-minute window to escape its view. The X76 can provide the speed but since you'll be traveling at an altitude of over seven miles you'll stand out on the satellite's radar like a missile launch. The timing may be too close; can you adjust your trip by three hours?"

Jack thought about the problem. "I don't think we'll have to make any adjustments. I've got it on a higher authority that we will be covered and invisible both coming and going."

Harrison laughed, "Well then, there is no problem. I'll have her ready for you when you're ready for her."

CHAPTER FIVE

Thursday morning as Jack was heading for the exercise room to work on his martial arts with Su Li and Laura, his cell phone rang. He answered it and heard Carol. "Jack, I have discovered an assault by demons and humans against the surface Portal in four hours. It looks like there are at least two squads or possibly three of twenty-four people, but I can only see where there are two demons."

Jack thought about the rationale for such an attack on the sovereign Nation of Israel and decided it would only be to see if they could flush the Crossfire Team out, giving proof of the location of their base. "Okay, Carol, get on your full combat gear and grab your sniper rifle. I'm about to sound an all hands alert. We need to respond to this attack in force, but do it so that they don't think we live here."

Carol said, "Yes Sir," and hung up.

Jack pushed the "All hands" button on his communications pack or CommPak on his belt. "All hands prepare for street combat with RHONE troops. Suit up with body armor for all hands and report to me at the air strip in thirty minutes."

Jack instantly sensed a soberer atmosphere that developed in the base after his call. The people that were training or exercising dropped what they were doing and moved with purpose to be ready in time.

Jack told Su Li, "I'll want you and Mike to have both of the V22 Ospreys ready for flight in twenty-five minutes."

Su Li looked at him with narrowed eyes but nodded as she ran off to accomplish this task.

Then Jack called the Mossad and told them of the impending attack. They had learned to listen to the team's advice and called the IDF for forces to counter this attack. Jack told them he didn't know exactly how the RHONE was going to get three squads of heavily armed troops into the Seaside Port of Tel Aviv, but indicated that there were probably going to be supernatural coverings, possibly from the waterfront. It was only six blocks to the area of the Portal, which was located inside of HaMered Highway.

Jack called Charlie and asked him two questions. When he answered Jack told him to talk to Su Li and Mike White and give them that information.

Jack pulled on his armor and webbing. He checked his weapons for full loads and all the other conditions necessary for combat. That brought a thought and he raced down to the Armory and opened the three tier safe they had installed there. Finally, an eye-print and a biometric scan allowed him to pick up two of the Force Generators they had stored there. He quickly relocked the safe and raced back to meet Laura. They ran out to the air strip in time to watch the others fall in and stand at attention.

Jack called Mark out and gave him one of the generators. Jack strapped the other one onto Laura and had her check the LED read-out. It was green as was Mark's unit. He had them shut them off. "Use these only if you really need to. I'm fairly certain that both the Mossad and the RHONE will be collecting video of this event, so we really need to keep these out of sight unless they're needed."

Mark nodded. "I take it that since we're using the Ospreys we are going to fly in from somewhere else rather than run out the Portal, right?"

Jack nodded and had the team break into two squads and board the two aircraft. Grabbing a seat Jack opened the "All Hands" comm-link. "All right folks, we are going to leave the base and appear over Jordan, just over the Israeli-Jordan border this side of Amman. We have thirty minutes' flight time over Israel, between Amman and Tel Aviv. We need to be here just as the RHONE attacks. When we leave, after we are victorious of course, then we will go back toward Amman and disappear into Jordan again. Eventually, we will arrive back at the Sea Base. Our enemy, the RHONE, is probably going to try to track us via satellite, radar, visually, and possibly audibly. Charlie, we need to make it seem like we are setting down somewhere south of Amman near the Red Sea in the desert of Jordan. Okay?"

Charlie looked at his portable control tablet for the entire COMSEC command back at the Sea Base. "We'll make it happen, boss."

The Ospreys were as stealthy as a jet/prop-powered Tilt Rotor could be. This wasn't a lot due to the giant propellers. One of the best ways to have stealth, regardless of the noise, was to fly nap-of-the-earth and blend in with the terrain until you wanted to be seen. Then you would pop up to a normal altitude of two to three thousand feet and turn on your identification markers, beacons, and lights.

Jack got up and came back to where Charlie sat next to the aisle. "Listen, the USAF has a top-secret spy satellite named "Megalith" that has really advanced radar capabilities. If you can work your usual techniques on it, I would like for it to change orbit to the west of the U.S. for the orbit over America on Friday morning. I know that's not a lot of warning and you might have to do a bit of work finding it, but, it would work to our advantage during that pass."

Charlie looked at Jack with his unreadable face and smiled, "No problem." I've been tapping into the video and radar feeds of that little piece of work for the last two months. You're right. It is formidable in its ability to detect even stealth aircraft. Does this line up with your quick visit to your company?"

Jack grinned, "Keeping secrets from you doesn't seem to work too well."

Charlie laughed, "I am a spy you know. But, truth be told, Linda discovered Megalith during one of her routine satellite sweeps. I had Crayton map it out and we had a fun time getting through the latest encryption. I think it took almost five minutes."

Jack nodded. "Just make sure it's looking somewhere else than the corridor between Colorado, and the Eastern Seaboard of the U.S. and Canada on Friday, from midnight Colorado time until the next pass."

Charlie nodded and made a note to his wife, Linda, to have Megalith take a Pacific holiday on Friday. "How about we have Megalith take a restful look at Hawaii during that time?"

CHAPTER SIX

Jack sat in the front row of the seats on the V22 Osprey and thought about the upcoming conflict. He realized that this encounter was not only to pinpoint the location of the Crossfire Team's base but to also determine their fighting capabilities. On that basis, he called Colonel Ephron of the IDF, the man who was in charge of this event. The Colonel answered quickly, "Yes, General Malone?"

Jack sensed a no-nonsense attitude of efficiency in the man. "Colonel Ephron, I believe that RHONE is making this surprise visit to establish two things. The first is whether or not the Crossfire Team is based behind that Portal and secondly, how would our Military response be against a numerically superior force. Do you concur?"

The Colonel agreed but had some questions of his own. "If they don't know for sure that your team is based there, why would they assume to attack Israel in this manner? And, if your team doesn't show up, then they know they will be counterattacked by the IDF. What purpose would that serve?"

Jack liked the man's quickness and straightforwardness. "I assume that they will try to kill three birds with one stone here. The two I mentioned and to serve notice to Israel that Marco Marino can do as he pleases in Israel. I would like you to let my team go up against them first and then have your troops contain the battlefield and come to our rescue if needed. That way, your troops will sustain fewer casualties. This is only right since it is my team that they are after and that way you will be able to reduce any collateral damage to Tel Aviv."

Colonel Ephron apparently agreed with Jack's reasoning. "I will use our forces to contain the action. We have quietly been evacuating a three block area around the Portal with as little fuss as possible to limit civilian casualties. I will add a two-block corridor from the sea front to the Portal. The Portal Troops have been reinforced and your design of the Portal will increase their chance of

19

survival during the initial attack. I will send you a map showing our intended locations. How are you going to enter into combat with these villains?" Are you going to exit the Portal before they get here?"

Jack explained their ruse to make RHONE believe that they weren't based there at all. He asked for an area near the Portal where two large V22 Ospreys could land vertically. We will be coming in from the area of Amman, Jordan. We will be getting there immediately after the attack starts and before RHONE can breach the Portal. My pilots have already gotten approval from your Air Force for the entry, over flight, and deployment at the site of the battle."

The Colonel was somewhat curious. "How could you know that they were going to attack the Portal in time to be ready and fly in from outside the country and still be there that quickly?"

Jack smiled to himself. "The enemy of man is already aware that we have access to many of their plans in advance. If we didn't get there quickly they would be surprised. Remember, one of the things they are doing in this raid is evaluating our Military response and capability."

Colonel Ephron laughed. "Okay General, are you going to lead your counterattack?"

Jack looked up at Mark. "Actually sir, the combat phase is going to be led by General Mark Connelly.

The Colonel said, "That is good. I'm looking forward to meeting you both after the battle is won."

Jack hung up and motioned for Mark to come over to him. "Mark, I'm going to defer to your greater Military expertise." He explained the IDF's role and agreement from Colonel Ephron.

Mark smiled, "I know "Bucky" Ephron. I met him during joint Military trials several years ago. We hit it off right away. He's a good guy as officers go and boy, can he drink. I learned the term "L'chaim," the traditional toast in Israel. Okay, listen, I've already set the troops order of battle. Your group of twelve will come in from behind them from the West; I will lead another twelve of our troops from the city side. I'm leaving the rest of the team as a force reserve to reinforce either one of our teams if we run into problems.

Jack nodded, "Make sure one member of each team keeps an eye out for demons and is ready to break off combat with RHONE troops and deal with the demon or demons. Laura will take it for my team and you do it for yours? Have Su Li do it for the reserve team?"

Mark nodded. "Remember this is real, dirty, human combat. They are going to be trying to kill every one of our team. I'm going to have two of the reserve team hang behind your team just in case the RHONE has the same idea of reserve troops that would come in behind you and flank the other two teams."

As Jack agreed his cell phone rang. Colonel Ephron told him, "You called it right, General. There are about eighty-seven RHONE troops, heavily armed, that just stormed across the beach and through the corridor we created. They should be attacking the Portal in about six minutes. Where are you?"

Jack looked out the windshield of the Osprey. "We are over Israeli soil and should be there to land in less than three to five minutes."

Colonel Ephron smiled to himself. "Then we've got them right where we want them. Good hunting General."

Jack hit the "All Hands" button on his combat commset. "Okay people, we will touch down in about four minutes. This is the real thing and it is us or them. Don't play nice. Let's get the job done neatly and quickly as possible. Father Yahveh, we ask your protection and your favor for each of the men and women of Your Crossfire Team as we battle the forces of evil. Give us encouragement and a holy anger about the enemy. Stand with us Yahveh and give us the victory in Yahshua's name we pray."

CHAPTER SEVEN

Su Li and Mark White flew over Tel Aviv toward the sea and converted to vertical flight by rotating the huge propeller engines from forward flight to hover flight. Both aircraft sat down at the same time and the team members disembarked quickly out of the back hatches that had been lowered as the aircraft sat down on the street. The first people out set up a perimeter to cover their teammates as they left the aircraft. Full automatic gunfire and explosions could be heard two blocks away to the East.

Jack and Mark got their twelve member teams together and set out at a run for their positions. The remaining troops split up and left two warriors to watch their back from the sea side. The rest double-timed it to a middle position so they could back up both of the forward troops. Four members of each sub-team had a M320 40mm grenade launcher attached to their M8 carbines and two of each group had the double drum attachment which allowed them to carry 100 rounds of the new 6.8 MM composite cases, with brass bases and polymer walls, which reduced the weight of the ammunition each person had to carry.

As they neared the battle they came under fire from some of the RHONE troops that were stationed away from the battle to deal with law enforcement or IDF troops that were summoned to the scene. Three of the Crossfire Team took rounds and went down. The others found cover and returned the fire. Two 40mm grenades took out the sentries and the Crossfire Teams continued to advance. Only one of the Crossfire troops was seriously injured thanks to the body armor they were wearing.

Sean Murphy quickly patched up the injured woman. She had a thru and thru round to her left arm. After he patched her up he escorted her to the next block east and gave her to the medical troops of the IDF. He then headed back to the battle.

Jack took a quick look around the last building between himself and the battle itself. The Portal was set back three hundred feet between two buildings that were at least twenty stories in height. The original designer for the Sea Base had planned on an all-out combat assault on the Portal and it was designed to handle tank fire if necessary. At this point it had taken a beating but was still resisting the grenades and ManPad shoulder-fired rockets and letting the IDF/Mossad troops inside, drive the assault back from the entrance.

Jack saw, roughly, fifteen RHONE troops on the ground, dead or injured. His battle-com blinked a green light in his goggles which indicated that Mark and his troops were in place and ready. Jack hit the "Go" button and waved his team forward. They all fanned out to Jack's right and found whatever cover that was available. There were small walls and statues leading up to the Portal that were usable as shields.

Jack had been watching to see which RHONE troops were leading the action and figured he had spotted their battle leader. He sighted on the man and triggered three rounds that knocked the man off of his feet in a spray of blood. Jack then just started shooting targets of opportunity as did the rest of the twenty-four team members. The initial counterattack against the RHONE took out sixteen more of their troops. The other forty some-odd RHONE soldiers split up into two fronts. Twenty or so kept attacking the Portal while the others turned back to fight the Crossfire Team.

It was typical combat with bullets flying everywhere and people getting hit on both sides. The superior 6.8mm rounds from the M8s punched through the body armor of the RHONE troops while the body armor on the Crossfire Team stopped or deflected the 5.56mm or standard.223 caliber M-16 rounds. The firepower that Jack and Mark's troops poured into the RHONE positions was quickly decimating the defenders of RHONE and the team members switched their fire to the remaining troops still trying to force an entry into the Portal.

Six RHONE troops ran for the Portal from their front positions and Sarah took them all out with a M320 40mm grenade that blew them apart fifteen feet from the Portal. Jack called for half of the reserves to move forward and engage the enemy. As the additional firepower came into the battle the remaining RHONE troops gathered together facing the Crossfire Team's attack and forgot about taking the Portal. There were only about ten soldiers left of the entire eighty plus RHONE troops at the beginning.

Somebody yelled "Grenade!" and everyone dropped to the ground and sought shelter. The grenade went off and Sarah and a SOG Sergeant were peppered with grenade fragments and rock debris from the explosion.

Three large demons suddenly appeared behind the RHONE troops and jumped over them to attack the Crossfire Team members. At the same time three more demons appeared behind the Crossfire Team and charged them from that direction.

Jack, Mark, and about eight other team members started praying and their silver and gold armors appeared along with their swords. Jack parried the first swing of the closest demon and executed a reverse body attack which caught the demon by surprise. Jack struck the demon but not hard enough to end its existence. The demon started leaking smoke from the small of its back but continued to fight. It struck Jack chest high and knocked him backwards. Jack chopped downward with his sword and cut the arm off of the demon. Unarmed, the demon roared its hate and charged Jack's position. Jack went to high guard and literally cut the demon's head, neck, and chest into two pieces. The demon collapsed and dissipated into ugly greenish black smoke. There were sword battles going on in a half a dozen places when Jack stopped praying and his armor disappeared. He pulled his M8 from where it hung on its sling on his back and targeted each of the demons for head shots. He was making great progress when the remaining RHONE troops all started firing at him. Jack took two hits which knocked him down but were stopped by his body armor. Still, it hurt, a lot.

Laura saw Jack's dilemma and turned on her force generator. She jumped over the wall in front of her and flanked the remaining RHONE human troops. Two of them turned and sprayed her with a dozen 5.56mm rounds. The rounds hit the field, stopped, and dropped to the ground.

Laura's rifle was synched to the field and she was able to open up with her rifle and terminate the remaining six troops. She then turned and fired single shots at each of the remaining five demon's heads. Three of them collapsed and started disintegrating into foul smoke.

Mark ran one of the last two demons through and turned to attack the remaining demon when Gail Turner, a SOG Sergeant cut it in half with her sword. Mark turned back to see a huge demon enter the human dimension and Mark stopped praying to get his rifle so he could shoot it. It hadn't come into our dimension legally because Carol had said only two demons were on the matrix and they had already killed them.

The immediate problem was that the big demon came out of the demonic dimension directly behind Laura. Its presence was unknown to her and the demon quickly raised a huge fist and brought it crashing down on Laura's far smaller body.

CHAPTER EIGHT

Mark yelled into his combat microphone to warn Laura but it was too late. The massive fist came down to crush the life out of her. Then, it stopped two inches above her. The demon looked perplexed and lifted its fist to hit her again.

Laura turned around and ripped off a nine-shot burst at the demon, each bullet blowing big holes through the beast. It wailed in anger but disintegrated into black smoke and disappeared.

Laura shook her head and walked back to where Jack was rubbing his chest and side to relieve the pain the bullets had imparted to his body through his body armor.

Mark ran up and looked at Laura. He saw the green light on her Force Generator and smiled.

Laura looked at him and realized her generator was still on. She switched it off and squatted next to her husband. "How's it going?" she asked.

Jack sighed. "I should have just kept the Armor of Yahveh on rather than try to shoot those demons. This is not only going to leave some big bruises but it is probably going to hurt for a while. He winched as he climbed to his feet. "Let's go see how the other troops are doing."

Colonel Ephron's IDF troops had flooded into the area, mopping up any surviving RHONE troops and helping any injured troops on either side.

Mark listened to a call from the IDF and nodded. He looked up and said, "Between the firepower from the Portal and our attack we eliminated all but three of their troops. We've got twelve injured, one critically, and three disabled but we didn't lose anybody. I think it's because we were better trained, more accurate with our firepower and primarily because Yahveh was protecting us."

Colonel Ephron walked up to them. He was in full battle gear, but smiling. He saluted the two "Generals". "I am glad to meet you all. You fought a good battle and I'm glad you were here to handle those demons. This battle has given me a lot of respect for every one of your people.

Thank you again for taking the brunt of the battle. My people will take care of your wounded. They have already been transported to a local hospital."

Mark asked the Colonel, "Would you assign enough troops to protect the wounded at the hospital?" RHONE has many employees and it wouldn't surprise me if they took a chance to eliminate our people while they are there."

The Colonel agreed and gave orders to two of his aides to see that the Crossfire Team members are given additional protection.

Mark assigned three of the SOG troops to accompany the IDF troops. He looked at the Colonel, "Not to usurp your command Sir, just in case the enemy wants to use demons instead of humans."

The Colonel's eyebrows went up at that. "That's a new concept for me. Thank you."

The three men and Laura looked around at the battlefield. Laura sighed and said, "So much death and damage. Such a waste. Maybe the RHONE will rethink their plans to attack us in the future."

Mark shook his head. "These men were expendable and sent here to either beat us or die. Now RHONE has an idea of our Military combat capabilities, they will just plan accordingly next time."

After saying goodbye to the Colonel, the Crossfire Team gathered together and walked back to the Ospreys. They loaded up and it was obvious that everyone missed the thirteen members left behind.

Su Li and Mark White lifted the V22s off of the street and into the air. They rotated and headed back toward Amman, Jordan. They were able to avoid the Jordanian Air Force and then blend into the desert and disappear from satellite view by landing in a remote part of the desert just as darkness fell. They waited until they were sure the satellite coverage was gone. They stayed nap-of-the-earth until they crossed the Jordanian Red Sea coast. Turning NNE, the choppers flew up the Gulf of Aqaba, across Israel and returned to the Sea Base. Charlie assured Jack and Mark that there was no direct observation of them from aircraft or satellites.

Mark said, "How can you be sure we're free of observation?"

Charlie smiled, "Computer magic. I created a phony set of Ospreys and kept them going west, deeper into the Jordanian desert while we slipped away unseen. Then I made the phony set of Ospreys fade out of sight. I predict that there will be a large number of RHONE personnel combing the deep Jordanian desert for some time. I also sent an anonymous E-mail to the headquarters of the Jordanian Air Force that the RHONE is violating their airspace. I doubt that Jordan can do anything because they gave their allegiance to the anti-Christ, but it's worth a shot."

Mark nodded and looked at Laura. "I don't get worried very much anymore. But, I felt a real stab of fear when I saw that last demon try to crunch you. You should have seen the confusion on its face when the field stopped its fist two inches above your head."

Jack listened to something he hadn't been able to see after being shot and knocked to the ground. "So the field also works to defend against demonic attack?"

Laura nodded. "Yeah. And I for one am very glad that it does. Of course, it is from Yahveh and He isn't a fan of the demonic."

The two Ospreys finally ended at the Sea Base and everyone lugged their gear into the base. After cleaning up their weapons and arranging for cleaning of their field gear and uniforms the team sought to wind down from the battle.

CHAPTER NINE

Jack and Laura walked into the living area of their Sea Base and ran into David Zahavy and Alexis, his new bride. After greeting them joyfully, Jack asked David, "Aren't you two back a little early?" David grinned, "Yes, we came back a few days early because, while we enjoyed our time together immensely, the time there was mixed with feelings of needing to return to duty."

Alexis laughed, "David is a delightful husband and would do anything for me. But, he is a dedicated warrior and, while masterfully hiding his desires, I could tell he needed to be where the action is. Frankly, so did I. Ergo, here we are."

Jack laughed, "All right, you've only missed a few attacks on us and a pitched battle with RHONE forces in Tel Aviv that left us with thirteen wounded."

Alexis nodded, "And the RHONE?"

Jack shook his head, "Only three wounded." He looked at them both, "And eighty-two dead."

David turned to Alexis, "See, I told you we were missing all the fun."

Alexis grinned and looked at Jack and Laura. "Give us a few minutes to unpack and get some real gear on and we'll join you in the War Room."

Jack watched them walk off to David's apartment hand in hand and commented to Laura. "I am impressed and very encouraged that they came back early."

Laura nodded, "Me too. Let's go to work."

Meanwhile, Charlie Wu was intently searching on his computer in his private office in the COMSEC department when there was a knock at his door. He stopped what he was doing and motioned for the COMSEC tech to come in.

Ethan Reaper opened the door and came in and closed it again. He walked over the cushioned tiles to Charlie's desk and asked if they could talk for a few minutes. Charlie nodded, "Sure Ethan, what have you got?"

Ethan handed over a printout he had printed. "I found this being floated on the internet via the mercenary network. I thought you'd like to see it."

Ethan Reaper was probably the last person someone would expect to be working for a Christian Military team, especially in the heart of the communications and security operations. He was fairly thin, had long hair, and his arms were covered in tattoos. Ethan was also an atheist. His choice in clothes was modern day grunge that even people known as Goths wouldn't wear. His red retro sneakers and torn jeans were overlaid by his camo shirt that had to be three sizes too large for him.

But Charlie knew several things about Ethan that many people wouldn't take the time to find out. First off, all his mangy clothes were always clean. He bathed frequently, probably daily because he never smelled. He was meticulous about his work area and never ate or drank while at his station. He never missed anything important and his knowledge was at least three levels above that of most computer gurus on the planet.

Charlie had watched this guy, who looked like he lived on the street; take six encrypted computer systems, in a Russian Military missile base, apart in less than an hour. That included some of the strongest firewalls and spy systems on the planet. Besides that, Ethan was able to get all the satellite information the team needed and ease back out without ever tripping an alarm. He left no sign that he had been there, either. Charlie had watched his keystrokes and mouse movements carefully and the guy was a genius, definitely better than Charlie himself. Over the last two years Ethan Reaper had more than lived up to his name in the Cyber World for the Crossfire Team.

Charlie examined the flier. Essentially it said "$100,000.00 US to the first person to provide the location of the Crossfire Team's base." It had an email address to supply the verified information to along with a place for an address to send the money to after the location was verified.

Charlie looked at Ethan, "Tempted?"

Ethan made a snide face. "Hardly, I make more than that in a year developing video game software on the side. Plus, I consider you guys my friends, if not my family. You might as well be my family considering I spend more time here than anywhere else. I also don't see the profit in calling down a Military raid on myself."

Charlie smiled, "That's a good point. I'll get the Core Team to look at this and see if there is anything they want to do about it."

Ethan smiled, "Want me to steal their hundred grand and leave them a big Trojan horse?"

Charlie shook his head. "This is probably a trap that would let them know where you were. Probably not a good idea regardless of how much fun it would be for you."

Charlie saw Ethan out and went down to the War Room. He found Mark Connelly and showed him the flier. Mark stared at it for a moment. "Why don't you give Mr. Reaper an anonymous laptop and let him tell them where the Crossfire Base is located. But do it from somewhere deep in the Jordanian desert. That should reinforce our being out there somewhere."

Charlie grinned, "I'll see to it. I happen to know of a secret Jordanian underground base that is developing chemical warfare weapons pretty much where we would want RHONE to think we are. I'll bet if they went in there in force, the Jordanians might resent it."

Mark nodded, "Especially if they were given a word about an imminent assault by outside forces at that base."

Charlie chuckled.

CHAPTER TEN

Charlie thought over what Mark said as he went back to the COMSEC area. He walked into his office and sat at his desk for a while. Then he opaqued the windows and door to his office and locked the door. He reduced the lighting to one mini-floodlight bounced off of a wall and got down on his knees to pray. He praised Yahshua and asked Yahveh to cleanse him of his sins, known or unknown. He then sang several songs softly in Chinese and English. He knew that Yahveh inhabits the praise of His children and that allows Him to enter into communion or worship with them.

He then laid out his plan for taunting and possibly hurting the RHONE with Ethan Reaper and the plan that the Chinese spy in him had come up with on the way back to his office. Charlie then relaxed and waited while he continued to worship. He sensed a presence and opened his eyes.

Charlie saw an imposing figure. The figure was probably seven feet tall. He had on the purest white robes Charlie had ever seen, and he had seen his mother create some really white ones. A golden belt and sash held a gold trimmed scabbard with a large sword. His golden hair fell to his shoulders and his eyes were gold and bright.

Charlie felt no fear and smiled at the figure. "Who are you and who do you call Lord?" Charlie asked.

"I am known as Caleb. I serve the Most High God, Yahveh. Your prayer has come to the attention of the Most High and He has sent me to deliver your answer.

God says, *"You have humbled yourself to ask and capable to do what you desire. Take your servant, Ethan Reaper with you. There will be danger and combat so be prepared. Also be prepared to answer questions of faith in My Son. You must do this very soon. Do not be afraid, be strong and courageous. I will watch over you."*

Charlie started to say "Thank you" but Caleb had faded out of sight. He climbed to his feet and opened up his office to find his wife standing outside his locked door. He marveled anew at her youthful beauty and unlocked the door.

She walked in and closed the door. She asked him in high Mandarin, "Who were you speaking with?"

Charlie shrugged, "The angel Caleb who came in answer to my prayers. Prepare yourself for a short trip into the desert and lay out my gear if you will, while I make the arrangements."

Linda Wu knew her husband very well and knew he was telling the truth, however unlikely it seemed. "Yes, I will prepare. Usual weapons?"

Charlie shook his head, "The usual weapons plus two M8s with M340 grenade launchers, several Claymore mines, and night vision goggles."

Linda didn't question his request but left to fulfill it.

Charlie called Mark and filled him in on the plan and the word from Yahveh that Caleb had brought to him. Mark thought for a minute. "Let me pray about this but I think you can use some backup. I know you and Linda are excellent at warfare but you might have to deal with sheer numbers. I'll get back to you in a few minutes. Go ahead with your preparations and I'll get Su Li to take you in one of the V22 Ospreys."

Charlie pushed an intercom button to ask Ethan Reaper to join him. Ethan walked into the office almost by the time that Charlie had disconnected the call. "Ethan, I've decided you had a great idea although we're going to have to take a trip to do it right. We are going to go out to a place in the Jordanian desert and send a message to that RHONE email address that they can immediately trace back to our location. We're going to tell them that the home base for the Crossfire Team is located there. One of the hazards that will make them feel it is real is that there is a hidden, underground Jordanian base there. The Jordanians are working on chemical WMD's in that base so they will very irritated if we are discovered. That means everyone that goes will have to be ready for a fire fight if we're detected."

Ethan inexplicably felt an urge to go regardless of the possibility of danger. So Charlie sent him down to the Armory to get properly dressed for the occasion.

Ethan had never been to the lower levels of the underwater Sea Base but found the Armory without a problem. Su Li was in there preparing for the mission and she looked up at Ethan. "Who are you, and what do you need?"

Ethan looked at the lovely young Asian woman standing in front of him and cautioned himself to act properly around her. Normally he played the class clown when he interfaced with women but he had heard many stories about this one and he really wanted to live to go on this adventure. "I really don't know, Ma'am. Charlie just told me to come to the Armory and get dressed for some desert doings."

Su Li smiled and told Ethan. "Strip down to your underwear. What size shirt, shoes, and pants do you normally wear?"

Following his earlier revelation about Su Li, Ethan hurried to comply. He gave her his shirt and pants sizes and then his shoe size. He felt nervous about standing almost naked alone with a pretty, but very dangerous, woman in the cavernous Armory.

Su Li came back with a stack of clothes and a pair of boots. She set them on a table. She looked at the long-haired, skinny, tattooed young man and pointed at the floor in front of her. "Come here."

Ethan quickly dismissed any hopes that she had any interest for him other than the business at hand. He walked over and stood where she directed. She picked out a light tan T-shirt and gave it to him. He put it on and she handed him a pair of pants. She laid a second pair on the table to one side. After he got the pants on she gave him a heavy duty leather belt for the pants.

Ethan quickly put the belt on and was surprised how well everything fit. Su Li handed him a tan camo shirt with pockets and more pockets on it. After Ethan had the shirt on and tucked into the pants she handed him a rip-stop nylon holster that snapped on the belt on his left side. Then she gave him a set of body armor which covered him from his lower neck to his groin. She had to show him how to fit it to his body so that it was comfortable.

Su Li gave him some thermal style tan socks and his boots. She pointed out a bench behind him and had him put the boots on and lace them up. When he stood up again she handed him a desert camo field jacket with built-in web harness. He put that on over his body armor. Su Li stood back to examine him so far. "Okay, Ethan, here is your helmet; try it on. Again she had to help him adjust it to fit properly. She gave him a clear set of eye glass-styled goggles that fit close to his eyes. She handed him a cool set of Ray Ban sun glasses that he stuck in one of the pockets in his shirt.

Su Li looked him in the eyes. "I assume that you have never been in the Military or on a battlefield, right?"

Ethan's eyes widened, "No Ma'am, I haven't, yet."

She showed him how to connect the clear goggles to a plug on the helmet. "Do not lose this helmet. Not only will they take it out of your pay if you lose it but that will probably be done posthumously because without it in a fire fight you will most likely be killed. Do you understand?"

Ethan nodded his head which felt funny with the helmet. She then gave him a set of gloves to match his desert outfit. "Put those in your pockets unless you're wearing them. Don't lose these either. You'll need them."

Su Li took Ethan out of the Armory and over to the shooting range. He felt like he was a large robot stomping across the concrete floor. Su Li flipped on the range lights and loaded a man-shaped target onto a wire and moved it thirty yards down range. She walked over to a rack next to the range and took out a .40 caliber XP auto-loader. She turned to Ethan. "Have you ever held or fired a pistol?"

Ethan nodded his head. "Yes Ma'am, my father was an avid shooter and he taught me wheel guns, auto-loaders, and black powder pistols. I was a pretty good shot at that time."

Su Li loaded two magazines and gave Ethan some earmuffs. She smiled when he tried to put them on over the helmet. "Take your helmet off, but, keep track of it."

Ethan took a modified Weaver Stance and quickly but carefully fired off all fourteen rounds. Su Li hit the button and brought the target in. It was actually fairly impressive. He had centered almost all of the rounds with only two fly-aways. She looked at the young man who was examining the pistol. "This is really good, Ethan. Three things you might keep in mind are that soldiers almost always wear body armor like you have on right now. With a pistol you need to think of head shots. Secondly, consider whoever you're shooting at as a moving target and lead them a bit. And lastly, I'll get you a magazine holder for your right hand side that will let you carry four additional magazines for your handgun. Learn to quickly drop your empty magazine and reload a new one. This could possibly save your life in a close-in fire fight. I'm sure that Mark Connelly will train you on this and the other things about combat."

Su Li took the pistol and slid a fully loaded magazine into the well inside the pistol's hand grip. She released the slide, loading a round. Since Ethan was left-handed, Su Li then walked to his other side and shoved it into the holster on his belt. She snapped the restraining strap over the pistol and explained the FBI-based requirement for "grip acquired" and the 21-foot rule. "Let's say your hand is not on the grip of your sidearm and there is a man with a knife twenty-one feet away. If he charges you, by the time you unsnap the restraining strap and draw your weapon, he'll already be close enough to knife you. If you have your hand on your weapon, you'll have him cold ten feet away. Always remember that."

She then went over and pulled an M8 Assault Rifle out of its rack and snapped a fully-loaded magazine into it. She showed Ethan the basics and the sighting system. He nodded and addressed the new target she put out there at thirty yards. He sighted on the target and quickly blew through the magazine of forty-five rounds. When Su LI brought the target in there was no head, just a big jagged hole. There were ten rounds dead center where the heart would have been. Su Li whistled, "Sweet!"

Ethan smiled a lopsided smile, "I've always liked rifles better than handguns."

Su Li nodded, "I guess so. Okay, you come back to the Armory and I'll get you those extra magazines and a duffel bag to put your second set of clothes, boots, and gear in. Why don't you bring that rifle with you? I can see that you two like each other."

CHAPTER ELEVEN

Back at the Armory Su Li gave Ethan a quick lesson on how to use his Night Vision Goggles and his combat camouflage makeup. Then they loaded up his duffel bag and Su Li grabbed her gear and they headed back up to the COMSEC floor. One of the other computer techs stopped in his tracks and dropped the paperwork he had been carrying. "Is that you, Ethan? Holy Moly, you look downright dangerous!"

Ethan smiled at his friend. "Shhh, this is my secret identity."

Charlie looked at Ethan and then at Su Li. "Wow, good job, Su. He looks like he is ready for desert warfare."

Su Li grinned. "Don't be too surprised, it's all new to him but he's a heck of a shot with an M8 or a handgun."

She looked at Ethan. "I will see you later." She then took off at a run for the V22 Osprey on the air field.

Charlie had Ethan drop his duffel and set his rifle on "SAFE" and put it in the corner of the office. He then brought out one more thing for Ethan to carry. It completed the integrated fighting system for individual infantry soldiers that provided enhanced tactical awareness, lethality and survivability. The systems integrated into this overall system were the weapon system, helmet, computer, digital and voice communications, positional and navigation system like those used by U.S. rangers, airborne, and air assault soldiers. This version had an excellent wireless interface communications capability so that the helmet didn't have to be plugged into the computer directly.

Charlie hooked the equipment up and showed Ethan how to use it. There was a special pocket in the backpack just for the computer. He caught on very quickly as this was his specialty. He especially liked the graphics that the system showed in the clear goggles connected to his helmet. Charlie looked at Ethan. This system will directly connect you to the COMSEC computers through your own position in COMSEC." Charlie then gave Ethan the laptop computer that they would use to contact the RHONE that would not give them any real information.

While they were talking, Ethan heard Jack Malone in his headgear. "Charlie and Ethan, you need to head on out to the Osprey."

Charlie quickly climbed into his desert camo gear and grabbed his rifle and duffel bag. The two men hastened down to the entrance and out onto the air field. Charlie looked at Ethan and commented. "You seem to be carrying your load without too much effort."

Ethan shrugged his shoulders, "What else could I do? I didn't want Su Li to think I'm a wimp. She had more gear than me and she just breezed along."

The giant black Osprey was already fired up with the main rotors whipping overhead as the two men threw their duffle bags on board and jumped into the doorway. Charlie showed Ethan where to stow his gear and how to strap into the seat next to Charlie's wife, Linda. Charlie sat down on the other side of Linda and strapped in as the Osprey lifted off into the evening air as the sun set over the Mediterranean Sea.

Charlie was surprised to see David and Alexis, Sean Murphy, and Carol Moffet strapped in across from him. David smiled and yelled over the rotor noise, "We're your backup for this desert vacation." Charlie grinned.

Su Li flew over Israel as the dark of night settled over the countryside. She then flew out over the Gulf of Aqaba and finally out over the Red Sea. She proceeded down the Eastern side of the Red Sea until she reached the point due west of their target. She then shed altitude like she was going to land on a ship or aircraft carrier. When she was below radar range she turned east and flew nap-of-the-earth until she approached the area of the hidden base. She slowed the aircraft down and converted from forward flight to vertical flight and carefully set the plane down using her NVGs.

David and Charlie checked with her. Su Li showed them the record of the flight. "See the overlapping radar coverages? We would have been seen at that point. We're about three klicks (kilometers) from the actual base. It is due east from here."

David made the decision to have Su Li accompany them rather than remain at the Osprey because it would be too easy to take out with a shoulder-fired missile and because of that, the aircraft couldn't give them any air cover. David got everybody out of the craft and they all helped Su Li drape camouflage netting over the entire aircraft. The desert tan netting made it very hard to locate the aircraft visually from the air or satellite and the material of the netting made it even harder to find visually on the ground.

Ethan Reaper had jumped out of the aircraft and helped hide it. He checked all the gear he had on and the computer link with the Sea Base. He looked around at the desert and felt very small. It seemed to go on forever in all directions. The cool of the evening felt wet on the exposed skin of his face. He sincerely hoped that he could keep up with these seasoned warriors when they marched toward their target. "A hidden WMD base. Good Grief!" He thought to himself. "Why not just run into the cave and poke the bear with a sharp stick?"

It was only nine thirty at night and the others were talking about their being able to make it to the area of the base and send their message without being detected, in about an hour. Then another forty minutes and they would be back to the Osprey and head home.

Ethan thought "That would be okay for me." He watched as the others checked and cocked their rifles and slung them over their shoulders. He did the same with his rifle. Su Li came over and helped Charlie check him out. Charlie nodded, "You're good to go Ethan. Just stay near me."

Ethan found walking in the sand was difficult but doable. The fact that it was in almost complete darkness on the moonless night was offset by the NVGs they wore. The night-vision-goggles made the whole world turn varying shades of green. It was very much like the single shooter video games he had played as a kid. Actually, he thought, "I still play those games every now and then. "Of course," he thought, "I can get killed in this game and I don't get any extra lives."

David led them through the valleys between sand dunes to keep their profile down and to make it easier to walk than trying to climb the dunes and descend the other side. The 1.6-mile jaunt actually covered more than two miles that way. As they neared the perimeter of the base they ran into their first security detail

Charlie heard it first and had everybody drop to the sand. A minute later a large, jeep-like vehicle with treads passed fifty yards in front of them, from their left to the right, on a perimeter route around the base.

When it was gone, Carol asked David, "Why do they do that? Wouldn't it seem odd, them circling around in the empty desert? Doesn't that give away the location of the hidden base?"

David shook his head. "It is probably only done at night to add to their daytime surveillance capabilities. The Jordanians are aware of the satellites orbiting above the Middle East. That's one reason we chose this time, because there are none over the area and won't be for almost the next four hours. There is also enough wind from the sea that their tracks will be gone by early morning."

Carol asked, "Can't they spot us with their own night-vision devices?"

David smiled, "They could, except that the equipment we're wearing cuts down our thermal signature significantly. Also, by lying on the sand it would only look like an anomaly on a screen."

Carol nodded her head, "What about UAV or satellite coverages?"

David looked at the young lady in a new light. He hadn't realized she was becoming so smart about the battlefield. "We would be exposed to a UAV or a satellite but there aren't any UAVs up right now or Charlie would have detected them and the next satellite coverage the Jordanians can use won't be here for a while and we expect to be gone by then."

Charlie checked his computer pad and decided they were close enough to fool anything but a direct overhead satellite view of their location. He and Ethan set up the laptop and Ethan typed in the message they had decided to send. He got an acknowledgement and signed off. He waited almost ten minutes before he saw the evidence of a reverse trace for location. He then shut down the computer completely and nodded at Charlie.

"Okay, we're done" said Charlie. "Let's get out of here."

CHAPTER TWELVE

The entire team started back for the Osprey when Charlie suddenly held up his right fist. Ethan had learned this meant "Stop Walking". Then Charlie opened his palm and brought it down by his leg. This meant "Get Down Right Now!"

Ethan watched as David cradled his rifle on his arms as he used his elbows and knees to crawl over to Charlie. Ethan was next to Charlie and started to move back to give David room when Charlie whispered, "Don't move." So it was more of a threesome. David asked Charlie, "What's up?"

Charlie pushed his computer tablet over so David could see it. There was a lot of data being displayed but Ethan could interpret it because that's what he did every day. The screen had eight green dots near the center. "That would be us" thought Ethan. To the upper left there were twenty-five to thirty red dots moving in a spread-out line toward the left of center. That meant that there were twenty-five to thirty people headed not right at them, but probably toward the hidden base.

Ethan knew that Linda Wu had sent a small autonomous drone into the air after they had sent the message. This was a display projected from the drone. It was being deciphered from the underwater Sea Base and shown on Charlie's tablet.

David risked rising up slightly and he used the magnifying feature of his NVGs to attempt to locate the other force. He crouched back down and whispered, "They are probably six hundred yards away from us. Do they have any air assets that can spot us?" Charlie shook his head. David continued, "Then I don't think they know we are here. Let's move to the North and West and see if we can't slide by them without being seen." David looked around. "Total silence." He whispered loud enough for everyone to hear.

David rose to a crouch and started moving to the right and forward. Everyone else copied his actions. There was no complaint or question, it was teamwork and leadership.

Ethan realized that moving quickly while crouched over was a lot harder than walking and he concentrated on not making any noises. They had managed to get eighty to ninety yards before Charlie hissed and went prone again. The smell of the sand was still warm but not unpleasant as Ethan kept his head down. Charlie crawled over to David and showed him the tablet again. Ethan was still close enough to see it. Ten of the red dots had moved toward the North and they would run into the team if they both kept going the way they were. Ethan noticed that ten more of the red dots were moving to the South, Southeast. David whispered, "They're sending out flankers in case they run into trouble straight ahead. The people ahead of us will be turning toward the base soon and we are going to be right in their path."

Charlie asked, "Can we move to the South and let them flank us and go by us?"

David shook his head. "Not enough room. We're going to have to deal with these guys without alerting the main body of troops. David signaled Charlie and Linda Wu, Alexis, Sean, Megan, Su Li, and Carol to crawl up to his position. He quickly explained the situation. Along with Charlie the others laid their rifles down by Ethan and each of them took off their helmets and backpacks. They pulled out a black ski mask and donned it. Then they pulled out their K-Bar combat knives. David told Carol, "Attach your silencer and take down any of them you can hit but don't forget we're out there, too."

Carol nodded and reached into a deep pocket on her pants and pulled out an eight-inch-long tube which she quickly screwed onto the end of her rifle barrel. David looked at Ethan. "Ethan, I know you are new at this and I really had hoped it would be an easy jaunt but I need you to protect Carol while we are gone. As a sniper she is focused on her targets and is unable to defend herself. I need you to do that for her. Understand?"

Ethan heard himself say, "You can count on me, Sir." He thought, "Wow, now I've stepped in it. I hope I'm capable of doing this."

The other people looked at the locations of the red dots in front of them and crawled away into the dark. Each one had a large black anodized blade in one of their hands. In seconds they were gone without a trace. Ethan thought back and realized that all of them were seasoned combat troops, with the exception of Sean and Megan, the others were combat-seasoned spies too.

His thoughts were interrupted by Carol. "Come on, I've got to get a little elevation."

They crawled about twenty feet up the side of a sand dune facing East and West. The enemy would be coming straight at them. Carol lay down and spread her legs apart to keep from sliding down the side of the sand dune. She had also clipped on a Night Vision Scope and took off her NVGs. She slowly scanned the area ahead and was able to see the heat signatures of the seventeen people about to collide.

Carol carefully made an adjustment for windage and range and then sighted on the last person of the enemy and squeezed the trigger on her rifle. There was a muffled cough and the target went down. She moved to the next last target and repeated the operation. Two down! She watched as the two groups came together and suddenly seven of the enemy dropped out of sight. She sighted on the last target and knocked it down. The other targets had disappeared and she could not find another enemy target. She watched as she saw seven shapes crouched over and running back toward their position. Over his combat headset, Ethan heard Charlie tell him. "Get back to the rifles. We'll be there in a few seconds."

Ethan and Carol also ran crouched over and found the weapons and backpacks lying where they left them. Ethan saw Charlie and David and the others rushing back to them. Everyone was silent as they found their backpacks and rifles and got ready to go.

Charlie held up his hand again and said, "Get down, now!"

Ethan hadn't gotten up yet so he just stayed down. He thought, "This is definitely the most exciting exercise program I've ever done."

Everyone was still getting down when there was a major explosion several dunes to their left. Then there were dozens of more explosions, all over the place around them. Each one shaking the ground and lighting up the sky.

Ethan had never been in combat and couldn't process the violence of the random explosions which scared and confused him greatly. Panicking, he grabbed Charlie's arm, "What's going on?"

Charlie showed Ethan his tablet. There still were roughly twenty red dots to their left and somewhat East of them. But, now there were about fifty red dots behind them and to the North of them. Ethan suddenly understood. The new dots were shelling the other red dots and the team was caught in the middle of the battle.

David said, "Let's move quickly." Everyone got up and ran to the West. Ethan was glad to see he wasn't in the back of the pack. All at once they stopped and dropped again. There were explosions among the new group this time. Charlie looked at his tablet and said, "Uh Oo".

Ethan scrambled over to Charlie and looked at the tablet. Less red dots in both places but there were strange swirling patterns among the newer red dots. He looked at Charlie. "What are those patterns?"

Something flew from the group of new dots and screamed over the team members. Charlie looked up, "Armed drone!"

Ethan urgently pulled on Charlie's sleeve again, "What are those whirling patterns?" He had never seen such a pattern in all his computing days.

Charlie shrugged his shoulders and looked directly into Ethan's eyes in the light from the tablet. "Demons."

Ethan shook his head and said, "Demons aren't real, they are a figment of somebody's imagination, just like Yahveh and angels."

Charlie sighed, "Ethan, you are wrong on all counts. All of those things are real and we've got some not far away from us. When they detect us, and they will, we will have to fight and hopefully destroy them."

David said, "We're less than a mile from the Osprey, let's see if we can get out of here."

Again they ran through the darkness and sand. To Ethan it seemed to go on forever and he was running out of wind and strength. He got a boost and started running faster when Sean Murphy grabbed the back of his load harness and lifted up on it. They ran in step for five or six minutes until everyone stopped again.

Charlie suddenly appeared next to Ethan. He was deadly serious. "Ethan, I know you're tired. It's because you haven't trained for this type of activity every day like the rest of us. Sit here and rest while we get the camo off of the Osprey. Now, listen carefully to me. If any of the demons appear I want you to shoot them in the head. There are two different types of demons coming into our dimension at this time. One type is legal and your shots won't affect them because they still have their attributes of protection. The other type is not here with Yahveh's permission and therefore is illegally in our dimension. Those you can kill with your rifle. You will be testing them all for us. Okay? We will take care of the bullet-proof ones." Then he dropped several extra magazines and was gone to help the others with the tarp over the Osprey.

Ethan wondered if they were pulling his leg or not. He hoped they were because if they were right, then everything he thought was right was wrong. The tarp was off of the aircraft and Su Li jumped into the pilot's seat to start the engines.

There was a loud crackling, crinkling noise in the air to Ethan's right. A horrible creature with a large black sword appeared on the sand. Ethan was dumbstruck because he couldn't believe it was real. But, being who he was, he raised his rifle and shot it through the head. His bullet tore a gaping hole through the beast's head and it crumpled to the ground. It started turning into a fume and it stank horribly.

Before he could analyze anything, three more of the things appeared and he set to work shooting them. One more collapsed but the other two didn't and both of them headed straight for him.

Ethan pulled the trigger on his rifle until the breach locked open. None of his shots affected them and they were almost upon him.

CHAPTER THIRTEEN

The fear Ethan felt made him taste bile in his throat as the horrible creatures pounded across the sand toward him with death in their eyes. He made a mental reversal and realized that he had been wrong. And now he was going to die that way.

As the first demon was almost on him there was a brilliant flash of white light and a silver figure stepped forward and cut the demon in two. The silver figure whirled around and blocked the attack of the second demon's black blade.

The sand dunes nearby seemed to sprout demons all at once and dozens of them charged toward the Osprey.

Ethan's basic mental faculties were pretty well fried at that point and he fell back on what he knew. He ejected the spent magazine and slammed a new one in its place. He then began to shoot every demon he saw in the head. He was rewarded by a number of them dying, dissipating, or melting, whatever the heck they did. He continued to carefully lay head shots on each of the remaining demons, but the bullets had no effect.

Ethan changed magazines again and watched as three golden figures and three silver ones battled the remaining demons. Several times he saw the gold and silver figures blur into a flashing ball of blades whirling in destruction through the demons.

The battles weren't all one-sided by any means. Several demons ganged up on one of the golden warriors and were beating the stuffing out of it. One of the other golden warriors joined that particular conflict and killed two of the three attacking the first golden armored warrior. The first golden warrior collapsed onto the sand while the other golden warrior finished off the remaining demon.

Suddenly, the last demon was cut down and four of the six figures turned and walked back toward Ethan and the aircraft. All of the armor and swords faded out of view and he recognized David, Charlie, Sean, and Linda. Alexis had helped Carol up and was supporting her as she limped back to the plane. Sean ran over and helped Alexis get Carol up the rear ramp and into the plane.

David helped Ethan up and shoved him and his gear gently onto the rear ramp and on up into the Osprey. The huge rotor blades were rapidly whipping around as the ramp came up. Su Li lifted the Osprey vertically off of the sand and tilted them over to the West and the Red Sea.

Ten minutes later they cleared the Jordanian Coast on the Red Sea and turned North toward the Gulf of Aqaba and Israel. Everyone had worked at cleaning and reloading their weapons and magazines. Then, one by one, most of them collapsed in the seats and rested.

Sean was working on Carol with Megan's help. Carol was in pain but Ethan didn't see any blood, which was a miracle after the beating she'd taken from the three demons.

Alexis looked over at a very confused Ethan Reaper and got up and came over to where he was. She sat down next to him and put her hand on his arm. She just watched him for a few minutes and then asked him, "Can you assimilate what just happened?"

Ethan looked at the beautiful woman and realized that she had just crawled out into the night and took at least one man's life with her combat knife and then changed into some kind of golden, avenging angel and killed one or more of the demons that did not die when he had shot them. And yet, here she sat, very sweet and friendly and definitely female. He shook his head. "No, I'm not sure I do. This is such a huge paradigm shift from what I knew it just doesn't seem to be real but, I do know that those demons were very real. I'm trying to fit it into my idea of how life is and it doesn't fit at all."

Alexis sat back and studied the young man. He looked to be a soldier and he had certainly carried his share of the combat by shooting every single demon that had attacked them. It had to have been extremely horrifying to see demons running at him with murder in their hearts as an introduction.

He had killed six or seven before they ever got near enough for her and the others to engage them in combat. Yet, his whole life looked to have been one of rebellion and working outside the box when others told him that wasn't possible. He was headed for a train wreck of his idea of life and reality. Yet again, he was very smart, bordering on genius and that was one of the things that had made him ignore the possibility of the real spiritual life that existed all around him. She silently prayed that Yahshua would give her the right words to open him up to the Holy Spirit and the reality of Yahveh.

She felt a leading that was simply "tell him the truth of the Gospel".

"Ethan, to understand what happened out there in the desert you need to believe that there is more to existence than just human life. A couple of years ago I also believed I made everything happen for me and all I had to work was the years of life I had while I was here. I thought I had made myself what I was and that I was in control of my destiny. I couldn't have been more incorrect. Yahveh is real and He is in control of everything. He is like us spiritually because he created us in his image. But, if I am comparing myself to Him it is like comparing a kitchen match to the sun."

She patted his hand to connect with him and assure his attention. "Yahveh created us so that He could have someone to love that would love Him back. Evil crept into the Heavens in the form of pride. That pride caused the highest manufactured being, an Angel named Lucifer, to envy Yahveh and to try and take over Heaven and make himself the Most High. Angels don't have a soul and they are spirit beings. According to the Bible, one third of the Angels sided with Lucifer and therefore Lucifer went to war to topple the Creator, Yahveh God."

"Because Yahveh is the Creator and the Angels are parts of His creation, His loyal Angels won the battle and cast Lucifer out of Heaven along with all the Angels that sided with him. Lucifer, now better known as Satan, became obsessed with destroying Yahveh and humanity because he couldn't be the Most High. He is not a creative being so all he can do is imitate what he sees Yahveh do. He became the essence of evil, the negative to Yahveh's positive. His role in life is to steal, kill, and destroy." Alexis checked and could see in the dim light in the aircraft that he was attentively listening to her.

"The Angels that fell from Heaven with him became evil themselves. Evil corrupts everything and that is why they are ugly and deformed. Exposure to ultimate evil has corrupted them completely. They are under Satan's control and they do his bidding. The limited time for us, before the Christ returns to Earth, is less than seven years away. Christ will rule Earth and Satan will be bound in an abyss for a thousand years. Right now, because his time to lure all of mankind away from Yahveh is almost over, Satan is breaking the normal rules of conduct for created beings such as himself. He is causing his demons to cross over from the spiritual plane to the human plane in a physical form which Yahveh forbids without His approval. Yahveh could stop him but then Yahveh would have to violate His own rules, which He will not do. But that is why you met your first demons today."

"There is no such word as coincidence in the ancient Hebrew language. So, the mere fact that you are with us tells me that Yahveh has chosen you to be a part of our team. Very, very few people know about us and fewer yet have the opportunity to join us. Consider yourself blessed."

Ethan thought about what Alexis had told him. "Where does your golden armor come from and why could you kill those demons that couldn't be killed by my bullets?"

"Yahveh has anointed the members of the Crossfire Team with a literal version of the Armor of Yahveh described in Ephesians 6 in the Bible. He has done this to compensate for Satan's overstepping his bounds. Normally the fallen Angels are far stronger and more capable than humans. The Armor and the Sword of Yahveh balance the tables and let us directly compete with the demons. As you saw with Carol, we can be hurt and even destroyed by the demons, even while we have the Armor on. We train constantly to be better at combat than the demons."

That was not too hard to understand. But, Ethan was still not clear on many things. "Why, if Yahveh is so capable, does He allow people to suffer illness and hurt? Why does he allow little children to die of cancer or other things?"

Alexis liked the way this was going. At least Ethan was considering a wider world. "Because when the original couple, Adam and Eve, were led to sin against Yahveh by

Satan, sin, disease, hurt, pain, and agony entered the world and has plagued humankind ever since. I don't know why Yahveh allows things to happen. But, I do know that since I gave my life to Jesus, Yahveh's only begotten son, I have the assurance that at the end of my life on Earth I will live with Yahveh in Heaven for eternity. While He was here on Earth, Jesus said, "I am the way and the truth and the life. No one comes to the Father except through me". That is in the Book of John, Chapter 14, and Verse 6."

Ethan shook his head, "I don't believe in the Bible because I've heard that it is full of errors and contradictions."

Alexis laughed. "I'll make you a bet Ethan. I'll give you a Bible. If you read it in context and not just take a little line from here or there, I'll give you a brand new CRAY computer of your own for free, if you can show me where it errs."

That made Ethan sit back and consider her challenge. "Okay, I'll take you up on that. But, what if I win?" Now he started sounding more like normal.

Alexis smiled a beautiful smile that lit up her face. "Then we will both be winners."

David keyed his combat mic and everyone on the team heard, "We're less than ten minutes out of the base. Make sure you clear your weapons, take all your gear, and clean it all up. Ethan, I'll have Su Li show you what that means."

Ethan nodded and looking up at the pilot's compartment at Su Li and said to Alexis, "I'd better do everything right or I may beat you out of this world yet."

CHAPTER FOURTEEN

After the Osprey landed and everyone except Su Li disembarked, Ethan went into an area the team called the Recovery area. Ethan was shown how to remove everything from his duffel and where to place it. Then he got a quick course from Mark on how to breakdown and clean his rifle and handgun and prepare them for the next use.

He was grateful that he had time to hit the restroom. Then Charlie called him into debrief him by filling out an After Action report on the computer. Ethan looked at the lined areas that were blank and looked up at Charlie. Charlie sat down next to him and had him fill in his heading information; his name, date, time, mission number, target, and mission name. Then Charlie pointed at the large open areas on the form. "Just summarize what happened and what you thought in brief statements. You know, like our form in COMSEC when you have to tackle a web site and then report it. It's the same thing."

Ethan was good at summarizing and was done quickly. Charlie looked it over and nodded, "Good, I'll put it in your mission packet and summarize it for the overall mission packet. You can go into the men's locker room and grab a towel. Get a shower and throw your combat clothes into the large hampers for laundry. The clothes you bring down here will be cleaned and placed in your locker. Oh, here's your locker key with the number on it. Here's a black felt tip pen, put your name on all of your clothing before putting them into the hampers."

Charlie reached out his right hand. "Congratulations Ethan. You were supposed to go on a fluff job to misdirect the RHONE, but instead you got the whole combat/demon run on your first trip. I'm proud of you. You hung in there even under attack by demons and didn't freak out. Many first-timers do freak out. It takes a little getting used to, I know."

Ethan grinned, "Mr. Wu, I did freak out, but only in my head. Alexis talked to me on the way back, when you were up in the cockpit with Su Li. Hey! I thought Su Li was going to critique me after we got back."

Charlie laughed, "Boy, you are a glutton for punishment, aren't you? Don't worry, she did critique you and you passed." Charlie slapped Ethan on the back. "Now, go get cleaned up. And, you are one of us now. Just call me Charlie when we're not in COMSEC, okay?"

Before Charlie walked away Ethan asked him, "My notes were real brief, does that tell you everything you need to know about my part in the mission?"

Charlie smiled at him. "Don't worry, everything you saw and did was video recorded by two cameras you were wearing. When you're dealing with supernatural creatures, it's best you have solid backup."

Ethan laughed."I guess it is." He then headed for the locker room.

Mark caught Charlie as he headed back to COMSEC. "How did Ethan do?"

Charlie nodded, "I think he did exceptionally well considering it was his first combat, first demons, and first outing from COMSEC. I actually think he will be willing to go out again, probably as soon as he can. He's a very good shot. The videos show that he never missed a head shot on some very active demons."

Mark nodded, "Okay, then he needs to come up to standard and that means training. I'll handle weapons, Jack can take him through sword fighting, you handle combat electronics, Su Li can train him in hand-to-hand, and David can handle his overall physical and combat training. I'll let Laura give him any help he needs in the Spiritual arena."

Charlie grinned, "I'll arrange his schedule so that he can attend the different trainings. I think he has a thing for Ms. Li. I'll bet he's even going to look forward to hand-to-hand with her."

Mark grunted, "Yeah, until after the first time. She's a strict task master and he'll have to toe the mark to keep her happy. Not an easy thing."

Charlie looked at Mark, "That's the way we like it in the Orient."

The two men went their separate ways and on the way to the War Room Mark met Laura. "Hello there. I think we're going to have you work with Ethan Reaper on Christianity and Judaism starting next week."

Laura looked introspective for a few seconds and tipped her head to the left. "Okay, I just talked to Alexis and I think she laid the ground work for me. He's going to have to come to his own understanding before we can do too much."

As Mark walked off he said, "Get Rose to help, she seems good at things like that."

Laura thought for a bit and then prayed that the Father would make that possible.

Laura then went to the medical area to check on Carol. As she walked into the area she found Sean working on a pretty battered Carol. Laura walked over to them and asked how they were doing. Carol grimaced and nodded. "I'm alright, nothing broken, cut, or missing."

Sean nodded his agreement. "Carol has some pretty big and deep bruising on her right side and arm, plus most of her back and right leg. I'm putting her on medical leave for ten days to give her a chance to heal. None of her injuries are life-threatening but she will have pain and stiffness for the next week or so. I'm totally amazed that the Armor works so well. I saw the power the demons put into the blows they were giving her."

Laura put down her things and took out her anointed oil. "Come on Sean, let's cover her in the blood of Yahshua and then pray for her healing."

Two more of the SOG personnel saw them and joined with them to pray that the Father would heal Carol's wounds.

CHAPTER FIFTEEN

After he had wound down and was allowed to sleep until eleven in the morning, Ethan had cleaned up again and gone to work at COMSEC. He thought back over the adventure he had just survived in the Jordanian desert and realized that for the first time in his life he had done something really meaningful.

He was on a break and was looking through the New International Bible he had anonymously downloaded from on line. It was quicker than the printed Bible that Alexis had given him. The more he studied the Scriptures the more he realized he hadn't been able to find any really overt errors, mistakes, or contradictions. He decided he would wait until he was off work altogether to really focus on it.

He had already worked through a lesson with Su Li in hand-to-hand combat and he was a bit sore in places. But, he'd learned a lot and he was looking forward to his next lesson with her. He looked at his task list on the side of his computer screen and noted that over the next three days he had physical education with David, weapons training from Mark, something about sword training with Jack, and, "Oh Oh! I've got a religion class with Laura today." he thought. He checked the time and he had eight minutes to get into the Conference Room downstairs.

Ethan ran to the staircase, jogged down the stairs and over to the Conference Room, beside of the War Room. He walked in and found that he was actually first this time.

Sitting down in one of the chairs at the conference table he collected his thoughts and arguments so that he could try to hold his own. Laura walked into the room. "Hi Ethan, how are you doing today?"

"I'm fine Ms. Malone, how is your day going?"

Laura smiled and Ethan noticed that almost every woman on the team was what would be called beautiful or definitely pretty. Laura sat down across from him. "My day is going well and I have been looking forward to this meeting, especially after talking with Alexis and reviewing the action reports and videos of your trip to Jordan."

She laid down her Bible and two notebooks and studied him.

Ethan was feeling a little nervous at this point and asked, "What will we cover in this meeting?"

"We are going to cover the basic mission for the Crossfire Team and how you are going to relate to it. Please understand, you are under no compulsion to become a born-again Christian if that isn't your desire. At this time all of the members of the team are born-again Christians because we feel it is the truth, because we have been tasked by the Most High God, Yahveh to do His will concerning combat against the enemy, Satan and his demons. You don't have to be like us. Now, as far as Yahveh and the world goes, how do you see yourself?"

Ethan realized that Laura wasn't going to avoid discussing the real reason for this meeting and he actually was glad. "Ms. Malone, I ..."

Laura interrupted him. "Ethan, you earned our respect by your actions in the conflict in Jordan. As a team we don't stand on protocol in our normal routines. Please call me Laura."

"Okay, Laura, I was going to say that I have never been involved or actually know very much about any organized religion. I guess that makes me an atheist or an agnostic, whatever the difference is between them."

Laura nodded, "An atheist doesn't believe in Yahveh or any religion, an agnostic believes in Yahveh but isn't sure about organized religion."

Ethan thought about that. "Okay, I guess I've been an atheist most of my life and I have considered things like angels and demons pretty much mysticism or fantasy. Either way, it didn't bother me. Now I have a problem with my paradigm. Demons are real, I know that now. That changes things; I suppose it means that angels, Satan, and God are probably real, also. I'm just not sure I can postulate a living God that would sacrifice His Only Son to take away my sins. And, for your information, what I just talked about I've learned from the computer and Alexis' Bible in the last twenty-four hours. I'm reading it because she bet me a brand new CRAY computer if I could prove that the Bible has errors in it, as I've always heard that it did."

Laura smiled at the young man. "I ought to tell you that you have been offered a losing bet and that many of the really on fire for Jesus Christians over the last two thousand years were originally skeptics like you who set their minds on proving the Bible wrong."

Ethan repeated what Alexis had told him. "I will admit it rung as truth in my mind, but I'm still not sure."

Laura asked "Okay Ethan, what can I do to help you solidify things, especially spiritual things in your mind and heart?"

"I know it's trite but could you show me any proof that Jesus or God is real or that Angels are real? I know that demons are real."

Laura smiled, "I think something could be arranged. Would you pray with me and ask Yahveh for proof? If you're right and He's not there, then no harm, right?"

Ethan frowned. "Sure, but I don't know how to pray, which is probably pretty easy to understand since I've never thought that there is anyone to pray to that would listen to me."

Laura leaned on the table and reached for Ethan's hands. She bowed her head "Lord Yahshua, I want to thank You for everything I am and I have. You said in Your Word that if I draw near to You, You will draw near to me. Please cleanse both myself and Ethan from any sin in our lives, remove any of our sins as far as the East is from the West. Father Yahveh, we come before you today to help Ethan find the one true basis for life and if it is Your Will, show Ethan a proof of Your existence and that of Your Son, Jesus, and also that Your angels exist and are real. We are but frail humans and we are subject to sin. In Ethan's case, Your Word says, "My people are destroyed by a lack of knowledge." Don't leave him blind and lost since such short time remains. I pray this in Yahshua's Name, Father."

Ethan really tried to sense a powerful entity like Yahveh would be but when Laura quit praying he opened his eyes and said, "I'm sorry but I didn't really get anything."

A voice of great energy spoke from behind him. "That, Ethan Reaper, is because you don't really expect to hear from Yahveh or even know what to look for."

Ethan spun around in his chair and beheld a beautiful angel in deep gold and fierce white colors floating between his chair and the wall. Rose smiled at the young man and moved to Ethan's left so that Laura could see her too.

Rose spoke to Laura. "Hello Laura, great warrior for The Most High. He heard your plea and sent me to be His proof for Ethan. Also I need to tell you that you are needed in the War Room. The RHONE is increasing the challenge against the team." She turned toward Ethan again. She held out her right hand and a sparkling white mist with bright motes of light in it transfixed him. It only lasted for two seconds but when it faded from view Ethan's eyes were wide open.

Rose said, "Consider carefully your proof, Ethan Reaper. You now have a vivid picture of Heaven, and another one of Hell. Choose wisely. Your mind and your heart will generate the faith you need to believe in the Most High."

"My name is Rose and I am one of the protectors of this team of warriors for the Lord. Call on the Lord in times of need and if we are needed we will be there for you. Remember, above all, the Most High loves you more than you can ever imagine. He will never leave you or forsake you. But, you must decide if you want to be with Him through true faith in His Son Yahshua. Yahshua's words were true then and they are true now."

Rose faded from view and Ethan feel sad for her going.

Laura looked at the stunned man and smiled. "We get to see her frequently. Is there anything else I can answer right now?"

Ethan sat there stunned and just shook his head. Laura picked up her things, and left the room.

Ethan was overwhelmed by not only the existence of Angels but by the views in his mind of Heaven and Hell. The indescribable beauty and peace of Heaven drew his soul like a magnet draws metal. He wanted that love more than anything he'd ever known. It was a rest of contentment and satisfaction beyond his imagination.

Hell on the other hand was almost too horrible to contemplate. The fire, the darkness, the insufferable heat and hate, violence against him that was horrible and unending. The worse thing was that there was absolutely no hope of relief, rescue, or even a break in the torture in that place, forever.

Ethan realized he had been given a major life-defining choice and he bowed to the inevitability of his eternal future. Pushing the view of Hell away and recalling the peace of Heaven, he got up and went to find Alexis and David.

CHAPTER SIXTEEN

Jack had made several long-distance phone calls before he sat down with Mark to discuss the trip to Denver. "I talked with Sensei, my Dad, Mom, and my Uncle Larry. They are all now ready to come to Israel. Dad and Larry got all their loose ends taken care of and the Sensei sold his school. Their problem is that the new Government is restricting travel, especially to Israel.

So, since we're going to have roughly, about forty-five extra seats on the X-76, I invited them to travel with us back from Denver. See any problems with that?"

Mark shrugged, "Nothing we can't work out once they are here."

Jack checked the time and it was closing on 7:30 A.M. on Friday morning. He and Mark grabbed their day gear and headed out for the airstrip. As they were leaving the base they ran into Sean Murphy and Megan Cole. Sean asked Jack, "Sir, Charlie tells me that you're going to make a quick visit to Colorado tonight. Megan and I are free for the next two days and just want you to know that if you need extra help we'd be honored to back you up."

Jack looked at Mark. "Well, I don't know. Mark, should we take the kids along?"

Mark smiled, "You never know when you're going to need extra hands to make the work easier."

Jack looked at his watch. "We take off in fifteen minutes; can you get your gear and be back here by then?"

Megan pointed behind Jack. Looking around, Jack saw their combat gear and rifles stacked on the ground.

Jack smiled, "Okay then, let's get on board."

The two young people grabbed their gear and headed toward the parked Shrews. Jack called them back. "We're not going that way this time."

With Mark leading they walked over to the Research Building. Inside they were met by an Ex-USAF Major who escorted them over to the X-76. Stowing their gear in back, they came up to the front rows and sat down. Jack keyed his combat microphone. "X76 boarded and ready for departure."

The hatch on the X-76 closed silently and a large screen Monitor lit up on the front bulkhead. It showed the large hanger door opening. The plane rolled out and lined up with the main runway. Several seconds later they accelerated down the runway and lifted gently into the air. They exited the tunnel up from the base and flew out from beneath the island and rolled to the right. The nose came up and the aircraft rapidly gained altitude until the sky turned deep navy blue, almost black. The Mach meter next to the screen showed the plane exceeding the speed of sound and quickly moved up to Mach 5 which is considered Hypersonic Speed. The monitor rose up to the ceiling as there was nothing to see at this time. The four people talked about operations for a while and then Megan frowned. "Is Su Li the pilot or Mark White?"

Jack shrugged his shoulders, "I don't know, why don't you two go up to the cockpit and see who is there." As they walked off Jack grinned at Mark.

Megan opened the cockpit door and stood stock still. Sean leaned over and stared over her shoulder. They closed the door and returned to their seats. Sean smiled, "There is no pilot. Are we on that UAV we took to the Arctic Circle about a year ago?"

Jack nodded his head. "Yes, we're on a UAV. The plane is totally autonomous and it is one very smart vehicle."

There was a chime sound and the Monitor lowered to its display position. It lit up and the Major who had helped board them was seated at a desk. "Hello, General Malone and General Connelly. My name is Tom Garlin and I wanted to make you aware of some of the improvements we've made to the Ghost."

Jack asked, "The Ghost?"

"That's our new name for the X-76. It fits it better. Since you used it to go to the Arctic Circle almost a year ago, we've added an upgraded CPU and control capabilities, two hundred Terabytes of memory, and a new sensor array. This array provides omni-directional monitoring of just about anything that is physical, especially anything that uses power. By the way, this sensor array is so new it hasn't been revealed to the USAF as yet. Considering our new accommodations and their change in allegiance, it most likely will never be revealed to them, either. These arrays are a power of twenty times more effective than even the sensor arrays on U.S. satellites. So, please test them out well and bring them back to us. I have arranged with the IDF for air-to-air refueling during your trip over and on your return. You should have more than sufficient fuel."

Jack asked, "Major Garlin, how are you funding all this? I know that you were black ops prior to relocating and obviously the U.S. isn't funding you and since they never knew about your operations there's no more money coming from that direction."

The Major chuckled, "Actually, we are being funded by the Israeli Government and by your organization."

Jack thought back and laughed. "Okay, now I understand the line item covering that rather large monthly expenditure for "base operations" that I've been signing for each month."

The Major smiled, "Don't worry General, your team's money is being spent wisely and overseen by Mark Connelly to make sure we don't ask for too much. Anyway, General, good hunting. Garlin out."

The monitor screen darkened, rose upward and parked itself in its enclosure on the ceiling.

Mark looked at his partner and grinned. "I thought that you knew that when the President authorized the research division to move to the Sea Base that we would be in charge of them and partially responsible for their funding, since we were going to use their products. Anyway, I learned a couple of things about this aircraft since we used it last. Watch this." He pushed a button on the armrest of his seat. "Ghost, show us the operational parameters for this flight."

There was no reply but the screen moved from the ceiling and rotated back to its position on the front bulkhead. The screen lit up and pretty much exploded with information. The flight path was indicated on a globe of the world. All the data about the flight was displayed, speed, ETA'S, direction, altitude, temperatures inside and out, and the entire bottom half of the screen displayed a three dimensional radar view of the world around the aircraft.

The aircraft was dead center and the space around it was shown along with tags to indicate what was shown. Horizontally, the view covered about one hundred miles forward, backward, and to both sides. Vertically the area was about sixteen miles in depth. The ground passing under the aircraft was indicated and since they were over open ocean they saw thirty or thirty-five ships on the surface and four submarines, two American, one Russian, and one British.

Everything on the lower display was moving as the aircraft traveled across the space at Mach 5 plus the movements of the sea craft.

Jack's eye widened at the display. "They weren't kidding about the new sensor array." Beside each of the ships and the subs were a list of detected radar and sonar emissions, and probable destination and speed, present heading, armaments, and probable number of crew members.

Jack noted that the "Ghost" had maintained its altitude at 70,000 feet and its speed at Mach 5, roughly 3500 MPH with the exception of a brief interruption to refuel over the Atlantic Ocean. With a travel distance of 6,860 miles, it was only going to be a trip of approximately two and a half hours with the half hour being speeding up and slowing down and an in-air refueling.

Mark asked, "What course are we following to illegally cross a dozen borders of at least six countries?"

Jack laughed, "Nothing new for us. It looks like we're cutting across Europe and crossing the Atlantic in a Northern global arc which will bring us across the lower part of Greenland and over Canada and finally into the U.S."

Mark shook his head. "I do hope this buggy is invisible to ground radar, because otherwise, at this speed and height, we would be considered a missile on a targeted strike on Denver and we would find out just how good the U.S. missile defense is at knocking down objects like us."

Jack said, "Tom Garlin thinks we won't register on their scopes and Yahveh said that He would cover us over and back."

CHAPTER SEVENTEEN

Thirty minutes later the Ghost suddenly slowed down below Mach 1 and the map on the bulkhead showed they were traveling over Canada from East to West and approaching the Northern border of the United States.

Mark studied the other air traffic from the display and laughed.

Jack said, "What?"

Mark pointed at the map, "Tom Garlin is probably right that we were not detected up to this point. But, we're about to cross into the U.S. and there is a very good vertically aligned radar web all along the Northern borders between Canada and the U.S. This is to stop terrorists or drugs from flying low and evading the normal radar systems. We're not invisible, just stealthy. The Ghost knows that and can detect the web of radar ahead of us. So it just timed it out so that we could jump into the radar shadow above an airline jet headed for Denver while we cross the border. See how the center of the display shows us and the jumbo jet at the same place?"

Jack studied the display and saw Mark had figured out the sudden slow down. They crossed the border and the Ghost slipped away in the darkness from the jumbo jet and accelerated back to roughly Mach 3. The altitude kept dropping until it was less than two thousand feet. The ground began to show the city of Denver and quickly came upon Jack's company which was pulsing in red on the display.

The Ghost's forward speed slowed completely and rapidly dropped vertically until it slowed at three hundred feet and then gently landed inside the Corporate Compound exactly where Jack wanted to be.

The side hatch popped inward and then rose up to open the door in the side of the Ghost. The stairs lowered automatically and Jack led the four-man party out of the plane. He was greeted by Bob Wexler; the plant manager, his Dad, Steve, and his wife, Donna, his Uncle Larry, and Sensei Grady.

After the reunion was finished, Dr. Clashire came forward and indicated the two large black soft containers on the pallet behind him. "Hello Jack," the Doctor said. "I packed all thirty-three generators myself. I know you've been very busy, and I can tell from your extremely advanced form of transportation, not to mention the hour, that your visit must be very short. So, I have put all of our research and development progress on these five DVDS for you to review when you are back in Israel. It is good to see you looking so healthy. How is your lovely wife, Laura?"

Jack pulled out his cell phone and showed the Doctor a recent picture of Laura and a group picture of the whole team standing in front of a large sign that said, "Bless you, Dr. Clashire, for your devoted work in Christ's name." Jack opened his briefcase and gave the Doctor several 8 X 11 photos that they had taken at the Sea Base and in the field. Jack even had a picture that had been taken when all of the Core Team was battling demons and in their armor. Charlie had added the demons as they would not reproduce on film or video. Jack also gave copies of that picture to the others there.

Sean and Megan had been introduced to everyone and then had loaded the Force Generators and the entire set of luggage that the three men and one woman were taking with them to Israel.

Mark checked his watch and made a circling motion with his right hand in the air. Jack saw it. "Well, it looks like we've got to be on our way. Stay safe, stay in touch, and pray for us."

The six men and three women boarded the Ghost and it wound up its engines and began to lift off of the ground. Suddenly it dropped back to the ground. Mark pushed the button on his armrest and asked, "What is the problem?"

The screen came down and lit up the display. On the display was an overhead diagram of the plant site and several blocks surrounding it. There were Military vehicles closing in on the plant and three different ground to air missile trucks that were using active radar to saturate the air around them. It was fairly obvious that the Government knew that they would be there. Those forces couldn't have just been standing by on the chance that there would be an intrusion by the Crossfire Team into Colorado.

Mark said, "Escape and evade."

The engines quickly powered up and the Ghost lifted up and moved forward enough to clear the nine-foot security fence around the plant site and then dropped almost back to street level. The plane immediately accelerated away from the plant racing down roads that had little or no traffic on them. It was a route that slipped through the web of the closing Military units. The view on the video display showed their aircraft flying at about two feet of altitude and moving at an almost frightening rate of travel down streets and roads heading South, Southeast from the plant. Several times they overtook vehicles on the road and lifted over them. Twice they also did that for two cars coming the other way. One of the drivers didn't like the landing lights on the Ghost and flashed his high beams at them. Occasionally the plane would detour over empty lots or fields so as to not be trapped on any particular street.

The display also showed the changing view from overhead with the radar/missile trucks and the other Military vehicles racing to box the plane in. That wasn't working very well so two of the trucks fired three missiles each toward the plane. The Ghost suddenly stopped and slid under an overpass. It only stopped for a minute while the missiles lost radar lock and overflew them. Then they were off on the high-speed road race again. A person's mind couldn't follow all of the turns and changing directions the multi-ton aircraft made as it navigated the streets. All at once the Ghost lifted up twenty feet and accelerated very rapidly. Everyone inside was mashed into their seats as the plane opened up the space from the Military vehicles.

Mark could see a dozen fighter jets registering on the sensor array and realized that the Ghost had been aware of them and stayed low until the movement of the aircraft gave it an opening it could use.

At sixty feet off of the pavement the plane broke the sound barrier and most likely quite a few windows as well. Then the plane tipped upward and continued to accelerate rapidly. The altimeter was advancing so fast the only numbers readable were the thousands of feet in altitude and the hundreds of miles per hour. They cleared forty thousand feet in less than three minutes and that put them out of range of the ground-based anti-aircraft missiles on the trucks. But, it didn't put them out of the fighter's range.

Still the Ghost lived up to its name and disappeared off of the fighter's radar scopes more than it showed. To accomplish the stealth disappearance, the aircraft rolled over upside down so that its exhaust was hidden from the fighters until it passed them in altitude and then it rolled back upright. The Ghost dumped several bunches of chaff which remained on the fighter's radar and drew them to places far behind the Ghost. When they reached two-thousand miles per hour the plane transitioned into its SCRAM-Jet configuration and rapidly rose to almost eighty-thousand feet and indicated a flight speed of four thousand miles per hour or, to put it in a way it could be understood, the plane was covering 1.1 miles every second.

Jack figured out that at the speed they were traveling they could cross the country from San Francisco, California to Washington, D.C. in forty-five minutes.

That immense speed and fifteen miles of altitude put them out of the range of the fighters, which by then were searching Southward while the Ghost had arced around and was going Northeastward.

Mark said, "We're coming up on the U.S. border and we don't have any aircraft to hide us this time. Whoops, we just crossed the border and I think we were so high and going so fast we didn't light up their screens until we were way out of their range."

Sean quipped, "They probably aren't too concerned about a missile attack from Denver on Canada."

Mark shook his head. "It looks like our flight path is going to arc over the globe like a satellite in a Northern Polar orbit."

Jack shook his head again. "A Polar orbit transition? That's gutsy because if anyone can track us they'll think we *are* an ICBM."

The Ghost continued to gain some more altitude and maintained its speed until it leveled out at its maximum of both. Jack couldn't believe the readouts. "You know we are at twenty-two miles of altitude and are going Mach 6. I had no idea this was a realistic operational range for any aircraft."

The Sensei laughed. "Well, it's good to see that things are still exciting for this group." Sean was talking to Jack's step-mother and checking her vital signs after the most recent part of the trip.

After another thirty minutes passed the Ghost dropped back down to its most efficient altitude and speed, 50,000 feet and 3,500 miles per hour.

They met the Israeli tanker somewhere over the Atlantic Ocean and refueled for the rest of the trip home.

The Ghost made it back to the Sea Base in just over two hours from liftoff at the Denver plant to the 10:30 A.M. morning landing in Israel.

Jack and Laura took the four new residents on a tour of the base and found them apartments, one each for the Sensei and Uncle Larry, and one for Steve and his wife Donna.

After everyone decided to "rest" for a while, Laura and Jack headed back for the War Room. On the way Laura looked at Jack, "Okay, what happened on the trip back that Donna was telling me about?"

CHAPTER EIGHTEEN

Once the Transatlantic crew had a restful day and a good night's sleep, Jack called an "All-Hands" meeting in the living room. After a prayer of thanksgiving for a safe trip for the people on the Ghost trip, Jack prayed for the Father's blessing on the team.

Mark had each one of the new members of the Core Team come forward and pick up a Force Generator. When the four new members each had one, he showed them how to put them on and told everyone to flip the operate switch. Then he asked, "Does anyone have a red light on their generator?"

No hands were raised. Jack stepped forward and explained the devices. "What you have on your hip is a God-created protection device that will keep you safe from any form of violence. Slow forces like a fist, knife stab, or slash. A fast force such as a bullet or a blast. Even an ultimate force like a nuclear explosion. But, to use one, you have to walk sinless before Yahshua or the devices won't work. I know every one of you and your walks with Yahshua. But, to convince you that only a true believer in good standing with the Lord can use these devices I have invited two of the COMSEC employees and two of our Jewish associates to help us in this demonstration."

Jack motioned two of the COMSEC personnel to join him. He looked at the first one, a middle-aged man named Scott Pangelli. He was a dedicated Buddhist. "Scott will you help me with this demonstration?"

Scott Pangelli nodded his head. Jack looked at the assembled troops and smiled. He asked the new core members, "I need a single volunteer." Sean Murphy held up his hand and walked forward at Jack's request. Jack smiled at the young man. "You have a green light on your generator?"

Sean looked down and saw a solid green LED glowing brightly. "Yes Sir."

"Would you turn it off and strap it on Scott, please?"

Sean turned the generator off and strapped it around Scott's waist. Jack asked Scott to turn the generator on. Scott switched it on and looked at the light. It was a solid red light. Jack had Scott turn off the generator and then he had Judah Maritz try it on. Again, it glowed a bright red. After he took the device off Judah's friend Aaron said, "You haven't gone to any classes with Mr. Zahavy, have you?" David was going to work with Judah on his salvation but had been too busy since then. Judah shook his head. "But I am going to see that we have those meetings after this."

Finally, Jack had Ethan Reaper try it. This time the indicator glowed a solid green. Jack looked at Ethan with one raised eyebrow. "Oh, really?"

Ethan smiled, "Sorry to mess up your demonstration. I came to the realization of the truth of Yahshua yesterday and gave my life to Him last night after praying with David and Alexis. But, don't I have to be baptized before I am a true believer in Him?"

Jack laughed and pointed at the green light, "Apparently not, but you still want to break off any negativity you've run into and, to break off any curses on you or your life. It is also a public statement that you are willing to die to the old man you were and to rise as a new man in Christ. So, rather than ruin it, you just sealed the demonstration,"

Jack looked out over the assembly. "I want to make clear an important point to each one of the members of the Core Team. If a person believes in Yahshua as their Messiah their faith is enough to get them to Heaven at the end of their life. But, if they aren't living a life that is fully committed to Him, they will block the blessings available for them here on Earth and their lives will show no victory.

"Each person that is anointed to use one of these generators needs to be leading a life that is as free from sin as possible, or asking Yahshua for forgiveness if you do sin. I know all of the Core Team members are because the green lights on the Force Generators prove that they are walking as Yahshua wants them to. Therefore, all team members will receive all of Yahveh's blessings while you are here on Earth if you ask for them. The man or woman who believes in Christ will get to Heaven. The man or woman that does as He asks will bring Heaven down here while they are on Earth. I want Him and I also want the blessings He has already prepared for me."

"I know that all of us have been anointed to use these generators during our battles with the RHONE. We will take the brunt of the combat and do whatever is necessary to protect the people we are anointed to protect and defend." Jack got a standing ovation for his statement and his stance for the Lord.

Mark stood up, "Remember, no one, not even a loved one can learn about these Force Generators. Because it can provide total protection from any assault, men will kill to possess it. Countries will have their armies attack anyone to possess it. One word about it could result in a new arms race. Most governments are secular; they don't really believe in Yahshua or even Yahveh God. So, even though Yahveh will never allow anyone to make or use a working unit outside of the ones we have here, and the other eleven teams around the world, they could cause world panic and massive evil, resulting in many deaths." He turned to the Core Team. "Shut your unit off, record the number on the unit, and give your unit to Jack or to me so that we can put them in the secure reserve area. We will pass out the units as they are needed. We also have additional units for the entire SOG when Yahveh gives us the command to have the SOG use them."

As the meeting broke up Laura came over to Jack. "That was good, Mr. Malone."

Jack grinned at her. "Why, thank you Mrs. Malone, I'm glad you approve of my presentation."

Laura hugged him and then stepped back. "I got a text from Carol." Tipping her head to her left toward the young lady, "She needs to talk to you immediately."

Carol limped up to the couple. "Jack, I've taken another look at the Matrix and found something that could be trouble for us. There seems to be a large concentration of demons that are going to transit to our dimension six days from now. They are going to enter somewhere in Jordan, probably where Charlie and company made them think we have our headquarters. I don't have a valid reason for this yet."

Mark and Sarah Connelly came up to the group. Mark said, "Well, I believe I have a valid reason for their mass insertion."

Jack looked at the set of Mark's jaw and nodded. "Okay, let's take this into the War Room."

Once the recorders were running and everyone was in their positions Mark took the floor. "I've been talking to the IDF and the Mossad and they have gotten some Intel. It seems that six days from now the RHONE is going to invade Jordan and attack that base that Charlie and David visited three days ago. It seems the entire Light Armored Division that was assigned to find us and kill us is going to sneak up on our underground base there and assault us. Charlie's ploy worked much better than we expected. The RHONE is bringing twelve tanks, eight APCs, and fifteen hundred troops. They also have artillery and mortars, snipers, plus twenty-five helicopters and bomber aircraft."

Laura asked, "How did the Mossad get such accurate numbers?"

Mark smiled, "They watched them move everything down to a port in Libya and start loading the mechanized units on a ship. How I know that they are destined for Jordan is the Mossad has a contact who is one of the Officers on that ship."

Jack thought for a few seconds, "And I expect that the Jordanians aren't going to complain or fight them, right?"

Sarah laughed, "Ten-Four. Marco Marino has ordered the Jordanians not to interfere with this "training mission". But, I don't think they know where the RHONE is going to "train"."

Jack smiled, "So, the RHONE thinks they've sniffed us out and the Jordanians haven't told Marino about their little WMD plant. I am concerned that the demons haven't told Marino where we really are based and about the Jordanian WMD plant. The demonic has to know these things. This should be very interesting."

Laura had another set of facts from her heavenly training open up in her mind. "The reason the demons haven't told Marco Marino is because Satan has commanded them not to. Remember that the demonic hates all humanity and it serves Satan's aims to have this conflict between us and the RHONE and the secret of weapons of mass destruction plant hidden from the OWG.

CHAPTER NINETEEN

Mark stood up. "I think this could be the time for us to take down the entire RHONE division using the Force Generators. Look at the situation. We have a combat stretch battlefield which is a huge chunk of desert, with no Israelis in the middle. We'll have limited observation concerning the generators. And, best and lastly, we can eliminate the entire fighting force the RHONE is fielding against us in one place."

Jack looked down for a moment as he thought about that concept. "I'm not sure I can shoot fish in a barrel like that. I'll take this up in prayer and let you all know what the Father wants us to do."

Jack and Laura went to their apartment to pray. Jack led them in sincere praise and worship and then placed their petition in front of the Lord for direction and guidance. They then rested in the Lord and waited.

When Jack opened his eyes he saw an Angel that he had never seen before. This messenger had a brooding look and a stern attitude. Jack asked, "Greetings, and who do you serve as Lord?"

The being looked directly at Jack. "I serve the most high. I have been sent to bring you the answer to your prayer. The most high says, *"You must do what I have instructed you to do. Utterly destroy all of the RHONE including their superiors. Use your skill and determination to win the day. Remember, I only allowed Gideon three hundred soldiers to win against thousands. This battle will glorify my name. Do not be concerned but be courageous and you will achieve great things."*

The angel disappeared and Jack thought about his message. Then he looked at Laura and shook his head.

Thinking about the directive he came to a conclusion. He shook his head, "I don't buy it. It makes no sense and Yahveh is the source of peace, not confusion. And, I am very confused by His permission to allow us to get the Force Generators for the battle, but now He doesn't mention them. Are we supposed to use them or not to use them against the RHONE?" He stared at his wife for a few seconds. "Do you understand these contradicting directives? They leave me confused with a bad feeling in my spirit."

He thought for a few seconds, "Let's pray for Yahshua to surround us with His angels and protect us and our communications with the Father. I smell a rat somewhere."

Laura nodded her head. "I agree. I also don't feel right about this last message. It stands at odds with everything we've been told before. But, didn't Raquel tell us that the enemy could no longer influence us here at the Sea Base. That the angels were protecting the base so that the enemy can't get to us here?"

Jack got down on his knees "Yeah, but when I asked this "angel" who he served he didn't say Yahshua or Yahveh. He only said he served the most high." Jack prayed that Yahshua would surround them both in a hedge of Heavenly protection to keep the enemy from interfering with their time with the Father. They then sang two songs in praise to the Father. They were about to lay out their concerns about the upcoming battle when suddenly their Heavenly armor and swords appeared. They both jumped to their feet as their room disappeared and they were instantaneously engulfed in a battle that was being waged between angels and demons.

Jack blocked a demon that thrust its sword at him. Turning on his heel Jack managed to turn inside the demon's strike range and smash the handle of his sword into the face of the demon. The demon recoiled but it was too late. The flowing glory of Yahveh spread from the hilt of the sword during the blow and fractured the demon's head as rivulets of light from the blow continued to spread further throughout its body.

Laura ducked as two blades met above her head. An angelic blade deflected a black demonic blade that had tried to smash Laura into the ground. Laura ran her blade through the middle of the demon and cut to the left freeing her sword.

Everything around them was chaos as the huge melee ebbed and flowed between the Heavenly forces and the demons of darkness. There were angels and demons crumpled on the ground. The demons were being consumed by the power of Yahveh and their bodies were dissipating into smoke while the angels would simply disappear suddenly from sight.

Both Jack and Laura were filled by a raging power of Holy Anger at the demonic attack. This power of righteous indignation was a heady fuel that propelled them both into battling the demons with everything they had. This all-consuming desire allowed them to focus every bit of their ability and training into their battling. Laura went into the time-compressing, high-speed techniques and simply slid through the crush of demons like a whirling ball of blades. She sensed the continual addition of more demons to the battle as a personal insult and it only made her determined to destroy as many of them as possible.

Jack was battling four demons at the same time and getting smashed and stabbed constantly. His armor and shield protected him and his intense determination let him battle back against overwhelming odds. He was about to go to the high-speed technique when two of the demons attacking him were destroyed and removed from the battle. The other demons attacking him lost their focus and turned to face other attackers. This gave Jack a chance to take out the two of them quickly.

Jack noticed for the first time that there were other human forces battling against the demons in the gloom. He saw more and more people in suits of gold or silver armor rushing into the battle. He recognized some of them as other members of the Crossfire Team but many others were strangers. He went to high-speed and started sliding between demons and cutting them down before they knew he was there.

The battle had suddenly shifted dramatically against the demons and they knew it. Jack dropped out of the high-speed technique as the demons begin to disappear in droves. Before he knew it there were none left in the area.

Jack saw Laura on the ground in the gloom and ran to her side. She waved him off and sat up. She looked up at him and grinned. "I ducked too low on that last pass and fell on my back side." Jack offered his hand to help her up and then they looked around the battlefield. All of the angels had also disappeared but the human combatants were still there.

Jack squared up to face one of the strangers who walked up to them. Jack's armor and sword disappeared at the same time as the other humans remaining in the dim area. The tall black man held out his hand and shook Jack's hand. He studied both Jack and Laura for a second. "My name is Marcus Trembold, and you would be...?"

Jack introduced himself and Laura. "I'm glad you showed up when you did, Marcus. The demons were becoming overwhelming."

Marcus smiled, "Don't they always try that?" He waved his hand around. "The shift to battle this time was much unexpected for me and some of my team." He looked around at the others congregating in small groups and talking. "I don't recognize many of the people here but see that they are equipped as we are and definitely fighting for Yahveh. Are all of these people part of your team?"

Jack scanned the dozens of people around him. "Some are, many are not. I am impressed that there are so many of us. Where is your team based out of?"

Marcus waved his arm and eight or nine people walked toward him. "We are based in Europe, primarily in Italy. Your team?"

Jack also waved his arm and the Crossfire Team members came his way. "We work out of Israel now but originally we were based in the State of Colorado in the United States."

Marcus stood back and grinned. "I've heard of your team! You were the ones in Africa that stopped the killing of Christians in Zyngola, right?"

Jack nodded as Mark and Sarah arrived. He introduced them to Marcus and then asked Mark. "How did you get drawn into this mess?"

Mark looked at Jack quizzically. "I was just going to talk to Carol when "zap", here I am fighting for my life."

Jack nodded his head. "Like you, Laura and I had just gotten a message from what I think, was a false angel, and were praying to Yahveh when suddenly we were thrown into combat here."

Marcus laughed, "I can clear up your confusion, I think. This, as the young people would say, wasn't our first rodeo." We've had no warning any of the times it happened. We were simply doing whatever and then we were suddenly taken by Yahveh to support His angels in battles against the forces of darkness. One second you are doing something else and then you're in the thick of it. Although, now that I think about it, never when we've been on a mission."

Jack smiled, "First time for us. Are there any rules involved we can understand?"

Marcus put his hand on Jack's shoulder, "There may be but I have no idea because we end up back at our headquarters just as suddenly."

Laura asked with a little urgency. "Marcus, do you have a phone number or an email we can use to contact you? You know, before we all disappear."

Marcus nodded and gave them his email address. He had just finished when the world shifted and the Crossfire Team found themselves back at the Sea Base where they started. Jack felt a heavy fatigue set in as the events of the last hour suddenly caught up with him. Taking a deep breath, he smiled weakly and used his phone to call Mark. "I suggest we rest for a bit and get together in a while to talk this over."

CHAPTER TWENTY

After they had rested for a few hours, Jack got out of bed and resumed his prayer to the Father. He wasn't surprised when a glow appeared in the bedroom and the angel Caleb appeared.

Caleb was in his young, dynamic form and his piercing gold eyes studied Jack for a few seconds. "I understand that I erred in my pronouncement that this base was free of demons. I apologize to you and your team for that error. Satan has dropped to new lows in his eagerness to stop all of our human teams, especially yours. He instituted an age-old time technique of his own to shift the times of my cleaning house, so to speak, and his insertion of demons below our covering. As I said, this is a very old technique which caught both me and Hugo almost completely off guard. Essentially, you were visited by both of these two demons before I rid the area around the Sea Base of any viable demonic activity. Satan just delayed the second visitation in your time. That is why this latest demon didn't mention the Force Generators, because they weren't involved at the time he visited you. It's complicated, but now that we know what he did and how he did it, we are instituting our own time management of the area and you should be free of these imitators. Your discernment is many levels above when you first started and we applaud you."

Caleb smiled, "The Most High has heard your plea and sent me to give you these words to clarify His commands to you."

"My son, I understand your reluctance to use the Force Generators to destroy the RHONE because it appears to you an overwhelmingly unfair advantage in your eyes. That is My compassion living inside you. You are wise to be compassionate, but realize that the generators are simply equalizers against a much larger force. I don't want you to totally destroy them but show them that they cannot defeat you because you represent Me. As they realize that you are invulnerable because you are protected by Me, most will withdraw from the combat with your team. It is

critical that you destroy the ones that are too prideful and keep attacking you. They would make a force that would never stop attacking you and the other teams. As to the ones that recognize that it is My power, rather than that of Satan that rules over them, let them live. Their leaders will try to force them to keep attacking you, which these soldiers know is foolish. I will put the fear of Elohim into these soldier's hearts and this will start the destruction of the RHONE from within. When this fear strikes them, the warriors of the RHONE will turn on their leaders and destroy them. These warriors will then spread the fear of Elohim to all of the other warriors of the RHONE. Go in My Name as you fight this battle."

As Caleb faded from view, Jack saw him look to his left and start to pull his sword out of its scabbard. The momentary glimpse was imprinted on Jack's eyes due to the brightness that flared from Caleb's blade.

Jack sat back on the floor and contemplated all that the angel had given him. He was startled when Laura said quietly to him, "This is a complicated thing that we have to do, isn't it?"

Jack had forgotten that his wife was in the room during his discussion with the angel. "Sorry honey, I got wrapped up in the communication with Caleb and forgot where I was. I didn't mean to wake you up."

Laura laughed quietly, "That's okay, and it was very interesting to wake up to an angel talking anyway. Maybe we need to give this information to the whole team since we will all be going to this battle."

Jack nodded his head and got to his feet. "I'm going to get a shower and then let you get ready while I jot down some notes for the meeting. Why don't you arrange an all-hands meeting for about an hour from now?"

The meeting started with prayer after everyone who was available gathered in the large living room area in front of the War Room. Jack had spent the last half hour with Mark, Sarah, David, Alexis, and Carol, putting a battle plan together that would meet Yahveh's requirements and let the team prove their point to the RHONE soldiers.

Jack then turned to Carol. "How are you healing Carol? I am reluctant to assign you to further combat until you are one hundred percent."

Carol studied Jack's face for a few seconds. Then she stood up and turned her back to Jack and lifted the back of her blouse. There were no marks or signs of bruising to be seen. Carol dropped her blouse and turned around again. "I expected I would dearly need the ten days you gave me yesterday but, you guys prayed for me and the Father healed me completely. I woke up this morning to do the Modei Ani and realized I didn't hurt anywhere. Thank you so much for praying for me. Jack and Laura looked at each other and just grinned.

Turning to the assembled company, Jack spelled out the message from the Father. Then he explained the plan of battle that they had worked out. "To make it clear to everyone, because everyone is protected by the Force Generators. The Core Team will be drawing the RHONE's attention by moving directly up the middle of the battle. We are not going to just walk around like targets at the carnival and let them shoot at us. At the same time, we are not going to casually slaughter all of the soldiers we are battling with from the RHONE."

"What we want to do is to quickly reduce their war-making capabilities effectively and efficiently. To that end we are going to issue side arms and rifles to all troops and assign heavy weapons to individuals and groups. I want Sarah, Alexis, and Carol to handle the sniper work with the BMG .50 caliber sniper rifles. The goal for all troops is simply to destroy their tanks, helicopters, armored personnel carriers, mortars, rocket launchers, and anything else that allows them to wage war against us."

Jack looked at the entire group. "Our goal is to remove their heavy weapons and support as quickly as possible with as few causalities to their soldiers as possible. Soldiers that recognize their inability to hurt us we will let live. Those that are so driven by demonic forces that they continue to attack us, we are to destroy completely as Yahveh has commanded us to do."

"The Core Team will take the battle up the middle to the RHONE. The other team members will have vehicles and will fill in around us and take care of aircraft, vehicles, and heavy arms from a distance. Remember, the RHONE survivors will be our troops, in essence, after they turn on their leaders. There will be fatalities and causalities on their side due to collateral damage from removing their war-making capability. If you blow up a tank the people inside are at risk, that can't be helped. So be it. If you use a rocket or a grenade launcher to eliminate a mortar site, the people manning that site could be killed, so be it. We are not to act charitable like Christians against these forces, but, since we are Christians we don't want to inflict more harm than necessary. If the soldiers fighting us surrender, throw down their arms, or retreat without shooting at us as they run, we let them live. Are we all clear on this?"

Jack looked around and saw smiles on many faces. "This way we will show them our capability to stop their numerically superior forces but we will let the Father put the fear of Yahveh into their hearts".

"Okay, we've got a whole day to get ready for this encounter. I want everyone to figure out how we're going to transport and position the heavy weapons and ammunition that we need to use. Mark will assign the weapons and the teams for larger weapons. The majority of the team, the SOG, will have the vehicle-mounted heavy weapons and armor. For the Core Team, most of their weapons will be man-portable. Therefore, let's work together to find the best way to carry everything and how to use it with the team members in your unit in coordination with the SOG units supporting us."

"This meeting is adjourned. Attention, Carry on."

Mark quickly made the assignments and the teams broke apart to get their weapons and to determine how they were going to handle their individual roles.

After the SOG was gone, Mark looked at Jack and Laura and smiled. "I've got a goodie for you two, come on."

The three of them walked down to the Armory and Mark went in and came back with a really large weapon. Mark smiled, "This is the FIM-12 Stinger Missile." Then he grinned. "Sometimes you just need a bigger gun. I figured we need a little more firepower than the normal lightweight mortars or ground-to-air missiles to get rid of those pesky enemy aircraft or tanks, or to punch through fortified buildings."

"This system is a man-portable, shoulder-fired, supersonic missile system weighting about 40 pounds. This system is designed to counter high speed, low-level, ground attack aircraft and is also effective against helicopters, unmanned aerial vehicles, and observation and transport aircraft. It can also be used against tanks, bunkers, etc."

Mark placed the device on the counter. "Once fired, this system, like other Stinger missiles, uses proportional navigation algorithms to guide the missile to a predicted intercept point. This is a true "fire and forget" missile, requiring no inputs from you once the weapon is fired. You can take cover, move to an alternate position, or engage additional targets. You've got a rate of fire of one missile every 3 to 7 seconds. It also possesses an integral identification, friend or foe (IFF) subsystem to assist you in identifying friendly aircraft, although I doubt that we'll need it in this case."

Mark picked the large device up and put it on his shoulder. "The launch motor ejects the missile from the launch tube. The missile coasts a safe distance, about 9 meters, from the gunner before the dual thrust flight motor ignites and provides a sustained 22 gravity acceleration that arms the missile. After the missile is armed, a sustained flight phase maintains missile velocity until the propellant is consumed. Then the missile enters a free flight period in which the motor has burned out, but the missile maintains a degree of maneuverability prior to interception or self-destruction."

Mark gave the launcher to Jack so he could shoulder it. "The warhead consists of a fuse assembly and the equivalent of four pounds of a newly developed, extremely high explosive, encased in a pyrophoric titanium cylinder. The warhead can be detonated by penetrating the target, impacting the target, or self-destruction. Self-destruction occurs 15 to 19 seconds after launch. What do you think of it?"

Grinning at Mark, Jack said, "I don't know Mark, don't you have anything bigger?"

Mark nodded his head, "Yes, but you need an armored vehicle to carry it."

Laura laughed, "Okay, we'll take this one."

Jack asked, "How many missiles will we have to carry in addition to the launcher?"

Mark shrugged, "They weigh about ten pounds each, and how many do you want to carry?"

Jack calculated the weight and probable need. "Give us eight between the two of us.

CHAPTER TWENTY-ONE

The evening began with a beautiful sunset over the Mediterranean Sea that left the sky over Israel peaceful in shades of light pastels in the blue range with lilac and pink highlights. The team and the SOG boarded the two VTOL aircraft. They left the peaceful sky behind and entered into the world of Military combat.

The two Ospreys lifted off of the sub-sea runway and exited the secret entrance under the lip of the Southern end of the island. By the time they gained altitude and headed South over the Mediterranean, the skies had turned to gray and black. The two aircraft approached their turn into the Gulf of Aqaba on their way to Jordan.

Su Li followed the lead of Mike White as he flew out over the Red Sea next to the nation of Jordan. She matched his Tilt Rotor as it dumped altitude until they were only a few feet above the water. They made the left turn and stayed on the deck as they crossed above the shore. Mike transmitted, "Feet Dry", to inform the Sea Base they had left the Red Sea and entered Jordan. As they crossed the coast of Jordan they saw the three Israeli LSTs offloading the vehicles for the team's use.

Everyone tensed up as the two aircraft switched to vertical flight and lowered to the sand. The two ramps were lowered and everyone grabbed their gear and the other supplies and disembarked quickly. After everyone was on the ground the two Ospreys lifted off and headed back toward the sea to keep the team's "footprint" as minimal as possible.

The SOG met with the Israeli troops and took command of the ground vehicles. The SOG moved the vehicles up to where the Core Team was and loaded the rest of the team members. They reached their advance bivouac and spent the few hours of the night resting in preparation for the upcoming battle.

The next day as they approached the combat, Mark stopped the vehicles and assigned them to their sectors. The Core Team split up and approached the battlefield on foot with their Force Generators on and showing green LED lights in the dawn's early light.

Mark took four of the troops while the others followed Jack. They headed for the location of the secret Jordanian underground lab about a mile from where they had deplaned.

Laura took several deep breaths as she marched through the sand toward certain combat. She looked down on her left hip and saw the hooded green LED glowing solidly. Even that didn't completely settle her nerves so she prayed and asked the Father for peace and assurance that she and the other team members were safe in His hands. Confidence flooded over her and she straightened up and felt her worries melt away into the Father's hands.

Charlie Wu was attached to Jack's team but was still handling the communications for the entire team. He checked his projected view of the surrounding area from a British satellite above them and sent a private call to Jack and Mark. "Generals, beware that the RHONE has detected our approach and is moving assets into place to interdict us."

Mark commented, "Thanks Charlie. Everyone check for your green light and prepare to take away the enemy's capability to wage war."

The first indication that the RHONE was out there was an explosion. Followed by many more explosions. Mortar and Tank rounds landed very accurately in the area of the Core Team. The explosions tore great holes in the desert and blew sand high into the sky but didn't affect any of the team members.

As they drew nearer to the RHONE troops, their Force Generators began to defeat a large volume of rifle as well as rocket and mortar fire. Still, there was no effect on the Crossfire Team members.

Jack saw a RHONE tank pulling out of a revetment in a sand dune as it angled for a clearer shot. He aimed the FIM-12 Stinger missile and fired it when his scope locked in on the tank. The missile tracked true and literally blew the turret off of the tank killing everyone in it.

Laura handed Jack another round and started to draw her sidearm as two RHONE troops ran from behind the tank with their rifles blazing directly at her and Jack. The two

RHONE troopers emptied their magazines without hurting either of the Crossfire Team members. One of them charged Jack with a bayonet on the barrel of his empty rifle.

Laura shot the man in the face with her .40 caliber XD auto-loader. The force of the bullet threw the man onto his back five feet away.

The other RHONE trooper threw down his empty rifle and raised his hands in surrender. Laura holstered her handgun and told him to go back to his camp and tell his Commander that the RHONE will never be able to hurt us. Then she and Jack walked toward the battle leaving one very confused trooper watching them walk through heavy machine gun fire and not even notice it.

A quarter of a mile north of Jack's position, Mark was directing his troops to knock out three main battle tanks with shoulder-fired missiles. He saw a helicopter preparing to fire a missile directly at him and two of the SOG warriors. Another one of the SOG team had been tracking the helicopter and had fired a FIM-12 Stinger missile which had already locked onto the helicopter and had been fired. Before the chopper could fire its missile it detected the Stinger and tried to evade without success. The helicopter turned into a large fireball that fell to the ground directly on top of one of the burning tanks.

Carol and Sarah were on top of a dune using .50 caliber sniper rifles to take out any mobile units in their area. The targets were becoming scarce as the RHONE troops were quickly retreating from the field of battle.

The thirty-one SOG team members were moving in a jagged semicircle around the Core Team and heading to the north. As word spread to the remaining RHONE soldiers that the Crossfire Team members were indestructible, it resulted in routing the remaining RHONE troops away from the area of the Jordanian underground lab.

The final RHONE soldiers turned and ran toward their transports. That left the Crossfire Team standing there watching the helicopters and trucks flee the area. Jack and Laura knelt and prayed their thanks to Yahveh for the victory and their ability to put fear into the hearts of the RHONE soldiers as the Father wanted them to do.

A message from Charlie alerted Jack and Laura to the approach of a Jordanian vehicle from the area of the secret lab.

Jack told everyone to stand by while he talked to the Jordanians.

The single desert personnel vehicle slowed as it approached the leaders of the Crossfire Team. The doors opened and several Jordanian Military Officers got out and walked up to Jack and Laura. The leader saluted Jack and smiled at him. Jack had a general knowledge of the Jordanian Army Officer rankings. This man was a Lieutenant General they called "FAREEQ". His rank was perhaps the rank with some general authority and more specific responsibility. It was usually given to a direct assistant to the leader of the Joint Chiefs of Staff of the Jordanian Military. Jack noticed the two crossing Arabic swords with a crown above them, and the red collar flashes along with other decorative signs that indicated his rank.

"I am Lieutenant General Mohammad. I don't understand why you battled the Military arm of Marco Marino on our soil. But, I want to thank you for doing so. Marco Marino thinks he can do as he pleases and it doesn't sit well with many people. I am so amazed how your few troops were able to rout such odds. Could you enlighten me as to any of these things?"

Jack considered the request and decided on the most effective answers. "Lieutenant General Mohammad, I represent the Crossfire Team. We serve the Elohim of Abraham, Isaac and Jacob, the Yahveh of our fathers, and the Yahveh of Israel. The Yahveh that glorified His servant, Yahshua, in this small battle against Satan and his earthly representatives."

"Marco Marino has determined that he cannot allow any Military force not under his control. He has commanded the RHONE to destroy us completely. We felt that this deserted desert gave us a good battleground that wouldn't include innocents. Yahveh gave the RHONE into our hands today and we were able to rout them without injury. I ask your forgiveness for using your land to accomplish this battle but, it was here or downtown Amman."

General Mohammad nodded his head. "I think I much prefer this area to that of any populated city. I will have to ask you and your soldiers to leave Jordan now that you have accomplished your goal. We will take care of the dead and their deserted equipment."

Jack was about to thank the General when Laura broke in urgently. "We are about to be attacked by demons." She had obviously gotten a word from either Carol or the Lord.

Jack asked the General to stand back and laid down his Stinger launcher. He stood up and started to pray earnestly to Yahveh God.

General Mohammad shook his head. As a devout Muslim he knew that the Christian faith was a sham and that the only Yahveh was Allah.

Suddenly Jack's armor, shield, and the sword of Yahveh appeared as it did for the other Crossfire Team members. With a creaking, snapping, and scraping sound like a thousand fingernails on a blackboard, several inter-dimensional rifts opened and dozens of obscenely ugly demons poured out. One of the larger demons materialized, individually, much closer to the Jordanian vehicle and began to slay the soldiers there with a large black sword.

General Mohammad back peddled and drew his handgun from his holster. He heroically stood his ground and fired six rounds at the demon with no effect. Laura ran over and engaged the demon to distract it from the remaining Jordanian soldiers. One of the soldiers still in the vehicle opened up on the back of the demon with a machine gun and raked the demon up and down several times and incidentally hit Laura at the same time.

The demon had the right to be there and the bullets did it no harm. But that attack did make it turn toward the vehicle with death in its eyes. Laura chopped off the beast's right shoulder and arm which dropped to the ground with its sword.

Leaking red smoke, the demon bent over to pick up the sword with its left arm and Laura beheaded it with one swipe of her sword.

Laura turned to defend the Jordanians from the demons when two normal-sized demons grabbed both of her arms and pulled them to each side. A third demon stepped in front of her and rammed his black blade directly into her unarmored face.

CHAPTER TWENTY-TWO

When the black blade slammed right at Laura's face it activated the Force Generator field and was stopped short. The demon pulled his sword back and with a mighty swing he tried to decapitate Laura. Again he was stopped by the field. Puzzled that attacking wasn't working, the ugly demon studied her to determine what was different.

Laura's sword distracted him because the power of Yahveh was flowing off of the blade. He noticed the Force Generator at her left hip. The power in the box equally drew him and repelled him, so he knew it was unique. As Laura fought to get loose from the two demons holding her, the third demon reached slowly toward her hip and pushed on the green light in an effort to turn it off. The demon couldn't stand to look at the thing because it seemed to be filled with the light of Yahveh and that weakened him and scared him at the same time. Suddenly, something from his left side flew at his face and he snarled and jumped back. It was the head of the demon holding Laura's right hand. The demon looked that way and found Jack swinging a powerful blow at his neck.

The demon quickly brought up his black blade to deflect Jack's blow. But, as the demon watched helplessly the bright blade with the Esteem of Yahveh sundered his black blade and cut his head from his body.

Laura saw Jack kill the demon on her right and then kill the one in front of her. The third demon let go of her left hand to strike Jack but she was already running her blade through its belly with her right hand.

Lieutenant General Mohammed stood still in shock as he stared at the whirling battles going on around him. The few Jordanian soldiers still alive were also dumbfounded. Completely out of context in the middle of the battle, General Mohammed's cell phone rang. He answered it to hear his superior officer asking him why he had not reported in on his approach to the strange invincible soldiers.

Mohammed tried to explain the large attack by demons but his superior would not hear of it. General Sayif told Mohammed that such things do not exist in the Koran, therefore, they are not real and do not exist. To believe in such beings was heresy and would end Mohammed's career in the army and quite probably, his life.

Mohammed realized General Sayif's dedication to the Word of the Koran would not allow the General to listen to him so he simply told his superior to come and see for himself. He broke the connection as he dodged another demon's blade. One of the Crossfire Team's SOG soldiers ran at the demon and killed it with one swipe of his glowing blade. Mohammed bowed to the man who nodded back at him and then turned to attack three more demons.

Dozens of more demons poured out of the two inter-dimensional rifts and attacked the humans.

Jack prayed to Yahveh for help to destroy the rifts or at least permission to close them himself. He didn't want to repeat his prideful actions of the last time.

He heard Yahveh tell him to continue to destroy the demons in the field. Yahveh said that He would contend with rifts created by the demons from the demonic realm.

The warriors were decimating the demons as quickly as possible but there were going to be too many of them soon.

Mark started pumping 40mm grenades into the groups of demons coming out of the rifts and killing many of them. Several other Crossfire Team members started doing the same and the pressure dropped on the sword fighters.

Suddenly there was a loud Heavenly word heard everywhere and the rifts disappeared with a flash of light.

The demons were dismayed but couldn't seem to go back to their dimension. So, they turned to defend themselves against the humans. Jack ran out of grenades for his M-8 so he started attacking the demons with his sword again. It was hard and normally it was actually very dangerous work because the demons would gang up on one warrior and try to bind them so that they could get their black blades around the warrior's armor. The Force Generators changed all that.

Jack noticed that he was sweating from the exertion of fighting with the demons. The constant high level of energy was draining him as he prayed continuously; he did nothing to dodge the enemy's blades, axes, clubs, and claws, and simply fought to strike correctly in every case.

Jack took out a major demon that had waded through the smaller ones and simply knocked them aside to get to attack him. Jack ducked the massive round-house swing and drove his shining blade through the exposed arm pit and out of the neck of the big monster. This disabled the demon's sword arm and cut through its spine at the same time.

Alexis attacked the demons around Jack from his right and as he turned he went into high speed time compression and cut down eight more of the smaller demons. Alexis chased three more demons across Jack's vision as he spun around looking for more targets.

Jack immediately noticed a dozen or so demons were attacking a Jordanian command vehicle and had gotten inside. Jack could see blood on the inside of the glass and knew it wasn't demon stain. He ran over and attacked the pack from the rear. Jack quickly destroyed the eight demons outside the vehicle. He slashed the back of the last demon and grabbed it and threw it backward out of the truck. He noticed a lull in the fighting. The team had destroyed the entire enemy force and there were no more demons to fight.

Looking into the shambles inside the vehicle he saw movement and an officer fighting to get out from under two Jordanian soldier's bodies. Jack's armor disappeared along with his sword and he reached in and grabbed the man's arm and pulled him out of the vehicle. The man was a major officer.

General Sayif was terrified on very basic level and was also covered in blood and demon stain. He was shaking so bad he couldn't talk. He was waving around a pistol with the slide locked back after it had run out of ammo. His eyes darted everywhere looking for more demons.

Seeing the man's distress, Jack prayed as he put his right hand on the General's left shoulder. "Heavenly Father Yahveh, remove the fear and incomprehension of this child of God. Replace it with your peace that goes beyond human understanding. I ask this in Yahshua's name."

CHAPTER TWENTY-THREE

As the anointing on Jack flowed over the smaller man's body, the Father removed the fear and dread that was reverberating in his mind and peace flooded him.

Jack watched as the eyes lost their dilated and panicked state and returned to normal. The General blinked several times and looked at Jack in awe. He bowed to Jack and thanked him in Arabic.

Jack smiled and stepped back and helped the General move away from the bloody vehicle. He could tell that the touch of Yahveh had greatly calmed the Genera and now he slowly looked at everything in the area. The man looked around in awe; like he was seeing the world for the first time. Actually, he probably was seeing the world for the first time through the peace of Christ.

Lieutenant General Mohammad stepped up and saluted his superior. The General smoothly returned the salute and then shook the younger man's hand and then stepped forward and hugged him.

The Lieutenant thought that the world had decidedly shifted strangely; but in a good way.

General Sayif smiled and shook his head. "Mohammed, I am at a loss to understand or explain these creatures or why these demons attacked you; but, I am glad that you survived. Please introduce me to this man." He tipped his head toward Jack.

Mohammed smiled back. "General Sayif, meet Jack Malone of the Crossfire Team. Perhaps he can clear up the confusion in the General's mind."

He repeated his request to Jack in English and mentioned that General Sayif spoke English, also.

Jack nodded to Mohammed and addressed General Sayif. "General, I apologize to you concerning this demonic attack. As a team we are a problem for the enemy of mankind, Satan. When we defeated the AntiChrist's army here, Satan launched an all-out attack on us from the demonic realm."

Jack pointed at the vehicle behind the General. "Unfortunately, you arrived at the wrong time and demons aren't too picky about who they kill. Like all demons their desires are to steal, kill, and destroy. I'm very sorry about your men and Mohammed's also. We tried to keep them protected but the demons broke our containment because there were too many of them for us all at once."

General Sayif frowned, "I too am sorry for our men. But, what did you do to give me this peace?"

Jack smiled, "I just prayed that Yahveh would take away the terror and fear and grant you peace and He did."

I have never, ever felt such love and care. This Hebrew Yahveh is real. I think I am going to have to consider my options because I can't deny the living God. I will probably lose my Military position, my family, and my life, but, now I know that it will all be worth it to know God."

Sarah had walked up and listened to the exchange. She suggested that Jack pray the sinner's prayer with the General so that he could continue on his path to know the real God.

Jack asked the General if he would like to do that and after some thought, he agreed. Mohammed asked if it would be acceptable for him to pray with them. The General smiled and stood next to his new friend. Jack led them in the sinner's prayer and welcomed them into the world of the brotherhood of Christ.

Mark came up to them. "We should be heading out. I'm getting calls from the IDF that they need some of our unique help back in Tel Aviv."

On the flight back Jack commented to Mark. "I'm wondering if the battle with the RHONE was important, but that the positive connection with General Sayif could be even more important in the near future."

Mark looked at his best friend in the world. "I don't know. The battle with the RHONE was necessary to get them off our backs and could go a long way with eliminating the RHONE all together."

As the first of the two aircraft touched down near the portal, Jack got a call from the IDF. "Mr. Malone?"

"Yes."

"This is Colonel Ephron. I am responding to a call from the Tel Aviv Police. They asked for our help when they ran into what they called "demonic activity" that they cannot overcome. Apparently my men have had no better luck with these creatures. I really need your team's help in this if you can spare them."

Jack got the address of the activity and asked Mark if he and Sarah could handle it. He needed to seriously pray and he knew that he probably needed to attend to that before anything else.

Mark nodded and keyed his microphone. He got Sarah and they quickly headed across town to the address in an IDF vehicle.

Mark's eyebrows rose when they arrived. He saw several IDF vehicles and two Police cars; but the address was an upper class hotel.

Running into the lobby they were urgently directed to floor six. The bellman running the elevator was taken back by the appearance of both Mark and Sarah. They were still in their combat gear with M-8s, grenades, and handguns, plus they still had the smells of battlefield combat with the associated grit and grime and demon stain. They looked so grimly professional and imposing that the bellman punched the sixth floor and decided in his mind that he would do whatever they asked without comment.

Exiting the elevator on floor six Mark and Sarah were suddenly buffeted by nearby gunfire, screams, and running people. Both of their spirits recoiled from several demons that were smashing their way down the hall toward the elevators.

Both Crossfire Team warriors began to pray and their armor and swords appeared. Mark took the lead against a large demon that resembled a botched medical experiment. It moved like an ape on its rear feet and its hands. From the waist up it was heavily built with large, strong arms and hands that were smashing and crushing everything it grabbed hold of. The head was grotesque with multiple eyes and a large drooling mouth full of pointed teeth. It was roaring and smashing IDF soldiers back out of its path.

Mark deliberately stepped in front of the creature and took a central guard position with his sword directly in front of him. The demon threw a large chunk of the wall at him and Mark stepped back. The demon used its extremely long arms and grabbed Mark's left arm to control him. Mark rotated his wrists to the left and brought the Sword of the Word down against the demon's right wrist. The sword bounced back without damaging the demon. While this surprised Mark it didn't affect his response to the attack.

Mark's arms were strongly muscled and he wrenched his arm out of the demon's grasp by stepping backward and doing a high circle rotation with his whole arm. As he broke free he switched hands with the sword and reached down and turned on the Force Generator.

The demon was now on him and it tried to bite Mark's head off. The Force Generator stopped the attack and Mark was able to ram his sword into the demon's black lined mouth. The sword came out the back of the demon's head and Mark twisted the blade to increase the damage.

The move caught the demon off-guard. It stepped back and pulled away from the blade. It was very irritated by the unexpected move and tried to jump on Mark to batter him to the ground. Mark continued to pray that Yahveh would give him to ability to destroy this spawn of Satan.

As the two squared up to each other, Sarah stepped forward and beheaded the creature with her sword. The body dropped to the floor with a crash and began to dissolve into foul-smelling green-black smoke.

A second demon that more resembled a human being, tried to strike Sarah with a black sword. Mark stepped around Sarah and ran it through from the side with his sword. That demon dropped immediately and dissolved. The third demon was confused as to which human to attack, which froze it in indecision. Both Sarah and Mark struck the creature and ended its confusion as it collapsed and dissipated.

Everyone was attempting to sort themselves out, tend to the injured soldiers, and quiet the terrorized hotel customers as Mark turned off his Force Generator. One of the IDF soldiers yelled to get Mark's attention and pointed to one of the rooms down the hall.

Mark and Sarah ran down there and stopped by the room. The soldier told them, "There are three disabled women in there with a demon. It locked the door. Mark turned and slammed against the door leading with his left shoulder. The door lock shattered and the door flew open.

A small, ugly demon was attempting to attack the three elderly American women who were confined to power chairs. It didn't have a sword but was attempting to grab the women so it could bite them. The demon displayed some serious dental work along the lines of triangular teeth and long, sharp fangs.

As the two warriors watched all three of the women whirl around and change places to confuse the little monster, one of the women smacked the demon backward with a cane, sort of like a game of motorized chair polo. The second woman was loudly praying for the protection of Yahveh for all of them and everyone else in the hotel. The third woman, an African-American woman with flowing black hair, shouted at the demon, "I rebuke you in the name of Jesus Christ, you slime of Satan."

The name of the Lord weakened the demon and the black woman took full advantage of that weakness. As she slammed into the demon with her power chair it clawed at her head and pulled the hair off of her head. She ignored the assault and kept her chair on full power. She carried the small demon across the room and smashed it into the far wall with the power chair.

Accompanied by shouts of "In the name of Jesus Christ and by His blood, you get him Jessica!" from the other two women, Jessica continued to reverse her chair off of the demon and then smash forward into him again. The demon was staring at the hair in its claws in confusion. It obviously didn't comprehend what a wig was. The little demon was slowly collapsing onto the floor from the constant wreaking by the Lord's name and the battering the black woman was giving him with her power chair. Jessica was grinning and yelling at the demon "I'm going to beat you down with an old shoe." The demon was weakening but wasn't out of action completely. It flung the wig it held across the room and tried to grab the woman's legs but couldn't catch hold of her in its weakened state.

Sarah stepped over and in front of Jessica's power chair as she backed up. Sarah ran her sword flowing with the Esteem of Yahveh through the demon which screamed its defiance as it dissolved into greasy black smoke.

Sarah stopped praying and her armor and sword disappeared. She turned to the astounded older woman and smiled. "We got him." Then she slapped a high-five with Jessica and walked back over to Mark. All three of the women were cheering and doing circles with their power chairs, high fiving each other. Mark shook his head in amazement, "I do believe that demon picked the wrong group to terrorize."

Sarah laughed, "You're so right. I think in this case it was the demon who was terrorized. It seems odd to me that they weren't scared of it."

Mark was praying about that inconsistency when he got a Word of Knowledge from the Lord. "They were full of the Holy Spirit who wasn't scared of the demon. These women have all given their lives to Yahshua and weren't frightened because of His peace."

As they walked back down the hall Mark became more serious and told his wife. I need to find out why these demons were attacking here and why my sword couldn't kill the first demon. Sarah nodded as they stopped to coordinate with the Police and the IDF forces.

CHAPTER TWENTY-FOUR

Jack went directly to his apartment in the subterranean base. He was surprised that Laura wasn't there already, but the call on his spirit was critical. He knelt next to his bed and entered into prayer with the Father of the Universe. He continued to praise Yahveh and Yahshua as he knelt on the floor.

Jack felt he had many questions which didn't seem to have any apparent answers. Especially after hearing from Mark. He felt a presence and opened his eyes to see the angel Rose floating several feet away. Feeling relief Jack smiled, "Hello Rose, how goes the battle?"

Rose stared at him for several seconds. Then a soft smile lit up her face. "The battle continues, Jack. How are you holding up?"

Jack thought for a few seconds and replied. "I am blessed and highly favored. I am where I am supposed to be, doing the will of the Father. I couldn't ask for more for myself, but, I do have some questions. Are you here in response to my prayers?"

Rose slowly nodded her head. "That, and some other things, also." She looked at Jack again. "Do you remember the time you were knocked out of an airplane and I caught you and brought you to Earth?"

Jack nodded as he remembered that event. As he fell, Rose appeared and surrounded them both with a bubble of energy. He'd felt that it was like she'd folded her wings around him. Except Angels didn't have wings. As the two of them came to Earth they had gone through three or four walls of a home, leaving perfectly clean seven foot in diameter holes. "We made a real mess of that house we went through."

Rose nodded, "That house belonged to one of the people that became one of the enemy you faced in the battle with the RHONE today."

Jack thought about that, "Well, in ancient Jewish wisdom there is no such thing as coincidence, and then this is part of the Most High's plan. What is the significance of that?

Rose looked at something far away. "Carl Rosteen is the man we are talking about. He is a financier that Marco Marino has selected as one of his world bankers for the One World Government. He is prosecuting the efforts to eliminate the Crossfire Team and was in the command post to watch the Team be destroyed. You will understand the spiritual connection in a minute."

Jack thought about that for several minutes. He knew that Rose was a messenger of Yahveh and also a warrior for the Heavenly realms. This angel had been a constant companion of the Crossfire Team almost since its inception. Rose had supplied essential information at key points in the team's development. He trusted the beautiful angel and her support for the team. He was aware that she had a great deal of information that she could not divulge to him because he couldn't comprehend the information in his four dimensional mind. He carefully asked her, "Rose, why did the demons attack the tourist hotel today?"

She smiled because she obviously understood that Jack was attempting to make the most of their brief conversation time. "Many things the enemy does are incomprehensible to us as well as to humans. The Most High understands all things but like the information I can reveal to you is limited due to your capability to understand, The Most High also has to constrain what He can, or will, divulge to the angels for the same reason. Some things are so complicated and intertwined we can't understand them. I am not privy to why they attacked that particular hotel when they did, but it will be revealed to both of us in time."

Jack nodded, "All right, I can easily understand those limitations. Can you tell me why Mark's sword could not defeat the demon in the hall but Sarah's could?"

Rose frowned slightly. "That question speaks to the complexity issue in all spiritual battles. All things in Heaven and on Earth are in constant motion and are being re-developed on both sides of the battle. The enemy of mankind is attempting to find a defense to counter the power of your armor and your sword which is a power of Yahveh. Your sword has a particular essence or frequency of the Most High's response to your prayers during battle. It seems that they have found a means to counter that power. But, only for one demon and only for Mark's sword. It didn't stop Sarah's sword in the least."

Rose floated closer to Jack and stared at him intently. "There are hundreds of constantly changing factors involved in such a match-up. I doubt that they could have a particular demon with that particular defense capability that would specifically battle Mark again. The mere fact that it didn't work against Sarah's sword will probably make it unusable to them for future battles and they will discard it. They aren't creative and don't have a lot of patience. But, remember, the enemy will continue to seek ways to blunt your team's capabilities, so beware."

Jack contemplated the immense number of possibilities involved in making just that one match-up in the dynamic variables of battle involving eleven or more dimensions. He realized his mind couldn't conceive of any usable information at the four-dimension human level. He decided to dismiss the "fluke" that allowed one demon to block Yahweh's power from one warrior in one instance. Realizing the capability of Yahveh and His angels to foresee things, he decided that he would ask Yahveh about any upcoming anomalies in the future.

He looked back at the angel. "Thank you, Rose, for your help. Does the Most High have any wisdom for us as to what we need to do at this point?"

She smiled, "In a moment we'll get to that. First, I told you that I would show you why Carl Rosteen is involved after we damaged his dwelling in your fall. Keep in mind that I could have caught you in the air and stayed right where I caught you."

Rose's eyes sparkled, "Carl Rosteen was an up and coming mechanical engineer with a family and a good job at the airport you flew out of that day. But, his heart was far from Yahveh and his demonically-induced passion was to rule. His marriage was very shaky because he ruled his wife like a slave and demanded utter obedience from her and his two children. Some of the "religions" on Earth espouse those characteristics. Because Yahveh knew that if they stayed as a family unit, Carl would eventually kill his family and destroy their futures for disobedience to his orders, the Most High directed me to save you and at the same time damage his home. When we fell from the sky and literally went through four walls of his house, we left four seven feet in diameter holes. Doesn't sound like too much, does it?"

Jack thought about that and couldn't see the future and therefore the rationale for the house damage.

Rose nodded at him. "After you left and Carl Rosteen came home, he found his home empty and his family gone in defiance to his command to stay at home. His wife had taken the children to her mother and left him a note that she was never coming back to him; and she had already filed for divorce and a restraining order. With the unseen urgings from the demon that watched us damage the house, Rosteen immediately was deceived into believing, in his mind, that the huge holes that destroyed his house were the reason she left."

"Actually, she had left hours before we got there. But, following his line of reason, and directed by demonic forces, he determined that the holes were caused by the Crossfire Team. He somehow decided that the entire blame for losing his family was due to the team. After that, it was easy for the demons to steer him into joining the RHONE and eventually to become a leader in the fight against you in Jordan."

Jack nodded, "Okay, but, why did the Most High have to allow all that to transpire?"

Rose smiled, "Because Carl Rosteen's daughter is destined to become a widely renowned source of Yahshua's mercy and healing for hundreds of very dangerously dysfunctional families during the tribulations. The Most High would not allow her life to be ended by her demonically controlled, earthly father because of her future value to the Kingdom. Do you see now that many things are intertwined to ensure the path the Most High has determined for the people that do, or will, love and serve Him and the Kingdom?"

Jack smiled, "I do, but I don't pretend to understand how the Father arranges situations and outcomes years in advance with the apparent randomness of humanity."

Rose absolutely grinned at him. "There is no sequential time in Heaven and the arrangement of events by the Most

High is too complicated for me to understand. But, He has been doing this constantly for all of the billions of people on the Earth since the Earth was populated. He created the Earth, the people, and time. I think, to the Most High, randomness is simply another pattern He controls or counters in advance."

These concepts left Jack in total awe of Yahveh. Jack nodded his agreement.

Rose let some of the fierce white color overcome the peaceful golden color and spoke the word of Yahveh. *"My son, begin to take the battle to the RHONE. I have started the internal upheaval and rebellion in the RHONE and your continued successes will further erode their leader's control. They have taken something of great importance to you. But, be brave and courageous as you battle for My Esteem and My Kingdom and you will overcome them."*

Before she faded from Jack's view, Rose added an important statement. "Jack, remember that as Satan's tool, the anti-Christ, Marco Marino, "wants to be" the head of the entire world. He is not and never will be an ultimate leader. There are many groups in the world that despise him and will resist him. Those groups will include a majority of Americans, especially in the Military."

Jack considered that and lowered his concept of importance concerning the man. He had begun to think of the anti-Christ as a direct competitor to Yahveh Himself on Earth at this time. Jack realized that Rose's statement was designed to adjust this thought in his mind to the correct balance. He tried to figure out what the RHONE had taken from him without success.

CHAPTER TWENTY-FIVE

Jack walked into the War Room to find Mark working with Sarah, Alexis, and David. The abbreviated Core Team was searching all available on-line sources for information concerning the present movements of the RHONE. Mark looked up at Jack and nodded to him. He suggested a ten-minute break to the other three warriors. They got up and headed for the kitchen and a snack. Mark rotated in his chair and smiled at Jack. "You look concerned. What's up?"

Jack summarized his encounter with the angel Rose. "Now that we were able to defeat the RHONE forces with a tiny percentage of troops compared to their numbers and equipment, we are now tasked to attack the RHONE wherever possible. We also need to discontinue our use the Force Generators for the time being."

Mark nodded his understanding. "I already collected all of them, except yours and Laura's, and returned them to the vault. I understood that they were ours primarily to prove the Father's might to the RHONE and their leaders during this one lop-sided battle."

Jack took his Force Generator unit and belt off and handed them to Mark. "Give Laura a call and have her bring her unit to you. I really don't have any idea where she is or what she is doing at present." He sat down at his station and started to run over all the status reports.

Mark keyed his combat microphone and called Laura. Not getting an answer he entered her name in the base locator. It came up blank which was unusual. Mark called Charlie Wu and asked him to locate Laura.

Charlie said, "Wait one." Fifteen seconds later he told Mark, "I can't locate her."

Mark frowned, "Will you check outside the base in Tel Aviv for me?"

Charlie was very serious. "Mark, I can't find any sign of her anywhere on the planet."

Signing off from Charlie, Mark got Jack's attention. "I think we've got a problem here. Charlie can't locate Laura at all, anywhere."

Jack realized Mark's concern. Charlie normally could locate anybody anywhere in the known Universe with the medallion they all wore. Thinking back in time Jack realized he hadn't seen his wife since the battle with the RHONE. He knew that he had been tied up with the Jordanians and from that he had gone directly back to the base. He had thought that Laura was on the other aircraft as the team returned to the base. He couldn't understand why he hadn't checked on her. Then he realized that the enemy had deliberately distracted him and had kept him from thinking about his wife's safety. Now he knew what the valuable thing was that the enemy had taken from him.

Jack told Mark, "Contact the other team members and see if they remember where they last saw her." His concern flared into a near panic based on fear for her. But, he recalled the promises of Yahveh and didn't give into these forces. He prayed for her safety and return and the fear faded. Nevertheless, his heart was hurt and he dedicated everything he had, into finding her and rescuing her.

Mark polled the other Core Team members and turned to face Jack. "Sarah remembers her battling the last of the remaining demons after the Father closed their rifts. But, she doesn't recall seeing her after that."

Jack considered the possibilities. "Well, I don't think the demons could have kidnapped her because they couldn't even get back to their own dimension. That leaves only Yahveh as the one capable of translating her off of this world."

Mark tipped his head to one side. "Why not human intervention?"

Jack grinned a harsh grin. "Because she still had her Force Generator on her and knowing her capabilities, I doubt that any human that was on that field of battle could have overcome her."

Mark wasn't convinced. "Don't you think Rose would have spoken of Laura being whisked off to Heaven again?"

Jack shrugged his shoulders. "Rose said that the enemy...no, she said the RHONE had taken something of great value to me." He thought for a few seconds. "I'm going to double check our apartment and pray for the Father's help in locating her."

Mark nodded and then thought of another possibility. Calling Charlie back, he asked if the computer guru could track Laura's Force Generator. It would be the only one, other than Jack's that was not in the vault."

Jack ran to their apartment and carefully searched it. Then as a dread worry tried to consume him, he dropped to his knees. As he prayed a heartfelt plea for the Father's help and entered into the closeness to the Creator, he realized that he was no longer fearful.

As he began to pray, his communicator announced an incoming call. Jack felt a stab of momentary irritation but forgot it immediately. "Hello?"

Charlie Wu's voice was also concerned. "Jack I know what happened to Laura. Can you come to my office, immediately?"

Jack agreed and told Charlie to also get the rest of the Core Team there by the time he got there.

Taking the elevator on the living room floor Jack shot up four levels and exited at the Comm/Sec floor. He went immediately to Charlie's office and found the rest of the Core Team already there.

"What do you have, Charlie?"

Charlie pointed at the large screen in his office. "I had Crayton identify the last time our cameras saw Laura. This is what I found."

The crystal clear video wasn't focused just on Laura but everyone that was battling the last of the demons in Jordan. Laura had just eliminated the ugly demon in her area. Her armor and sword faded from sight and she was just turning away from where the rifts had been when she disappeared from sight.

Charlie ran the part where she disappeared, back in slow speed and stopped the video as Laura started to turn to her right. It advanced one small division at a time, probably less than a tenth of a second. Laura suddenly faded from the video, starting from her back, and three tenths of a second later she was gone.

Jack was beginning to get exasperated. He barked at the computer guru. "Charlie! What in Heaven's name is going on?"

Megan Cole spoke up. "I see what's happening here. Mr. Wu, would you run that last part again but stop when Laura is only half disappeared?"

Charlie did as he was asked and Megan stepped up to the computer keyboard in front of him. "May I?" She asked.

Charlie slipped out of his seat and nodded to her.

Megan typed a short series of commands and the picture stretched horizontally. When it did this it developed a thin gray line running just from over Laura's head and going all the way to the ground. Megan nodded her head. "Take a close look at this line." She pointed at the abnormality. This is a neat little trick called a "sand trap" in spy talk. Apparently there was a person or a device lying in wait and it tripped when Laura's armor faded from view. This is a Mylar net that looks exactly like sand and that's why you can't differentiate it from the sand all around her unless you look very closely."

Megan turned around to face Jack. What it did was to hide Laura from our view. I can only assume that the operator of this device was able to subdue Laura almost instantaneously because she doesn't struggle. They probably used a stun-gun charge or some fast acting gas."

She typed some more commands and the picture enlarged Laura's face. Megan was nodding again. "Look at her eyes. They are rolling up and her mouth is starting to drop open. Probably a contact gas that works in milliseconds to render the person being caught unconscious instantly.

Megan advanced the picture two more clicks and it was obvious to them all that Laura was completely knocked out by whatever the attackers did to her as she disappeared behind the netting.

Megan reset the size of the picture and stepped the video forward enough to allow them all to see the net collapsing back to lie flatly on the sand around Laura and seem to become just part of the desert again.

Jack's face was hardened and his eyes were an icy green. "All right, first, who did this?"

Mark spoke up. "I believe that the only groups that could do this would be the RHONE or the Jordanians. I would have to lean toward the RHONE because they were the only ones there long enough to set such a trap in a place near where the demons appeared."

Sarah asked him, "How would they know that the demons were even going to be there?"

Mark pointed out that the demons ran the RHONE soldiers and could have let them think that it was their idea to put it there.

David shook his head. "Let us assume it was the RHONE and they just waited until we left before they spirited her out of there. We have to find where they took her and very quickly, too. Remember, she was wearing a Force Generator unit and now the RHONE has possession of it."

Jack looked at Mark and Mark shrugged his shoulders. "It won't do them any good. They can't make it work regardless of what they do."

Jack shook his head. "True, but, they could severely damage or possibly even kill Laura in an attempt to make her show them how to operate it which she can't do anyway."

Charlie had been thinking about Laura's capture. "Hang on a minute. Just because we left that doesn't mean we can't see what they did after we left." He gently pushed Megan out of his chair and sat down. He typed very quickly for several minutes. He waited a few minutes and then said, "Look at the screen."

From the clarity and angle of the picture it was obviously being shot from a KH-11 Keyhole Satellite. The area of desert was deserted and the shot was covering a large area when there was some activity near the closer, right hand edge of the picture. Charlie refocused the view on that area and brought it closer. Sand was being moved from below and suddenly a ten-foot ditch opened up as the cover was thrown over to the side. Two men emerged from the large, grave-like hole carrying a body bag between them. They laid the body bag on the sand and proceeded to refill the hole very quickly.

They rolled up what had to be the Mylar netting and laid it next to the body bag. One of the men squatted down next to the bag and unzipped it a few feet. He reached in and kept his hand and arm in the bag while he consulted his watch on his other wrist. He nodded to the first man and re-zipped the bag.

At that point a large vehicle pulled up next to them. They loaded the bag into the back seat of the vehicle and got in themselves. The vehicle pulled away as Charlie widened the area of coverage. Charlie sped up the video until they had followed the truck to the beach and watched as the men loaded the bag onto an LST and took it out to a freighter sitting off-shore.

Charlie was just able to see the two men take the bag into the ship before the satellite coverage moved too far away from the area and out of range to see anything more of those movements. He backed the coverage up until he could see the name on the back of the ship. The name was the "Condor Pride" and the ship's registration was American.

CHAPTER TWENTY-SIX

Jack thought it through and then prayed for guidance. He felt led to proceed as he desired. At least the Father didn't tell him not to do what he had planned. He looked at the intense faces in front of him.

"Okay, here's how it is going to go down. Charlie, find the "Condor Pride" and keep us apprised as to where it is going and when it will get there. Also, see if you can get sufficient satellite coverage to ensure that the RHONE didn't off-load Laura as they sailed."

He looked at Mark, "Okay buddy. I want to hit that ship with everything we can to rescue Laura. Everybody that can volunteer is welcome. That includes the IDF, the Mossad, and our SOG. I need a plan in less than half an hour. We can't use our Force Generators but we can be soldiers. Work that out as you prep for the assault. Get Su Li and Mike White to commandeer two of the Israeli F-22s and have them give us maximum air cover. This whole thing could be a trap and if it is, I don't want anybody from the other side left alive to tell about how it wasn't sufficient to stop us from getting Laura and her Force Generator off of that ship."

Sarah just nodded her head and stood up. "Then let's load up."

Jack tipped his head to the right. "Don't you think we should give your husband some time to develop a workable plan?"

Sarah shook her head. "He's already got the plan. We go find the ship and kill everybody on it except for Laura. That's the basis for all of his plans. Or, haven't you noticed?"

Mark stood up. "It's a good plan, I like it. Let's go get Laura back."

David grinned. "This is just like a U.S. Marine T-shirt I saw in Tel Aviv a few days ago." He quoted the saying on the shirt. "Join the U.S. Marine Corp, visit exotic foreign lands, meet interesting people. Kill them."

Alexis nodded her head, "I like it, too. Get me one."

Again, Jack was amazed at these people he thought he knew. They were willing to put their lives on the line against unknown but probably heavy odds, and do it with a smile. "Simply unbelievable" he said.

Twenty minutes later the team broke into two groups and loaded onto two black MH-53J Pave Low helicopters they had "borrowed" from the Israelis. The Pave Low's mission was to perform low-level, long-range, undetected penetration into denied areas, day or night, in adverse weather, for infiltration, ex-filtration and resupply of special operations forces. They had been decommissioned in 2008 but still worked fine for black ops missions.

The MH-53J Pave Low III heavy-lift helicopter was the largest and most powerful helicopter in the U.S. and Israeli Air Force inventories, and it was also the most technologically advanced helicopter in the world in its day. Its terrain-following, terrain-avoidance radar and forward-looking infrared sensor, along with a projected map display, enable the crew to follow terrain contours and avoid obstacles, making low-level penetration possible. This would be critical to their mission this time.

These two helicopters were also equipped with armor plating, and three .50 caliber machine guns. The choppers could each transport 38 troops and easily contained the forty-six members of the Crossfire Team.

Having gotten gently but firmly rebuffed by the Israeli Air Force as to "borrowing" two of their multimillion dollar F-22s, Su Li and Mike White were piloting the two Pave Lows.

As the two aircraft exited the aircraft corridor and flew out into the gathering darkness over the Mediterranean Sea, they headed south and slightly east to fly down the Gulf of Aqaba and over the Red Sea. They could quickly intercept the "Condor Pride". The flight would only take an hour and fifty minutes.

Mark connected his communications gear to Jack's and told him the plan. "We are going to come in from both the front and the back at wave top level. These birds are quiet enough that we will be on them before they know it. Three things are going to happen immediately. First, we are going to use two LAWs to remove the antennas from the ship so they can't call for help. Second, we are going to kill everyone in the pilot room and its wing stations. Third, we're going to disembark half the troops at either end of the ship."

"Since we're going to make a big bang at the start, we don't have to worry about being stealthy after that. We just need to keep the survivors off-balance long enough to let us get into the ship and find and rescue Laura. After that we can sweep the ship and eliminate all the rats."

Jack shook his head. "I don't know, Mark. Yahveh told us to put the fear of Him into these troops so that they will start the internal revolt that will eventually destroy the RHONE. If we kill them all off, how is that going to accomplish Yahveh's plan?"

Mark smiled, "Something you don't know. The Mossad told Charlie who told me that there are only about two hundred men on this ship along with Laura. Also, the Mossad informer is also not on this ship. The other twelve hundred troops were moved to another transport ship that left later. That ship is several hours behind this one."

Jack thought about the new situation. "Okay, do we just cut down two hundred armed men?"

Mark was about to speak when one of the Israeli Air Force machine gunners tapped him on the shoulder and pointed at his ear.

Mark detached his comm gear from Jack and replaced it into the ship's comm service. He listened for several minutes and spoke one word. He then hooked up with Jack again. "Several new things have come up."

"First, the "powers that be" in Israel have decided that they like Laura better than you and therefore they are weighing in on the side of a precision rescue rather than my rather clumsy effort. We are to hold back while some of their Special Ops boys clear the way for us. Then we will be "accompanied" by a force of fifty IDF Spec Ops personnel as we sweep the ship for Laura."

Jack smiled at Mark, "I have to give way to a superior directive."

Five minutes later the choppers leveled off just above the waves and a different set of Pave Lows flew past them.

Jack took off his back pack and pulled out his combat tablet. He put in a call to Charlie Wu. "Charlie, the Israeli's are going to prepare the beach for us. Can you penetrate their communications and get us the pictures of their attack?"

Charlie's affirmative was followed immediately by a video feed to Jack's tablet. Mark moved over beside Jack and watched with him as the Israeli choppers approached the slowly steaming liner. The two Israeli choppers rose up to deck level as they reached the rear of the ship. Their cameras showed several silenced rifles decimating the deck crew and the lookouts. Then an orange/green laser flashed out and cut off anything that looked like an antenna while the silenced rifles eliminated the crew and the captain of the ship in the pilot house. Then the two helicopters settled to the fore and aft decks and troops jumped out and advanced on the passenger and crew areas.

Mark smiled, then got up and did the "stand up" signal. Jack stowed the tablet and joined the others waiting to disembark. There was a heavy thump and the rear loading ramp dropped to the deck. The troops surged out of their aircraft and formed up.

Quickly joining up with the Israeli Spec Ops personnel, the teams moved quickly into the superstructure of the ship which continued to steam along even though there wasn't anybody at the controls.

Jack and Mark split up with ten men and women each and headed for the passenger deck, the most likely area to find Laura. They let the silenced rifles of the Israelis eliminate any of the enemy they ran into. Mark was sure their combat time would soon come.

Jack and Alexis opened a door and caught an officer literally with his pants down. Jack asked the only important question. Where was Laura?

The officer looked confused. "Who is Laura?" he asked. He told them he had no idea if there was a "hostage" or where they would be held. Mark told him to put his pants back on, and watched him carefully. With twenty heavily-armed American and Israeli forces right behind him he wasted no time in showing them the basically deserted cabin areas. Mark was about to handcuff the man to the closest object when gunfire rained down at them from above. Jumping back to the shelter of the decking above them Jack and many of the troops were safe from the guns. Several of the Israeli troops hid behind the structure on the deck and returned fire. The battle was short-lived as several more of the Israeli troops ran up the starboard stairs to the next level and ensured that no RHONE troops lived up there anymore.

A major gun battle erupted on the crew deck with gunfire and grenade explosions shaking the ship. It lasted less than eight minutes. The Israeli officer in charge got a comm message and told Jack that the ship was theirs and the enemy had been eliminated to the last man. There were several injuries to both the Israelis and Crossfire Team personnel but none were life-threatening.

Jack's comm unit pulsed for his attention. He answered and listened to Charlie Wu. "Jack, I've just gotten more information. Laura is not on that ship. I was able to tap into the American satellite, Megalith, and its coverage after our Keyhole flew out of the area. It's obvious to me that the RHONE knew about the Keyhole coverage and played us with it. In less than two minutes after we lost the Keyhole picture, the RHONE troops brought Laura back out and loaded her onto a helicopter which lifted off and headed back toward the Jordanian coast. I'll track it and find out where they went."

Jack sighed, "Okay Charlie. We'll be airborne in a few minutes. Get us a destination as quickly as you can."

Jack had told the Israeli Spec Ops officer about the new information. "It seems we just killed a lot of people without suitable cause. This isn't going to play well in the News Media. They tricked us into attacking this ship. I think this might have been a trap or a diversion to distract us from finding Laura."

Jack shook his head. "We're going to try to track the helicopter they took my wife away in and then go get her. We really appreciate your help and I apologize for falling for their trick. Tell your High Command that I will accept the blame for this debacle and we'll keep your presence here secret.

The Commando just nodded. "I'm afraid that you won't be free of us quite that quickly. I have relayed this information to our base. The word there is to stay with your troops until we resolve the matter."

Jack realized that the Israeli Military wasn't caving into the anti-Christ and wasn't going to allow indiscriminate

Military attacks on their citizens without an adequate response. "I, and all my troops, am very grateful and appreciative of your bravery and dedication on behalf of our interests. You do realize that we might run into even greater odds where we are heading?"

The Commando grinned. "I hope so. The less of these RHONE troops in the world the better", He said. Then he used his communications mic and talked in Hebrew for several seconds. He looked back at Jack just as the ship lost headway as the engines died. "Get your troops loaded, we just opened several new bilge gates to the sea. This ship will settle to the bottom of the sea in the next half hour and take its story with it."

CHAPTER TWENTY-SEVEN

After a solid headcount all four choppers lifted off the already slanting deck and formed up in a four-on-one flight and headed South toward Jordan. Looking back as they gained altitude Jack could see the ship was rapidly sinking at the rear where the weight of the engines multiplied the weight of the water flooding into the bottom of the hull. As the troops fell to cleaning and reloading their weapons and tending to their injured, Jack made a call to Charlie.

"Tell me you have found that chopper and where it is going." Jack's voice reflected the concern he had for Laura.

Charlie came back with, "Yes Sir, I have video of the chopper with Laura on it after it left the ship four hours ago. I am following the video of it as it flew toward Petra, Jordan. I will keep a close eye on it to ensure that they didn't do another swap. Here are the coordinates for Petra. I'll update them as time changes." Jack rang off and thought about why RHONE troops would take their hostage to Jordan. That just didn't make sense. He gave the coordinates to Su Li and she advised the other three aircraft. She adjusted her compass heading and was matched by the changes in the other choppers. They lost another twenty minutes refueling in air.

Jack was about to tell Mark about the direction when his phone chirped again. He picked it up and keyed it. "Hello?"

Charlie's voice sounded frantic on the phone. "Jack! At a point in the video, two hours and thirty minutes ago I saw the crew throw Laura out of the helicopter. They were at four thousand feet when she was ejected. She fell to the desert right into an area that is under fire between several groups of Jordanian nomads."

Jack shook his head, "How sure are you that it was Laura?"

Charlie softly said, "She was out of the body bag and I could see her face. Strangely, it looked to me like she was smiling."

"Give me the coordinates and still track that chopper. I want to know where it goes."

Su Li locked onto the new coordinates and with barely controlled anger; she told Jack that they would be there is less than thirty minutes at the rate they were flying. Jack's heart sank as he realized that by the time they got there Laura would have been on the ground for over three hours. In the middle of a fire fight between tribes. He sat back in the web seating and closed his eyes. He prayed that the Father would protect her. He had no confirmation that she was still in the world of the living but was intrigued by Charlie's comment about her smiling.

Jack got on the all aircraft comm line and told the others what was happening and what he wanted to do. "I will take flights two and three with me to where she fell. There seems to be some inter-tribal warfare going on at that location. Chopper flight four stay on that RHONE chopper. I want their heads!"

Mark came on the line. "All troops check your weapons and stand by for ground combat."

Less than twenty-two minutes later all three choppers landed near the place where Laura had fallen and moved out in a three prong attack formation. The main group headed for Laura's position while the other two groups moved in flanking movements to the right and the left of the center column.

Jack was about to speak to Mark when their column came under fire from somewhere ahead of them to their left. Everyone hit the ground and sought whatever shelter they could find.

Mark checked and found that three people had been hit in the first volley. Body armor had taken the sting out of that. He then started troops hop-scotching forward. One group would lay down suppression fire while the other group advanced. Then they would switch and the second group would pass the first one while it provided covering fire.

Contact with the tribal fighters happened suddenly and there were a lot of bullets in the air. Several minutes later the only firing was from the advancing force. The rest of the troops moved forward cautiously. The small group of tribal fighters had been overwhelmed by the superior fire from the commandos. Jack saw that they were poorly equipped with old rifles and no body armor at all.

Even though it was a dark night in the desert the troops fanned out looking for any sign of Laura. He looked up and realized that the fourth helicopter had returned from looking for the RHONE helicopter. As they advanced, Jack sent out an all troops call for coordination of the search. He was about to set up a grid search when he got an incoming call on the combat communications web. He was shocked when he heard, "Jack, this is Laura, can you please come and get me? I'm about six hundred yards in front of you and I'll try to fire a flare."

Jack was so relieved and a flood of joy overrode any caution. "Laura, thank Yahveh you're alive."

She came back with, "I'm alive, but only through the Father's Mercy and Grace. I've got at least a half dozen Bedouin tribesmen trying to haul me away on a cart. So get the lead out and stop them, please."

Jack told Mark, "She's alive and communicating. About six hundred yards ahead of us."

Su Li overrode Mark's answer. "Jack, I just overflew the group you're referring to. I'll try to stop their forward motion and not hit Laura."

Jack saw a triple track of .50 caliber tracers' lance down out of the sky just ahead of them. He took off running toward the fire from the sky. Everyone in their group raced after him through the dark. They had brought NVG gear for the assault on the ship and were able to make progress without running into obstacles in the sand.

Mark had kept pace with Jack and warned him, "There are people just ahead of us on the right and they're firing at the helicopter."

Jack hit the all troops switch, "Take them out selectively. Watch out for Laura."

There were less than eight fighters and they died almost without knowing what killed them. Jack had fitted a flare round into his 40mm grenade launcher and fired it almost straight up, the flare suddenly lit up the area like daylight. Sarah found Laura and the cart first. Laura was sitting on the cart with multiple ropes over and around her. But none of the ropes were actually touching her.

Sarah ran up to her and stared at the captive woman. Laura keyed her comm and asked Sarah to cut her free. Jack and Mark and two of the Israeli commandos arrived and helped cut and remove the ropes.

Laura grinned and jumped off of the cart. She rearranged herself and hugged Sarah. Then she jumped into Jack's arms. Jack realized how much he had been afraid of losing her and held her tight.

Mark called all eighty of the troops together and radioed for pick up at his green flare which he threw to the ground about twenty yards away from them.

Jack asked her, "How are you? Did they hurt you?"

Laura was obviously very tired but shook her head. "No, they tried to hurt me but I did a lot more damage to them after I woke up." Mark smiled, "This I gotta hear about."

The four helicopters landed and the troops reloaded onto their original rides. Before they left, Jack again shook hands with the officer leading the Israeli Commandos. "I can't tell you how much we owe you and your people for helping us rescue my wife. I am in your debt. Please convey these feeling to your leadership. Also, have them set up a meeting so we can coordinate as to any discussion about today's activities."

The Israeli Commando smiled. "We are glad that you got your wife back and anything we contributed to the activities was a small piece of repayment for your efforts for Israel over the last few years. I will file a complete report to my leadership but the only meeting that may happen will be to determine how she survived her ordeals. I, for one are curious as to how she survived a four thousand foot fall without being hurt. As far as the rest of the world is concerned, our activities tonight never happened. Stay well and Slalom, Shabbat."

Jack replied, "Shabbat, Slalom my friend."

The two men ran to their helicopters and all four aircraft lifted off of the sands. One of the choppers started taking ground fire but the .50 caliber machine guns responded and shut down the shooters.

The four choppers avoided the Jordanian radar and a flight of war planes and flew for the next two hours taking them back to Tel Aviv and to the undersea base.

CHAPTER TWENTY-EIGHT

On the flight back Laura had fallen asleep in Jack's arms. When they got to the base Jack got her to their apartment. She woke up long enough to shed her combat clothes and take a quick shower. She then climbed into bed at 6 A.M. Saturday morning.

Jack watched as she woke up around three p.m. the next afternoon. He grinned at her when she noticed him sitting in a chair near the bed. Thirty minutes later she had showered and fixed her hair and makeup. Jack waited patiently and then escorted her down to the War Room. Everyone that saw them smiled at her.

Smiling back, she went to her work space in the circular desk. She clicked on the recorder and started her debrief with many rapt listeners.

"I had just finished fighting some of the last demons on the battlefield in Jordan and my sword and armor disappeared. I was starting to walk back toward where Jack was when everything went black. I don't remember much, maybe some weird half-dreams, until I woke up as a captive on a helicopter. The first thing I did was a quick inventory. The captors, who I think were RHONE operatives, had taken all my weapons and strapped me into a web seat. When I woke up two men were watching me intently. One of them started interrogating me and trying to find out how we had been able to survive the heavy combat in the desert. I told them that it was the protection of Yahveh."

"They didn't like that answer and were pretty ticked off at me. I didn't want to mention the Force Generator for two reasons. First, it wouldn't do me any good because they couldn't use it. And, second, they hadn't taken it off of me, probably because it was small and the LED was dark. Actually, I think that the Father blinded their eyes to it."

When they were distracted by a sudden sideward jerk of the aircraft, I reached down and turned it on. There was no difference except I could feel that weird, all-over, minute electric current feeling when I'm wearing it and it is active. Knowing that they could possibly restrain me so that I couldn't take advantage of the field, I started releasing the straps holding me in the seat."

She stopped to take a drink of water and collect her memories. "I had cleared the last strap when one of the two men saw what I was doing and threatened me with a handgun. I stood up and ignored him. He fired six rounds at me which the field absorbed and then tried to grab me. I was angry by now and snap-kicked him into the far wall of the chopper. I was almost to the door of the aircraft when the second man smashed into the field attempting to capture me again. His weight and force were sufficient to knock me through the door and out of the chopper. He also fell out of the aircraft and just like me, he didn't have a parachute."

She smiled at Jack. "The fall reminded me of the one we deliberately used in Zyngola a while back. I wasn't even a little worried while I was falling. I hit the sand of the desert directly in the middle of a raging fire fight between Bedouin tribes. The field took all of the energy of the fall and I created a hole in the ground about ten feet deep. I must have blown sand a hundred feet into the air when I impacted the ground."

She smiled. "Of course, I was trapped in the hole and within a few minutes I had a dozen rifles pointed at me. I ignored them and sat down to await events. The tribal leader decided I was offensive and had one of his fighters shoot me. Needless to say that didn't work. After a lot of work, they decided to bury me in the hole. This wouldn't be good because they would cut off my supply of air. I stood up and started to move in any direction I could. I started widening the hole I was in and apparently I was on the side of a sand dune because one side of the hole collapsed and I was joined in the hole by three fighters and the tribal leader. Talk about panic! They personally dug the hole out the side of the dune and I walked out right behind them. As soon as I emerged they threw ropes around me so that I couldn't continue to move."

Laura laughed, "We were in a stalemate. I had no way to hurt them, they couldn't hurt me. So they decided to take me back to their village and see if they couldn't find a way to figure out what was going on with me. It had gotten dark by then and it took another two hours to get a cart and tie me down on it. We started moving slowly because they didn't have any night vision gear. There were several fire fights with other tribes which I sat and watched as bullets killed several of my moving group. Then all at once my comm device, which the RHONE people had also somehow missed, got an all-troop call from Jack. I responded and he and the rest of the team, along with some Israelis, came and rescued me."

Jack nodded, "That was definitely the Grace of Yahveh that they didn't see the Force Generator unit or your comm unit. Actually, that is very much unlike them. It had to be God. I would have thought that they would have taken everything off of you while you were unconscious."

Mark commented, "I believe you are right and that was a further demonstration of Yahveh's Will to show the RHONE that they cannot beat Him at anything. Otherwise, there is no way they would have missed those things."

Megan Cole smiled at the leaders of the Crossfire Team. "I would like to add my agreement about Yahveh's part in saving Laura. I would think that a four-thousand-foot fall would have resulted in a really severe deceleration when she hit the ground."

Jack shook his head. "No Megan, the field doesn't work that way. The field absorbs energy, including the energy related to deceleration. I can personally attest to that fact, as can Mark, David, and Sarah."

Megan grinned, "Than I'd like to try that someday."

Mark nodded, "Maybe one day you will get the opportunity."

CHAPTER TWENTY-NINE

Jack called Charlie Wu. "Charlie, did you continue to track that chopper after Laura exited it?"

Charlie's disembodied voice was heard by everyone in the War Room. "Yes, I did. But, it turned out to be a dead end, literally. It seems that when Laura went out of the body of the chopper along with the person who was probably the chief pilot of the aircraft, their weight caused the helicopter to tilt to that side. As they exited, Laura apparently hit the rotor blade tip, since the rotor disk was down on that side. Reviewing the record of the incident, Laura is knocked in the direction of the rear of the helicopter by the contact and the rotor blades began to wobble."

"Unfortunately for the remaining crew, the damaged rotor got them about two miles further on and then disintegrated completely. Since the rotor is the wing for a helicopter, the body of the chopper fell the same four thousand feet that Laura had several miles before and made a similar hole in the desert although it was accompanied by smoke and fire."

Mark spoke up, "So, do you have anything to follow?"

Charlie's voice took on a brighter tone and you could almost hear the smile. "Aahh, which would be a yes. Crayton was still following my programming and after the first ship sank and the helicopter crashed. Crayton continued to track the second ship to where it docked in Egypt. The RHONE troops and what you left of their gear is being unloaded prior to being trucked, I think, through the desert toward Tripoli"

Jack chuckled, "Thanks, Charlie. Give Sarah those coordinates and let us ponder an adequate response for their kidnapping of Laura."

Mark raised an eyebrow. "What have you got in mind, O' Great Leader?"

Jack prayed for guidance and came up short in his planning when he listened to the Lord tell him that Yahshua would repay the RHONE for Laura's abduction. He looked at

Mark, "I really don't have anything in mind at the moment. Yahveh says He will take care of the RHONE for taking Laura and that was the end of the message. Do we have anything cooking anywhere?"

Mark shook his head, "Not right now. I think . . ."

The COMSEC line lit up and one of the programmers announced visitors at the Portal on the surface.

Mark finished with "And,...I think our Heavenly Father will probably give us something to do."

Jack stood up and pointed at various members of the Core Team. "I want you and Sarah to accompany Laura and I to meet these visitors. While we're on the way up, I want you, David and you, Alexis, to video capture the faces of the visitors and run an ID program to confirm who they are. Let us know what you've got before we get to the surface if you can."

The two couples walked out and exited their own security gate onto the subterranean ground level. Taking a cart, they rode the quarter mile over to the elevators and selected one. They had just gotten in when Charlie Wu phoned Jack.

"Jack, the three-member team of visitors are who they say they are. They are three of the top Rabbis in Tel Aviv, or possibly the entire world. They are very instrumental in guiding religious state policy from Yahveh's viewpoint, for the Prime Minister and the Knesset. This is a power meeting so please tread lightly. I think all three of these men had to approve our being here and the base we are in right now."

Jack acknowledged the information and hung up. He relayed Charlie's findings to the others. The elevator reached the surface level and the four team members walked down to the reception room. Jack checked in with the Mossad team guarding the base and was granted permission for the four of them to join the visitors. The guard team had been instructed by their supervisors not to bother the visitors or restrict their right to enter the surface level of the base.

As the team entered the reception room the oldest of the teachers stood up and came forward. He said "Shalom" as he hugged each one of the team members and then introduced himself. "I am Rabbi Simon ben Chanan and these two Rabbis are my associates." The other two Rabbis nodded to the team.

Jack and Mark sat down at the conference table across from the three Rabbis with Laura to Jack's left and Sarah to Mark's right. Jack asked, "Rabbi Chanan, how can we be of service to you and your associates today?"

The Rabbi smiled faintly. "Mr. Malone, I have studied the records of your team's activities and discussed them with David Zahavy at great length. We are here today to determine the truth that we can understand of those activities. The Torah doesn't discuss demons and the rabbinical references tend to be someone's ideas, which were probably Persian to begin with, as to our sacred scriptures. Many people feel one way and many others a different way. Since it seems that your group runs into these creatures frequently we would like to understand what they are, what they want, and why your group runs afoul of them all the time."

Jack looked at Laura who shook her head slightly and gave the opportunity to respond back to him. Jack prayed silently that Yahveh would give him the right words to tell the Rabbis what they needed to know.

"Rabbi Chanan, I would like to give you a short answer to your questions which we can discuss at greater length afterward. Is that acceptable to the three of you?"

All three Rabbis nodded their heads. Jack felt led to explain things carefully but accurately. "The Crossfire Team was founded several years ago in Denver, Colorado, in America. Initially my wife and I were thrust into a dire situation requiring us to turn to Yahveh for salvation. Mark Connelly was with us at that time. As events unfolded, Sarah Cohen joined us in combating world terror. Eventually, an angel named Hugo explained to us why we were constantly in combat with demonic forces, in the form of physical demons, present in our dimension."

Jack couldn't tell if his story was getting a good review or not because the three Rabbis did not show any emotion but sat there listening.

"Hugo told us that several years ago the enemy of all mankind and the enemy of Yahshua, Satan, had started defying Yahveh by creating physical bodies for his demons and having them enter directly into our dimension to create terror and to separate men from God. As I understand it, demons represent the fallen angels at the time of the Great War in Heaven. Association with Satan, the source of all evil, has warped them into gross, evil-looking spirits that translate that ugliness into their physical forms."

"Now, Father Yahveh could stop this illegal activity but to do so would require Him to break his own rules, which He will not do. Therefore, He caused teams to be created to counter these illegal incursions into the human domain. Now, demons are here to do only three things. They steal, kill and destroy everything of Yahveh's that they can. We run into them all the time because the Father arranges events so that we can stop them from terrorizing the human race. We have "killed" thousands of demons which represents only a tiny fraction of their forces but, it has blunted their efforts and that was what the Father developed our team and eleven other teams around the world to do."

Rabbi Chanan pursed his lips and said, "I noticed that you stressed the word "killed". Why is that?"

Jack shrugged his shoulders. "Like angels and humans our spirits are eternal and can't be killed. Neither can the evil spirits of the demons. We destroy their "bodies" in our dimension and they are sent to the Abyss just as when they were commanded by Yahshua in His time on Earth."

The Rabbis held a mini-conference is hushed whispers. Then Rabbi Chanan asked Jack, "I know that we cannot see angels and they cannot be captured on film or by camera. Is this the same for demons?"

Jack nodded, "Yes Rabbi, even their Earthly dimension bodies will not show up on film, yet the human mind can clearly see them. That is one of the properties that Satan grants them. Once gravely injured, the demon body becomes inoperative, or dead, but it dissipates into foul-smelling smoke or mist."

Jack realized that the Rabbis were not convinced that there were actually demons roaming the Earth today. So, "Is it all right if we pray for Yahveh to enlighten you concerning these enemies?"

The Rabbis huddled again. Finally, after some fierce disagreement, they agreed.

The four team members closed their eyes and prayed together. Jack remembered that it was an earnest prayer for enlightenment from Heaven so that the Jewish teachers could honestly appraise the team's efforts.

After they prayed, they waited for an answer. Nothing was forthcoming so Jack decided they would just have to let the Rabbis determine the team's efforts from their words.

Laura suddenly shook and grabbed Jack's left arm. She looked at him with wide eyes. "There is something terrible coming."

Jack pushed his chair back and stood up along with the three other team members. They begin to pray in their prayer language. This went on for several moments.

CHAPTER THIRTY

Jack felt the icy threat approaching them that Laura had sensed. He turned toward the wall of the large conference room to his left and stepped to his left so that he was next to Laura. Rabbi Chanan was asking Jack what was happening. Jack looked over his shoulder. "We prayed for the Father to show you about the reality of demons. I believe that you're going to see one or more demons for yourself in a few seconds."

The air suddenly seemed charged and a tremor shook the building where they were. All four of the team member's armor and swords exploded into being and they all stepped into a high guard position with their swords held by both hands above their right shoulders.

The Rabbis were more than astonished by the appearance of the gold and silver armor and chrome swords. They could actually feel the essence and purity of Yahveh flowing off of the sword blades. All at once Rabbi Chanan felt very apprehensive.

A loud crackling and snapping accompanied the destruction of the wall the team was facing. What it revealed caused them all to step backward.

Wreathed in fire and smoke, a being half as large as the wall smashed its way into the conference room. The beast emanated palatable waves of evil and fear as it advanced. It looked like a large flaming mass with multiple claws, fangs, arms and swords. Everything was bright orange or red and it faded in and out of the flames as it moved. The creature uttered a horrible hissing scream that raised the hair on the humans there.

Laura took a deep breath and continued to pray her prayer of power, "Yea though I pass through the valley of the shadow of death I shall fear no evil."

All at once, two of the Mossad guards rushed into the room from Jack's left and proceed to empty their assault rifles at the beast without effect. Jack yelled at them to retreat but he was too late. Three arms of the beast snatched the two men up and literally tore them to pieces. Their brief screams were quickly stilled, but still horrible.

Filled with a Holy Anger, Jack charged the beast and went into the time management mode that let him move many times faster than normal. He swung his sword and sliced one of the beast's arms from its body. The beast let out a scream that shook the entire Portal as red smoke flowed out of the creature where the severed arm had been attached.

Jack continued to stab, slash, and block as he moved closer to the nine-foot tall body through the flames. One of the other arms swung a black sword at Jack but that one was blocked by the gleaming blade swung by Mark.

Laura was uttering a war cry that probably had its origin from the Moors of Scotland as she slashed another appendage from the creature.

Sarah ran past Jack and leaped up at the beast and swung her sword at the creature's chest. The sword penetrated the beast's chest and huge amounts of red smoke exploded outward hiding everything.

Jack kept moving forward destroying anything of the creature he could hit. Something smashed into his shield and the front of his armor. The force of the blow knocked him backward off of his feet and onto his back. He quickly rolled over to his right and avoided a large black sword which smashed into the floor where he had been lying. As he rose back to his feet he had a glimpse of the three Rabbis kneeling and praying. Jack turned to charge back into the battle.

By then, everything was just about finished. Mark had cut off two more arms that had been swinging swords and then went into high speed mode and was able to decapitate the creature. The huge beast dissolved into red smoke and demon stain. Part of the ceiling collapsed where the wall had been damaged as the flames died out with the creature's demise.

Jack turned and limped back to the table and the Rabbis. Laura walked up beside him followed by Mark and Sarah. Their armor and swords faded out and they quit praying. Finding their original seats all four of them sat down gratefully because the battle had tired them out.

Jack took a deep breath as he looked at the ashen face of Rabbi Chanan. "That, in a nutshell, is what we fight against."

The Rabbi rose and took his seat. He was shaking somewhat. "I had no idea how horrible a demon could be. I must apologize to you for our doubtful attitudes about your activities. I just confessed the sin of doubt and asked Yahveh to forgive us of the sin of doubt and to bless all of your people with his protection and his love. I ... I am at a loss for words. Thank you for saving us because we knew, without any doubt that creature was here to kill the three of us. I had no idea that such concentrated evil could exist in this world."

Mark nodded at the befuddled man. "Rabbi, this is just one of the billions of enemy demons. I now believe that we probably shouldn't have asked for proof to remove your doubts. I apologize to you for subjecting the three of you and those two brave Israeli guards to such evil."

Rabbi Chanan nervously looked at the fallen wall part of the room and asked, "Can more of those things come at us through that gap now?"

Laura shook her head. "No Rabbi, only in this one instance did Yahveh allow the enemy a chance to attack you. We were able to defeat it in battle. You are normally safe because Yahveh protects you constantly as you walk with Him. Never forget that, because the unsaved do not have that protection. All they have at this time is ourselves and the teams like us. We, on the other hand, will probably get to fight more of these fairly soon."

One of the Mossad Portal supervisors entered the room and spoke quietly with Jack. "What was that thing?"

Jack described the demon and asked the supervisor to forgive the team for this event that cost his men their lives. The supervisor shook his head. "You are all forgiven. It was our responsibility to defend you all and we let you down."

Jack shook his head. "Your men could not have known that their weapons were ineffectual against the beast. They died exhibiting the bravery we have seen from Israelis everywhere."

At that point several groups of men arrived. A forensic team attended to the fallen men and others began to replace the wall and clean up the mess. As the team and the Rabbis all rose to leave, Jack asked the Rabbis if they would like to accompany the team members on a tour of their base.

Rabbi Chanan shook his head. "Thank you very much Mr. Malone, but even though you four did all the fighting we are spiritually drained. We need to return to our synagogue and spend time praying to clean our spirits of the evil and violence. We admire you for your ability to stand against things like that."

"We, unfortunately, are made of softer stuff. I will be praying for a long time to forget the events of today. Daily we shall pray for your team's protection from these evil beings that Yahveh has you defend against. But, I promise you that we are going to stand with your team and we will support you, and your team, in every way possible. Shalom."

After the Rabbis had been escorted out of the Portal, Mark looked at Jack. "Memo to us all, let's not ask for such proof again."

Laura had been praying and she turned to Mark. "Show me," she said.

Mark sighed and pulled his shirt up on his right side. The huge bruise was already turning from red and blue to an ugly black color. Mark gritted his teeth when Sarah touched him there. Laura prayed for the damage to be covered in the blood of Yahshua. Jack joined the two women in praying for the Father's healing of the physical damage to Mark's side and he suddenly felt pain in his own body demanding attention.

Stepping away from Mark, Jack pulled his own shirt up and examined himself. There was a similar bruising to his abdomen and lower chest. It must have happened when he was knocked down. He suddenly convulsed due to a wave of nausea and dizziness. He tried to grab the back of a chair but missed and instead he collapsed onto the floor.

Laura had seen him going and grabbed his arm to break the fall. She lifted his shirt and started praying the blood of Yahshua over his wounds.

As she prayed, Jack's mind slowly spun into a state of fuzziness and Laura's voice faded out as he passed out. It wasn't uncomfortable but it was disturbing for some reason.

Laura used her combat microphone and called for transport to get both men to Bnai Zion hospital in Haifa immediately. As she kept her hand on Jack's belly she prayed with great passion for the healing of both men and sought the Father for an explanation as to why they suffered such damage through their armor.

CHAPTER THIRTY-ONE

Twenty minutes later, Doctor Alan Goldberg, a trauma doctor at the Bnai Zion Hospital in Haifa, in the north part of Herzyila, finished examining the damage to both Jack and Mark. He ordered X-Rays and quick Cat-Scans for both men. As they were stabilized by the medical team and moved to the X-Ray department, the doctor sought out Laura and Sarah.

After he introduced himself to the two women he asked, "What happened to them? I've never seen such deep bruising over such a wide area in my entire career."

Laura sized up the doctor and determined that he was a no-nonsense secular physician who wouldn't do very well with the disclosure of physical damage by a demon. "Doctor, we are part of a unit that works with the IDF to defend the Nation of Israel. These two men were hurt during a brief battle with an enemy force. Can you tell us how badly are they hurt?"

Doctor Goldberg frowned and shook his head. "These wounds concern me because of the large area of the impact bruising on both men. There is wide spread surface damage with considerable internal bleeding. I've ordered X-Rays and Cat-Scans to try to define the internal damage. What type of damage hurt them?"

Sarah spoke to the doctor in Hebrew. "They were struck by a massive force which apparently exceeded the ability of their body armor to stop the force. Without the armor they would have surely died. Can you tell us if those wounds could be life-threatening?"

The doctor frowned again. He answered her in Hebrew. "I can't say yet until I see the results of the tests. What group are you with?"

Sarah smiled slightly, "I'm sorry, but that information is classified and I can't reveal it."

The doctor frowned and shook his head again. He then walked off towards the ER.

Laura looked at Sarah. "What did he say in Hebrew?"

Sarah told her what they had discussed. Laura retreated to a quiet place in the waiting room and sought the Lord in prayer. Sarah joined her and bowed her head. Both women were deeply concerned by the damage to the two most important men in their lives.

In the middle of their prayers Doctor Goldberg returned with two security guards. He stared at the two women for several seconds. He then sat down on a small table facing the two women and looked at Laura face to face. "Ms. Malone, I need more information about your group's activities and the exact nature of these wounds. I have contacted the Military because of the nature of the damage to your husbands. Please forgive me for doing this but there are so many factions attempting to wage war on our Nation and your reluctance to be open with me about these injuries leads me to question your "group's" authenticity as defenders of Israel. These men are going to take you both to a secure location for questioning. I wouldn't resist if I were you."

Sarah saw the anger flare up in Laura's eyes.

Laura exhaled to relieve some of the stress. "Doctor Goldberg, for your own sake and that of your men here, I recommend you contact the office of the Prime Minister and verify our status immediately."

One of the security men said in Hebrew, "I don't think you have any support from there because they don't back terrorists." The man had pulled out his nightstick and slapped it into his other palm to stress his ability to control them.

Laura looked at the Doctor. "If you don't want more casualties for your services you need to curb your security men."

The doctor smirked slightly. "Don't resist these men. They are authorized to arrest both of you and are highly trained in combat."

Sarah looked at Laura who nodded at her. In one fluid motion Sarah rose out of her chair and used an upward Axe-Hand strike to the groin of the man closest to her. He doubled over in agony as the ex-Mossad assassin rotated around the doctor and grabbed the other security man by the arm holding the night stick.

Twisting the man's arm upward, Sarah struck the beefy man in the throat hard enough to shut off his air. She then swept the man's legs out from under him and dropped him on his head on the tile floor.

Continuing her spin, she bent over and brought her elbow down on the neck of the first man who was on his knees throwing up. The blow rendered him unconscious and he fell into his own vomit.

The first man had hit his head on the tile and that blow had knocked him out. Sarah returned to her seat before the doctor could react to her moving.

The doctor looked down at the two unconscious guards and attempted to stand up. Laura kicked him in the knee which dropped him back down onto the table he had been sitting on. She reached out and grabbed his shirt and smock and pulled his face to within inches of hers. She said softly, "If you don't understand that we are serious then I will have the Prime Minister remove you from your position at this or any other medical facility in Israel."

Keeping her eye contact with the Doctor, Laura used her left hand and keyed her combat microphone which connected her directly to Charlie Wu in the COMSEC group at the sea base. "Charlie, contact the office of the Prime Minister, in my name, and get someone in authority to Bnai Zion Hospital within the next twenty minutes. Jack and Mark have been injured and the doctor here is attempting to label us as terrorists. Have the PM authorize a squad of IDF Commandos to be here at the same time to protect the four of us."

Charlie's answer was brief. "Will do Laura, some of our people are on the way as we speak."

Laura's anger hadn't completely dissipated and her hold on the Doctor's clothes became tighter. "My husband and his friend have put their lives on the line for the people of this country. DO NOT interfere with their medical processing or attempt to interfere with us again. Do we have an understanding?"

The doctor nodded his head and Laura released him. As he tried to stand up both women rose in unison.

Three security men appeared in the hall headed in their direction. All three of them were armed with drawn pistols in their hands. Sarah squared up with the approaching force and an automatic appeared in her hand.

Laura looked the Doctor in the eyes. "I don't think you'll have to work on these new men because Sarah shoots to kill, not to wound, as do I."

Laura then spun the Doctor around as a shield and pulled out her own handgun.

The three security men ran into the room and stopped ten paces away from the women with their guns up and demanding that Sarah and Laura drop their weapons. Sarah smiled, "Not on your life."

Sarah suggested, "Why don't you and your men lower their weapons and we will do the same. Then we could resolve this situation."

The lead man shook his head. "We can't allow armed personnel in this hospital. There are too many innocents here."

Sarah spoke in Hebrew. "I know; we defend the innocent of Israel every day. I'm sorry you don't understand."

The standoff ended suddenly when three of the Crossfire Team's SOG warriors in full body armor appeared behind the three Security men. Each team member had their M-8 assault rifles laser locked onto one of the three security men. Megan Cole spoke authoritatively to the Security Forces. "Stand down, now."

The lead security man looked over his shoulder and realized that they were severely outnumbered and outgunned. He told his men to obey the order. The Security Forces lowered their weapons and put them on the floor. Megan said, "Kick the weapons away and get on your knees with your hands behind your heads with your fingers interlaced." From the ice in her voice there was no doubt in the Security Leader's mind that they would shoot without remorse to protect the women in front of him. When the Security Force had done what she told them, she added, "Cross your ankles."

The men obeyed and the three warriors approached them and shackled them with nylon cuffs.

Sarah and Laura put their weapons away and Laura released the Doctor.

There was a noisy disturbance in the hall outside the waiting room and then a fourth SOG warrior escorted a half dozen IDF forces and an Officer into the waiting room. These men were accompanied by an Official from the Prime Minister's office.

After establishing his authority, Ezra Boaz had the security forces released and all the combatants and the Doctor moved to a conference room down the hall. Sorting out the details quickly, he had the Security Forces take their two injured men to the ER and assured the SOG forces that they could stand down also. After talking to Laura, Ezra spoke to the Doctor. "Doctor Goldberg, speaking for the Prime Minister I can absolutely vouch for Ms. Malone and Ms. Connelly and assure you that they have the full backing of the Prime Minister and his office."

He smoothly complimented and chastised the doctor in one sentence. "With all the terror activities today, I understand why you reacted the way you did, because of the circumstances, but I do recommend you refer future actions like this to our office before you single-handed start your own personal world war. Are we clear on that?"

The Doctor nodded and turned to Laura and Sarah. "I apologize for my mistaken actions and ask you to forgive me. I need to leave now to attend to your husbands."

Ezra put his hand on the Doctor's arm and stopped the departing physician. "Israel does expect that Mr. Malone and Mr. Connelly will get the absolute best service possible."

Doctor Goldberg saw a short future for his career if he wanted to argue so he only nodded his head and walked out.

CHAPTER THIRTY-TWO

In the quiet of the aircraft hangar on the surface level of the Undersea Base, Su Li was enjoying herself inspecting one of the team's two primary aircraft, both nicknamed the Shrew. She liked the fact that, in nature, the actual Shrew was a most innocent-looking mouse-like creature. Yet, in reality, it was the most voracious creature on Earth. Ounce for ounce the Shrew could defeat anything it came up against. Owls were fifty times the size of a Shrew but if they didn't kill it when they grabbed it with their razor sharp talons the Shrew would start eating the Owl from the leg up.

Perhaps the need to eat its own weight in food every hour of its existence had everything to do with its viciousness, but, Su Li liked the use of the little creature for the name of her disguised Fighter-Corporate Jet. It was a superb work of art. It looked like a Citation X corporate jet on steroids but actually concealed the engines, avionics, and the weapons of an F-22 Raptor fighter jet. "Yep", She thought, "Poke at this Shrew and you'll lose a finger up to your armpit."

Her cell phone chirped and she looked at the caller bar. It was from the Mossad. "Crossfire Team, can I help you?" The caller was young and nervous.

"Ms. Li?"

"Yes, what do you need?"

"My name is Meiling Yong. I have just arrived in Israel today. I have important information for your team concerning you. I ended up being directed to this office. I need to meet with you as soon as I can. I know that the MSS (Chinese Ministry of State Security) is trying to kill me before I can relate this information to you."

Su Li thought for a second. She spoke in Mandarin, "How do you know me and what is this information you have that is so important?"

Meiling replied in the same language. "I was Thor's youngest sister. When he would visit our mother he would tell me about you and showed me your picture. I started to attend an MSS training school and during an exercise on the computers we were supposed to look up known criminals. I looked up my brother and found a file on you. Under recent items I discovered this information." It sounded like she was weeping.

"It records how you killed members of the Chinese Navy when my brother was killed. You dropped a bomb on one of their ships and it killed thirty-three crewmen and officers. It included a notice of termination by the MSS. It indicated that you were presently in Tel Aviv, here in Israel, and that they have a two-man team that is preparing to execute you."

Su Li wasn't surprised, "Go on."

Meiling Yong paused. "I didn't know if they had already killed you or not. Three weeks ago one of my fellow students told me that I had been "tagged" because I had read that file and then tried to find out where you were today. I fled the school and was able to get to the city of Hong Kong where an old school friend smuggled me onto a ship. The "Trailing Wind" docked at Haifa this morning. I hope the information helps to alert you to this situation. I do have the photographs of the team that was sent to kill you. But, I probably can't go anywhere you might be known to be because the MSS will find me and kill me. I could leave the photos here but they are starting to look at me with suspicion. I have to leave now."

Su Li thought about that. "Where are you staying?"

Meiling softly said, "Nowhere. I'm not even in this country legally. The crew of the Trailing Wind helped me to enter the city without going through customs. I don't want to endanger you after all you've been through. I'll take care of myself. Goodbye."

Su Li said, "Wait. I know of a small restaurant near where you are. I can meet you there in about thirty minutes. You can give me the photos and I can pay you for your efforts. Go west two blocks and you'll see a small shop that has a sign showing a smiling bagel. That's the sign for the "Happy Bagel" cafe. I'll see you there in thirty minutes. Okay?"

Meiling seemed conflicted. She obviously wanted to meet Su Li, but she didn't want to endanger her either. She finally gave in and said, "All right, but if you're not there soon, I have to leave and find...something."

Su Li told her, "Go now."

She checked her watch, she could barely make it if she ran. She ran for the elevators and called Charlie's number. Charlie's phone went into voice mail immediately. Su Li decided to call him back in a bit.

Coming out of the elevator she ran to the Mossad office but everyone was busy. She shook her head. "I don't have time for this" she thought to herself as she exited the Portal and took off on foot for the restaurant.

Twelve blocks weren't too far and she made good time, even against the lights. She slowed down a block before the restaurant to regain normal breathing. She pushed open the door and stepped into the small eating area. She turned around and observed the street. Nothing seemed out of place. She casually looked at the three customers eating at little tables. There was no one of Meiling's age there. She picked a rear table with her back to the wall. She checked her time and saw that there was still two minutes until the time they were supposed to meet.

A minute later a small Chinese woman carefully pushed the door to the restaurant open and looked around. She saw Su Li and her face lit up. She scrambled into the diner and headed directly for Su Li's table.

She slid into the other seat in the booth and reached out to hold Su Li's hands. "I'm so glad to meet you, even under these circumstances."

Su Li clasped the young girl's hands and smiled at her. She could remember when she was this young and this eager. "I'm glad to meet Thor's sister and I'm sorry about your having to lose him at such a tender age."

Meiling Yong looked around and then opened the big purse she had on a strap over her shoulder. She took three photos out of her purse with frosted plastic wrappings. "I didn't want to get them scratched." She took the first one out of the wrapping and passed it to Su Li. It was five inches by seven inches and definitely a computer printed picture. Su Li looked at the man in the picture and didn't recognize him at all. She waited while Li Yong took out the next one. Again, she didn't recognize the man in the picture. The young girl took out the last picture and passed it to Su Li.

This one also wasn't anyone she'd ever seen either, but she was sure the facial recognition software back at the base would give them names. She looked at Meiling and was startled. The young woman's eyes rolled up into her head and she crumpled onto the table like she was boneless.

Su Li went on high alert scanning for anyone with a dart gun or a gas generator. Nobody in the restaurant seemed to notice what was going on. Su Li carefully slid the photos in front of her to take a picture with her cell phone when everything went blurry and her fingers went numb so that she couldn't hold her phone anymore. Everything faded to black and her head followed her phone to the table. The last thing she remembered was realizing that she had been set up. But, by whom, why, and...?

CHAPTER THIRTY-THREE

As Doctor Goldberg studied the internal damage to Jack Malone, as shown in precise detail by the X-Rays and the Cat-Scans he tried to determine how to correct the deep tissue damage to Jack's organs and his epidermal layers. He used a new modeling software package that allowed them to conceptualize the impact that caused the damage. That way they could have a better idea how to treat the injury.

He had run the software three times but couldn't change the image of the cause of the damage. It looked very much like a giant ax head had impacted his patient at a very high rate of speed.

Doctor Goldberg concluded that Jack had been struck by a vehicle traveling at least forty miles per hour. The knife edge front of the vehicle had apparently slammed into his patient and then threw him down on his back from the shock of the impact. The man had a ruptured spleen, a severely compressed large and small colon and extensive tissue and epidermal compression.

After discussing his findings with several other doctors he came to the conclusion that he needed to do a surgical procedure and take biopsies of the damaged flesh and organs. He called down to the operating floor to arrange for the surgery.

The doctor thought at least the other patient, Mr. Connelly hadn't suffered any organ damage and the bruising would heal over time. There wouldn't be any surgery necessary for him.

Jack floated in a place where the neutral but pleasant temperature didn't affect him. He felt that he would be happy if it wasn't for the nagging pain in his middle. He wondered how long he had been floating this way and why he was dreaming about floating anyway. Then he could see the angel Caleb floating above him and he watched as the angel reached down and touched him where it hurt. The hurt went away and he felt sleepy again.

Laura had heard from the Lord and she headed to Jack's room. She walked in and found him sedated and asleep. She carefully lifted the hospital gown he was wearing and examined his stomach area and his lower chest. She ran her fingers over his flesh and smiled. There was no swelling, no discoloration, and no fever heat. It looked like he had never had an injury there at all. She walked out of his room and got the floor nurse to accompany her back to Jack's room. She showed the woman Jack's body where he had once had the bruising. The nurse looked at Jack's chart and then called Doctor Goldberg.

Several minutes later Doctor Goldberg arrived at the room and listened to the nurse's explanation. He looked at Laura and then checked Jack's injuries. Except for the fact that there were no injuries evident on his body.

The doctor wrote on the chart and then carefully disconnected the sedative drip. He told the nurse and Laura to wait there in the room because Jack should wake up in the next ten minutes or so. He had an urgent case in the ER he was handling and would make his way back up to Jack's room as soon as he could.

Jack started to come around after fifteen minutes and was fully awake in less than twenty minutes. The nurse prodded and pressed on Jack's belly and asked, "Does that hurt at all?"

Jack shook his head. "I can feel you pressing on me but there is no pain whatsoever."

After recording all of Jack's readings and values, the nurse disconnected the various sensors, catheters, and leads attached to his body. Freed of the cords Jack sat up and put his feet on the floor. He stood up and slowly twisted his body. Finally, he bent over and touched his toes. He looked at Laura, "No pain! I feel great."

Laura went to the closet and got Jack's clothes out. Jack dressed quickly and sat in the chair in the room and put his shoes on. Finished dressing he sat there and talked quietly with Laura until the doctor returned.

Dr. Goldberg walked into the room and was obviously surprised to find Jack out of bed and dressed. He asked Jack if he could verify his improved condition and Jack shook his head. "There is no need for further medical checks, Doctor. I'm in good health and sorry I took so much of your time."

The doctor leaned against Jack's bed and stared at him. "I'm not sure how to write this sudden health up in my reports. When I checked your injuries two hours ago I scheduled you for surgery in about another two hours. Your spleen and large colon were so badly bruised that I felt we would have to remove both of them to save your life. Yet, here you sit completely well. How do you explain it?"

Jack looked at the perplexed Doctor and told him, "I was damaged by a large black sword swung by a demon. After we dispatched the demon I passed out from my injuries which were what you saw earlier. While I was sedated I dreamed of an angel, named Caleb, who came and touched my wounds and Yahveh healed me."

The Doctor shook his head, "Like that is going to happen. I can't put that in my report. It's fantasy instead of scientific. I'd be the laughing stock of the hospital if I did that."

Jack shrugged his shoulders, "And yet, here I sit without damage."

Jack got up and shook the Doctor's hand. "Perhaps you should try prayer and see if Yahveh will explain this minor miracle to you."

The Doctor was still shaking his head as the couple left the room.

Stopping at the room that Mark was in resulted in Mark opening the door as they were about to knock on it. Mark smiled at Jack and Laura. "Hi guys, did you have a visit from an angel, too?"

The four of them went to the front desk and signed Jack and Mark out of the hospital. Then they released the IDF soldiers from guard duty and headed back to the Undersea Base.

On the way back Jack called Charlie to let him know that both he and Mark were all right and headed back to the base.

Charlie was relieved. "That's great news. But, I have some bad news for you, too. Su Li has gone missing and I can't locate her anywhere."

CHAPTER THIRTY-FOUR

When Jack, Laura, Sarah, and Mark were in his office; Charlie told them what he knew about Su Li's absence. "Mike White couldn't find Su Li seventy-five minutes ago. My computer tracking program showed that she left the Sea Base roughly two hours ago. I checked the Portal cameras and she left through the main Portal at 5:27 P.M. Tel Aviv time. She took off running East along Trumpeldor at a very fast pace. She wasn't jogging, that's for sure."Jack shook his head. "Do you have any idea why she took off or where she was heading?"

Charlie shook his head in response. "Not really. The electronic log shows that she got a cell phone call from a Mossad number just before she left, but, there is no log of the conversation. Also, as she was leaving she tried to call me but I was routing some of the SOG troops to the hospital at that time."

Jack frowned, "I don't like this. Charlie, keep looking to see if you can find out anything else about her leaving or where she is now. Mark, talk to the Mossad and see if they know anything about that call or about Su Li."

Ten minutes later they knew that there was no record of the call conversation on the Mossad's end and that she had left no information with anyone about what she was doing when she left.

Precisely at 8:00 A.M. the next morning Ethan Reaper showed up at the workout area for his three times a week martial arts class. When ten minutes passed without any sign of his instructor, he called Charlie Wu and inquired about Su Li. "Charlie, this is Ethan. I'm down here in the gym waiting for my third beating of the week. Would you happen to know where Su Li is this pleasant morning?"

Charlie sighed. "Ethan, I'm sorry I didn't let you know. Su Li has disappeared from the base. I've been tasked with finding her. And, I've attempted to find her. You'd think it wouldn't be hard to locate a young Asian pilot here in the Jewish homeland. It seems she's vanished without a trace.

Do you know any reason Su Li would leave the Sea Base around 5:30 yesterday afternoon?"

Ethan thought back. "I remember seeing Su Li in the morning when she was headed out to the hanger to work on the aircraft. But after that I was into the elusive Russian transmission that apparently came from the moon's surface and had my head stuck into a computer until around 1:00 A.M. this morning. Do you have any idea why she left?"

"She got a cell phone call from a Mossad number which turned out to be a dead end. The number was a desk phone in a Mossad neighborhood office about two miles from here. No one remembers seeing who used it although one of the operatives remembered a young Asian woman asking to use that phone yesterday afternoon around 5:00 P.M. They let her make a local call but the next time they looked she had left. It wasn't Su Li. I sent a COMSEC employee down there with a picture of her to make sure."

Ethan thought about that and asked, "What was the address of that office?"

Charlie gave Ethan the address on Trumpeldor. Ethan asked, "You probably have done a search for her cell phone or her medallion without any results, right?"

Charlie grunted, "Yeah, it's like she fell into a big hole. Look, Ethan, I've got to go." Charlie hung up.

Ethan thought about Su Li and realized that he seriously liked the woman and it really bothered him that she was gone and probably kidnapped. He decided he wanted to try to find her. Charlie was a top spy and a smart guy but Ethan thought he could do a better job of looking for the diminutive Asian pilot than Charlie could. After all, before the team had moved to Israel he had been taking a heavy-duty on-line course in computer investigation and crime investigation. He also knew how to look for people using the computer that even Charlie probably didn't know.

Ethan checked the time. Su Li had been missing for less than a day so her trail was probably still out there somewhere. It was only thirty minutes until he was off duty. He brought up his time sheet and checked his vacation time available. He had over three weeks coming and there were no urgent cases except the hunt for the missing pilot on the board. He clicked over to his time management form and asked for the next seven days for vacation. The system came back immediately with an approval.

Ethan finished his shift and clocked out on the computer. He got up and walked back to the room he had in the COMSEC living quarters and grabbed a glass of Orange Juice from his refrigerator.

Sitting down at his personal computer he logged back in to his work position. He thought out his search and began checking Su Li's path as she left almost twenty-four hours ago. He brought up the Portal camera and captured Su Li's image as she was leaving the base Portal exit. He was able to record all four views of her and he put them into a search data base.

He then went out to an Israeli police-only web site and logged in as a Chief Inspector Clueso, a false persona that he had created a year ago. He entered the proper password encryption and was accepted. Selecting the "City Street Camera" file he began to refine his search to the Trumpeldor Street in the area between the Portal and the Mossad office. He clicked on the identify camera location file and was rewarded with over eighty-two functioning cameras that viewed at least a part of the street.

Entering a search criterion of the approximate time after 5:20 P.M. the day before and selecting his stored images of Su Li, he then clicked on "Active Search Archive".

Three minutes later he was rewarded with multiple views of Su Li as she ran up the street. The last camera video of her was her walking out of the camera's range two blocks away from the Mossad street office.

He recorded the videos and then eliminated the search. Next he selected "Shop and Business Cameras" and then he selected only the three blocks on Trumpeldor Street on the west side. He found five businesses in that area with internal cameras but none of them included video of Su Li.

Ethan wrote down the businesses that had been eliminated by their cameras and then eliminated that search.

To be thorough Ethan ran through any Police Vehicle or Police Helicopter videos that might have been in that area at the right time. Two more negatives.

Removing all signs of Chief Inspector Clueso from the database he printed out both front and side views of Su Li's head and shoulder pictures. He logged out of the Police network and logged off his own computer.

Changing from his super casual duds into a dark business suit he then placed the photos into a small leather case and put it into his inner suit pocket in the suit jacket. He went down to his locker in the Armory. He took out the .40 Springfield XD auto-loader and a shoulder holster. Loading a full magazine into the hand gun he racked the slide back and chambered a round. He put the gun into a butt-down Italian Bianchi, spring-loaded holster under his right arm and balanced it with two more full magazines on his left side. He took out the K-Bar combat knife and put it into a side-to-side scabbard at the small of his back. Lastly he took his Ray-Ban sunglasses and put them on. He shut and locked his locker and turned to leave. As he walked out he threw a sketchy salute to the ever watching security camera on the wall of the Armory.

Checking out of the base he rode the elevator to the top and exited the Portal. Walking swiftly, he took less than twenty minutes to reach the place the last camera had recorded Su Li's progress. He looked at the businesses on the west side of the street and eliminated the stores that had cameras but no shot of Su Li in the block the farthest from the Mossad office.

There were only three businesses left. There was a clothing store, an auto repair facility, and a bagel shop. Ethan started with the clothing store. He walked in and went straight to the sales desk at the back of the sales area. He took out the pictures of Su Li and laid them on the counter. Flashing an authentic-looking silver police badge and identification card he asked the sales lady if she had seen this woman yesterday around 6:00 P.M.

The sales lady shook her head and looked at him. "We closed early at 4:00 P.M. yesterday. There were no customers in here at that time."

Ethan smiled at her and thanked her for the information. He exited the store and went to the auto repair place. No one in that store had seen her.

Repeating his performance in the bagel shop he got another negative from the young man at the counter. As he was getting ready to leave, an older man came up to the counter from the back of the store and asked what Ethan wanted. Ethan repeated his request and showed the pictures of Su Li to him. The owner spoke much better English than the young clerk and he stared at the pictures for several seconds before saying, "Yes, she came in here yesterday around that time, but, she didn't buy anything."

Ethan asked if the owner had any more information about her. The owner shook his head. "I saw her come in but when I looked out later she was gone."

CHAPTER THIRTY-FIVE

Ethan asked the man where she sat. He showed him the corner booth. Ethan couldn't see anything that showed that Su Li had been there. He turned and looked across the few small tables in the shop. They were all empty at that time. He felt like he'd come to a dead end in his search. He remembered some of what Laura Malone had been teaching him about the Holy Spirit of God, "I wonder if He would show me what I need to do." He looked around but no one was watching him.

He closed his eyes and prayed. "Holy Spirit, would you help me find Su Li and show me anything that I am missing here in this place."When he opened his eyes he found himself staring at an old, dirty, and broken-looking wall-mounted video camera, its dark lens staring back at him. There was no little red light on it to show that it was working. It looked like another dead end. Ethan though, "Still ..."

Walking over to the owner he asked, "Does that old camera even work?" as he pointed at it.

The owner nodded his head, "Yes it does, it doesn't look too good but I leave it that way on purpose so no one will steal it.""

Ethan asked, is it linked into the internet or is it on a wide-area network?"

The owner grinned a big toothy grin. "No Way! That's my private camera. I keep it only on a looping tape for my information."

Ethan smiled back. "Could I see the tape that recorded the time that the young lady was in your shop?"

The owner agreed and took him back to his small office. He selected the correct tape and put it into the tape player. He ran it fast forward until he got to roughly 6:00 P.M. Then he hit play and held down the fast forward button again until Su Li entered the shop. Ethan watched as Su Li looked out the window for a few seconds and then selected her seat.

There was no audio but it showed when a young Chinese woman or girl came into the shop and almost ran over to Su LI. They held hands for a few minutes and talked. Then the new girl took some papers or something out of her purse and, one by one took them out of the plastic they were in and passed them to Su Li.

Ethan watched as the girl's head fell to the table followed almost immediately by Su Li's head. They had both been knocked out by something.

Ethan watched as the two men at the middle table looked around. Getting up they threw their trash from their meal away and quickly walked over and picked up both women and carried them out of the store along with all the paperwork or what looked to be pictures the women had been looking at before they passed out.

Ethan stared at the owner like he might be in on the snatch and grab. The owner was starting to sweat. He looked at Ethan and shook his head. "I had nothing to do with that. I swear it. I didn't look at the tape when I changed it this morning. Believe me!"

Ethan stared at the man as he brought out his cell phone. The man quickly put his hand over the cell phone and asked Ethan not to report him. Ethan acted like he was thinking about it. Then he closed his cell phone and told the owner. "Make a copy of this tape, right now. Give me the original and keep the backup tape. If you'll do that, I'll try to keep you out of jail."

The owner turned to his tape equipment and selected a box of tapes. When he opened it he found it was empty. He turned and showed it to Ethan with his other hand raised in a universal expression of, "it's not my fault."

Ethan took the original tape and put it into his pocket. He looked at the owner. "I will return this after the investigation into the disappearance of the woman is finished."

The owner shook his head quickly from side to side. "No, no, you keep it; I don't want it back, really."

Ethan took out a notebook and asked the owner for information about himself. He jotted down the man's name, address, phone number, and physical description. He then took out his cell phone and took pictures of the man, his shop, the camera, and the booth that Su Li had sat in.

Then he left the bagel shop and headed back through the dark night to the Portal.

Back in his room he captured the video on his computer. He got several good shots of the faces of the two men. He went back into the Police computer and ran facial recognition on both of them.

While the computer was chewing on that Ethan went back to the street cameras and was able to get a long distance shot of the two men hauling the two women out of the shop and placing them into the back seat area of an American Chevy Tahoe. Then the men got in and drove away. Ethan captured the vehicle and its license plate and set the computer to find all street cameras that saw that vehicle for the rest of the evening of the day before this one.

As it was running Ethan went back to the facial recognition program and realized his mistake. The computer had identified the two men and opened up several more files which showed an on-going investigation into one of the men by the Police.

Ethan immediately captured all of the files, disabled the search, and backed out of the investigation completely. He switched back to the vehicle search and captured the one hundred and ninety-six video clips of the vehicle in its travel from the bagel shop. Again Ethan backed out of the search program and misdirected the reflex search for Inspector Clueso.

He went into the Police administrative files and removed all references to Inspector Clueso including his interest in the man in the Tahoe. Finally, Ethan sanitized the Clueso history and passwords. While the Police computer was trying to trace Ethan's connection, Ethan sent it on a wild goose chase into darkest Africa.

Clicking out of the Police server, Ethan was able to physically remove any trace to the Crossfire Team's computers involving this case.

The Police would see tiny traces of the searches and of the Clueso persona but everything would be a dead end.

Breathing a sigh of relief that he had prevented a run-in with the Israeli Police, Ethan read the files on Victor Chemolov. He was definitely an evil man. Ethan shook his head, "And Su Li is in this guy's clutches."

CHAPTER THIRTY-SIX

Ethan called up the videos of the Tahoe as it traveled across Tel Aviv. He arranged all the videos into time sequence. He worked through the videos and removed the duplicates and coverages that didn't show enough to help. He tracked the Tahoe from the Bagel shop to a warehouse district two miles north.

He watched as the outside cameras on a bonded warehouse caught the Tahoe as it parked outside of a small warehouse with the number 56 on the door. Ethan was happy that he was able to enjoy the night vision capabilities of the bonded warehouse cameras. It had turned dark by the time the Tahoe had reached its destination. But, with the NV camera it was like watching a daylight image with a lot of green shades.

Ethan watched as the two men carried the unconscious women into the warehouse and shut the door. He located the Police link to the bonded warehouse cameras and watched warehouse 56 throughout the night and into today. Around nine in the morning one of the two men exited the warehouse. He took the Tahoe and left. He came to the present time and the Tahoe had not come back as yet.

Turning off his computer Ethan thought for a few minutes. He decided to make sure that Su Li was still in the warehouse before he brought the rest of the team in on what could be a false alarm. But, he also knew he could make mistakes and get both himself and Su Li killed due to his pride if he rode in there like the Lone Ranger hoping to save the damsel by himself.

After all, he had only been on one mission and only two weeks of training to be a warrior. But, if he could prevent her from harm he would do what needed to be done. As a safety backup he put everything he'd learned including the video clips and what he was going to do into a file that he put into a delayed posting to Charlie Wu's Email. Ethan set the delay post for one hour.

He got up again and checked his weapons. He put the Ray Bans on his desk and left his apartment. He rode up in the elevator and asked the Mossad security detail for a vehicle and a driver.

Since Ethan wasn't one of the usual Core Team the man in charge of the Portal asked him what he needed the car and driver for.

Ethan smiled, "I've got a clue as to where our missing pilot might be and I want to check it out. See, she's my teacher in hand-to-hand combat and I am really worried about her."

The Mossad leader told him to wait just inside the exit doors and he would get a car and driver for him.

After Ethan left, the man called down to the Mossad base across the airfield from the Crossfire base. Getting the man he wanted, he explained what Ethan had asked for. The voice on the other end of the phone asked, "Do you think he is on to something?"

The leader laughed, "Yes, actually I do but, I'm not sure this man is up to the task in his own right."

"Okay", came the answer. "I will get a car and meet him at the gate."

After he hung up the leader smiled. Mr. Reaper didn't know it but he was about to get one of the top Kidon, Mossad's ultra-secret assassination unit as a driver.

Ethan saw the Chevrolet SUV pull up at the curb beyond the crash barriers and jogged out to it. He opened the front door on the passenger side and hopped into the seat. The driver stuck out his hand, "Hello, I'm Elon, you are Ethan?"

Ethan smiled and shook Elon's hand. He immediately noticed that the man's hand was calloused and strong. "That would be me." He handed Elon a piece of paper with the warehouse area address on it. Elon nodded and pulled out into traffic.

Ethan checked his watch and saw that it was after 10:00 P.M. in Tel Aviv and that should remove day-time personnel from the action.

Elon asked him, "What are you doing out tonight?"

Ethan thought about the casual request and decided to go with his gut-level feeling about the man. "One of our personnel left the base yesterday and then disappeared. I did some digging and think she might have been taken to a small warehouse where we are headed."

Elon looked over at Ethan, "What are you going to do when we get there?"

Ethan thought that was a bit of an intrusive question for a driver but, again, what the heck. "I'm going to see if I can verify her presence in this place."

"And then?"

"I'll either call in our team or I'll see what I can do to facilitate her escape from her captors."

Elon nodded his head. "Okay, how many captors do you think you'll be facing?"

Ethan shrugged, "Don't know for sure. I know one man for sure; possibly two if the second man I know of has returned by the time we get there. I don't have a clue as to any more people that may have already been there. That's why I'm going to see what intelligence I can get about the operation."

Elon smiled, "Sounds like a good plan. What do you want me to do?"

Ethan looked at the man. "I don't want to get you into our trouble, or in this case, probably my trouble; so why don't you wait for me with the SUV. If I'm not back in twenty minutes you might give my group a call. Here's the number." Ethan gave Elon a card with Charlie Wu's name on it. "Just tell the guy on the other end that Ethan's bit off more than he can chew. Charlie will understand, he's my boss."

They reached the warehouse area and Ethan had Elon do a drive by first. The Tahoe was back. Ethan shook his head, "Looks like at least two bad guys." He pulled out the paper with Chemolov's picture and rap sheet on it.

He handed the paper to Elon, "This is one of the two guys in there and he's a really bad guy."

Elon looked at the paper. His face was normal and expressionless but his heart jumped. The Kidon group had been looking for this man for months. He had killed three Rabbis and a hand full of children during an escape after he'd executed a Mossad agent three years ago. Elon made an executive decision. Normally he worked in a team of four to seven operatives but this fortuitous find needed to be handled now.

Elon looked at Ethan, "Looks like a tough character. You want some help?"

Ethan smiled, "I probably need it but like I said, I don't want to get you involved in our problems. If it looks tough, I can get people here in less than fifteen minutes." Ethan opened the door and stepped out of the SUV. "I'll be back soon." As he thought to himself, "maybe, maybe not."

CHAPTER THIRTY-SEVEN

Elon watched as Ethan moved carefully from shadow to shadow as he approached Warehouse 56. He placed a call to his unit leader and told him about the operation that was going down and who was probably in the building. The unit leader told him to assist the Crossfire member as needed. A flying squad was already on its way to that location.

Ethan carefully surveyed the building but couldn't see any cameras or watchers. He searched the warehouse and found it didn't have any other doors or windows. It only had just the skylights on the roof which were all closed and the front door. Moving up to the building he carefully scanned the wall until he found a wire that ran through the wall about two feet above him. The hole was bigger than the wire and a small amount of light showed through the little hole.

Reaching into his jacket pocket Ethan took out a little adaptation of his own. It was a video camera lens chip on a long, thin, flexible leader. He plugged the cable from the other end of the flexible cable into his cell phone and selected "Video" on the phone's keypad. He got a good picture. He reached up and slowly slid the flexible leader into the building.

As the camera lens reached the inside of the warehouse building Ethan could see some of the interior which was well lit up by bright lights. He checked to see if there was anyone near enough to see the little lens. He didn't find anything to worry about. He pushed the lens in further and was able to slowly rotate the lens and turn it this way and that as he twisted the flexible lead.

He finally saw past some large crates and saw the back of Victor Chemolov who was looking at something in front and below him. He looked to be shouting but there was almost no sound through the little hole and his video didn't have any sound capability. Then Chemolov raised his right hand and swung it downward sharply. The man then turned to his right and walked out of sight. What his absence showed drove a dagger of fear through Ethan's heart. Su Li sat tied to a chair facing him and her face was cut and bruised badly. But she hadn't given up. Even from forty feet away through his little lens Ethan could see the fire in her eyes.

Deciding he needed help he reached for his cell phone. A quiet voice behind him said, "Don't make a call."

Ethan looked over his right shoulder in the dark as his left hand slid over the handle of his pistol under his jacket. Elon shook his head slightly. "Don't get heroic Ethan. You can't draw your pistol before I could shoot you, if I was a bad guy."

Ethan dropped his left hand and whispered, "What are you doing here, Elon?"

The Kidon agent laughed quietly. "I am here to help you. Did you find Ms. Li?"

Ethan showed the Mossad agent his phone picture of Su Li. "Yes, and I've got to get some help to get her out of there before Chemolov kills her."

Suddenly another figure silently appeared next to Elon and spoke quietly in Hebrew. Elon quietly fired off a bunch of orders in Hebrew and gave the new man Ethan's camera. He then turned and took Ethan's right arm in his left hand and led him to the front of the warehouse.

Ethan's eyes grew wide when he saw three more Israelis setting up a string of putty-like substance about an inch in diameter around the door in the front of the warehouse. The four men moved away and Elon pulled Ethan back. Suddenly the det-cord exploded and blew the entire door and its frame out of the building. All four men rushed into the building with their short, silenced, Galil assault rifles up with laser beams looking for targets.

Ethan pulled away from Elon's grip and pulling out his pistol. He moved into the warehouse behind the four men. They went four different directions but Ethan made a bee-line for where he knew Su Li was tied to the chair.

There was a sudden hushed chain-saw sound as one of the Kidon agents unleashed a flurry of shots off to Ethan's left. Ethan reached the big crates that he had seen from the outside and carefully glanced around the crate. His teeth clenched when he saw Chemolov standing next to Su Li with her hair in his left hand and a handgun pointed at her head. The big man was looking past Su Li toward where the gunfire had been. His back was to Ethan.

Ethan didn't know what to do. If he shot Chemolov the man could trigger his gun and kill Su Li. But, if he didn't do anything she might die, anyway.

As Ethan debated what to do, Elon appeared to Ethan's left. He snap aimed his pistol and fired one silenced shot directly into the base of Chemolov's brain where it met the spinal column. Chemolov dropped to the floor next to Su Li without a sound and looking for all the world as if he was boneless. Chemolov's pistol fell to the floor unfired.

Ethan put his pistol away as two more of the Kidon agents came toward them dragging the body of the other kidnapper. He quickly got to Su Li and pulled his K-bar knife from its sheath at his back. In three quick swipes he had cut her cords and released her from the chair. As he helped her get the bindings off of her legs and arms he smiled at her. She looked good even though her face looked like she'd been in a car wreck. Ethan held out his hand to help her get up from the chair.

Su Li staggered a bit as she moved forward. Ethan grabbed her left arm to keep her from falling. She moved close and clutched Ethan. Due to the damage to her lip she mumbled, "What took you so long?".

Ethan smiled, "I had to stop for bagels first. No, actually, I'm not even supposed to be out here. I wasn't assigned to your disappearance. Charlie doesn't even know I'm out looking for you."

Behind him he heard Charlie's voice, "You sure of that, Ethan?"

Turning around Ethan saw Charlie, Mark, Laura, and Sarah standing there in their combat gear with their M-8s in their hands. Behind them he saw Jack talking to Elon.

Taking a tough tone, Ethan said, "I'm sorry I interfered in the case Charlie, but no one takes my teacher away from me and my lessons!"

Mark looked at the two bodies on the floor, "And it doesn't look like they will ever do that again."

There were more lights and more people showing up. The Israeli Police walked up to Elon and spoke to him for a few seconds. Then they came over and asked Su Li to answer some questions. She told them everything she could remember but it wasn't much.

The Police officer asked her what the kidnappers were questioning her about. Su Li shook her head. "Same old thing. They wanted to know where the Crossfire Team base was. I didn't tell them a thing."

Two Paramedics came in and sat Su Li back down in her chair and went to work on her face and hands which were also bloody.

Ethan slowly stepped back from the action and leaned against one of the crates. Elon and Jack came over to him and he straightened up. Jack smiled at him. "You continue to amaze me, Ethan. I have a billion dollars worth of computers and spies looking for Su Li and you find her in less than two hours work, get the Mossad to help you and rescue her before we even know what you were doing. Good work."

Elon reached over and shook Ethan's hand. "Thank you for leading us to a cold blooded killer of Hebrew children that we've been seeking for the last three years. I'm sorry I stole your action by shooting Chemolov but I just couldn't resist it."

Ethan smiled at the Israeli agent. "No, thank you for helping me save Su Li and actually, I didn't know what to do so that he wouldn't kill her. You solved that problem nicely by the way. I still have a lot to learn, apparently."

CHAPTER THIRTY-EIGHT

After coordinating with the Kidon team, the Crossfire Team was transported back to the Sea Base in two large SUVs, again, courtesy of the Mossad. Once back home, Su Li was accompanied by Laura and Sarah to her apartment. Laura made sure she was comfortable when Sean Murphy knocked at the door. Sarah let him in and he checked Su Li's injuries.

After he checked her out he sat down and took her left hand in his and looked directly at her. "Su Li, you took a major beating and it's going to take time to heal. We'll pray for you that the Lord will restore your beauty. But, the good news is that you didn't get any broken bones so that we don't have to do any reconstructive surgery."

Sarah smiled, "I have a feeling Chemolov was just softening you up in the attempt to extract information. The next stage would have been more damaging, both physically and psychologically."

Sean added, "Both of your eyes are in good shape and the loose teeth will reset themselves because you're young and were healthy to begin with."

Standing up Sean said, "My prescription is that you spend today resting but I'm putting you on limited duty until you feel ready to resume your routines. I also would recommend you use swimming to restore your strength because it will help your skin heal in the process. I'm glad you're back with us." Sean got up and patted her on the shoulder, then he left the apartment.

Sarah fluffed up the pillow Su Li was leaning against on the couch. "How do you feel?"

Su Li sighed, "I feel fine but my face and hands hurt. I'm not really physically incapacitated but I am tired. Even though I was unconscious I apparently didn't get any real sleep or rest. The thing that bothers me the most is that I'm deep down mad. I've prayed against this anger, confessed it as a sin of unbelief in Yahveh and repented of it. Yet, I'm still mad!"

Laura suggested that the three of them pray against the anger. "Heavenly Father Yahveh, we are your children and we stand in awe of your being, your strength, and your love. We come seeking your love and healing touch for Su Li's spirit and body. The abuse and violation she suffered has opened a door for the enemy to attempt to stoke the fires of anger in an attempt to make her sin in her anger. She has prayed for forgiveness and repented of any sin involved with this assault. We pray that you will cleanse her soul and spirit of unforgiveness and anger. Wash her in the blood of Yahshua and shut any doors opened by the enemy."

Laura prayed in her prayer language and listened for the Father's words. She got a definite leading. "Su Li, this encounter may have opened an old wound. You need to again repent of your anger when Thor was killed because deep inside you saw it as abandonment, even though he didn't want to leave you. It is still a stronghold for the enemy to cause you to want to scream in anger at the loss you felt at that time. Repeat after me. Dear Most Precious Father in Heaven, I confess the sin of anger and unforgiveness against Thor when he was killed. You are my life and my support and my love. Please forgive me for harboring this sin and release me from it forever. I ask this in Yahshua's name. Amen."

Su Li sat there for a few minutes with her head bowed. Then she looked up at Laura. "My anger is gone! I feel so free and released. Oh, how I wished I had known about this before."

Laura shook her head. "Hurts that deep take time to get to and cut loose. It's a lot like peeling an onion. One layer at a time. You look so much happier." She gave the smaller woman a gentle hug.

Sarah asked, "We saw the video that Ethan found of your meeting with Meiling Yong. Do you think she was part of the effort to kidnap you?"

Su Li slowly shook her head. "No, the RHONE apparently worked with the MSS to set Meiling up. The MSS deliberately let her see the file on me and the recent update that indicated that they had sent killers to Israel to find and kill me. She was shepherded all along the way to find me and bring me to where Chemolov and his partner could get me. I still don't really understand how they made both Meiling and me pass out."

Sarah made a small face. "It's an old spy trick. They treated the pictures they "let" her find. Those pictures that were so conveniently already wrapped in plastic sleeves to prevent damage in transit. Actually, they had treated the pictures with a combination drug. When you handled picture one, or two, and then picture three you activated the drug which knocked you both out. If she had been part of the plan she won't have been knocked out. Seeing that could have prevented you from actually handling the last picture."

Laura asked, "Su Li, do you know what happened to Meiling?"

Su Li nodded; her voice was flat, devoid of any emotion. "Chemolov shot her in the head. He killed her to show me that they meant what they said about killing me if I didn't give them the information they wanted. Then they threw her body into a sewer in hopes that it would make me talk. It just made me angrier." Su Li looked very sad, "She was another innocent and probably the last contact I'll ever have with someone from Thor's family."

Laura called down to the on-duty SOG personnel that were doing kitchen duty and arranged a light breakfast for all three of them.

Downstairs, after filing their after-action reports and cleaning up, the rest of the Core Team had moved to the War Room taking Ethan with them.

When they had the recording system running Charlie asked Ethan, "Explain what you did and how you knew how to do it?"

Ethan explained about his training back in Colorado on investigative techniques because he had wanted to improve his computer sleuthing abilities. He also explained about his virtual Inspector Clueso. "As I saw it, the problem was that we didn't know why or where Su Li had gone. Since I had set up this computer persona it was a natural path for me to use the Police capabilities with the cameras to see if I could track down where Su Li went. I made a mistake when I left the facial recognition program running unattended. When the software identified Chemolov, it automatically triggered an alert and I was almost caught peeking in their files. I think I got out and cleaned up my trail sufficiently so that the team won't be charged with snooping in their private stuff."

"Several times I thought I would tell you or Jack about what I'd found. But, I was concerned that they might have moved her and therefore not lead to anything and distract you guys from what you were already doing for Su Li."

"By the time I found her I was in too deep with Elon and the Kidon assassins to get a message to you. I mean, other than the file I left you before I went to the warehouse. Really, I was only going to make sure she was there and then call you."

Jack listened to Ethan as he related his advanced search techniques and his single-handed attempt to locate Su Li. When Ethan was finished talking he spoke up. "You do know that if Yahveh hadn't protected you there were many places where you could have been captured or killed and we wouldn't even know about it."

"That's why we always work as a team. We work together joining our individual talents with the others to achieve our goals. While that is true, it does not minimize the effort you made to find Su Li. You were brilliant in deducing the quickest way to locate her. You just need more seasoning to avoid traps in which your enthusiasm can expose you to."

Ethan now fully realized he had endangered himself and Su Li and he had to admit he was too eager to solve the mystery without realizing the danger they were in. He realized that he was probably going to be put on a short leash for a while. But, Yahveh had protected him and he would make the effort to endure his wrist-slapping until he was more skilled.

Jack then asked Ethan to go up and check on Su Li and then come back and tell everyone how she was doing.

After he left, Jack asked everyone there for their opinion of Ethan and his actions in this matter.

Mark chuckled, "The kid showed me some things and I'm a professional investigator married to a spy. I think we need to incorporate him into our Core Team operations and let him do any investigating for us." Mark still missed his friends, Stan and Debbie Hargrove, who had been killed recently. They had been the Team's investigators before that event.

Charlie, David, Alexis, and the others agreed with Mark. David added that they still needed to keep an eye on him until he was better trained and had several more missions under his belt.

Jack nodded, "Okay,

Ethan walked in and sat down. "Su Li, Laura, and Sarah were all talking at the same time and I couldn't get a word in edgewise." He grinned. "I finally called Laura on her cell phone, although she was only four feet away from me. As to Su Li's condition. She's fine and is going to take today off. Tomorrow she will return to duty on a limited basis."

Jack thanked him for the report. "Ethan, we've been discussing your efforts over the last twenty-four hours and we have come to a decision that affects your future with this team."

Ethan had to force himself to breathe. He was sure that he had over-stepped his bounds and now it could cost him his job and his income. But, he didn't try to plead for another chance or for favor. He just sat there and waited to hear what his future held. He realized that now that he had given his life to Yahshua he wasn't fearful or resentful or even worried how things would work out. He had a destiny that he wasn't in charge of and he realized he liked it that way.

Jack smiled at him. "Even though we have some reservations about how you accomplished your quest we all are agreed that you showed us some real grit and inventiveness. If you are willing, we would like to move you into a full-time position on the Core Team. You will function as our lead investigator, especially on cases that are mysterious."

Ethan realized that he hadn't taken a breath throughout Jack's message and he let the pent-up breath out of his lungs as quietly as he could.

Jack said, "Charlie agreed that your computer talents would be a good addition to the Core Team operation and he will have a hard time replacing you in COMSEC. He did reserve the right to call on you if he gets too overloaded."

Ethan nodded his head. He was elated with their decision. "Thank you for the vote of confidence. I'll try to live up to your standards. I know I tried to save Su Li on my own and that was not really intelligent. I appreciate the chance and would have been very disappointed if I had to go to work somewhere else."

CHAPTER THIRTY-NINE

The meeting broke up and Jack went with Ethan to his room in the COMSEC barracks. After collecting his belongings and his computers, Jack brought him back to the escalator up to the apartment level. He took the twelfth hallway and opened the door to the suite.

Jack placed Ethan's suitcase on the settee at the end of the king-size bed. Looking at the younger man he said, "This is now your apartment, is it okay?" Ethan realized that he was truly amazed and blessed by the upscale furniture and appointments in the large apartment. Looking around the room he admired the professionally decorated suite. Artistic paint mixed with silk wall coverings. There were automatic light systems in the living room, bathroom, closets, and of course, the main bedroom. He smelled the beautiful scent of ozone in the air which smelled like a rainstorm had just passed through. The furniture was seamlessly joined to walls or the floor and large mirrors expanded the already large room.

He walked over to the floor to ceiling windows on one wall that showed the sea with its waves marching into an unseen shore below his sight level. He could see foam blowing off of the peaks of the waves. It was truly beautiful and very restful.

Ethan looked at Jack in awe. "How do you get this window looking out over the sea while we are at least a half-mile below the water?"

Jack grinned as he joined the young man. "This is the one feature I never get used to myself. Actually, my father invented this and my company developed it. We call it the "Viewport". There is actually more than a mile of water, rock, and sand above that wall and the view it shows. My company in Denver, Colorado both manufactures the Viewports and has contracts with other companies to do the same. While I understand the physics of it, I am not sure I really know how it works. Everyone loves the views it can provide. You should be used to this. All the windows in COMSEC are Viewports."

"You want to see something else that will stun you?" Ethan nodded his head. Jack told Ethan to lie down on the bed with his head on the pillows and close his eyes. Ethan did as he was told. After he closed his eyes, Jack picked up a remote control and pushed two buttons on it. He then told Ethan to open his eyes. When he opened his eyes he said, "Oh, my God."

The room was gone except for the bed, and the two of them. The sea and the sky spread out in full splendor in every direction. It was as if they were in floating on the sea with no ship or buildings anywhere near them. Ethan could actually feel and hear the cool sea breeze as it blew the waves along. He could see the sun setting over the Western horizon. It was very pleasant and relaxing. He could hear sounds of the distance in all directions over the water. There was a gull circling above them and he could not only hear it's call but he could hear the echoes from the sea. It was the most incredible things he had ever experienced. He looked at Jack with amazement in his eyes. He felt that if he got off the bed he'd probably have to swim to stay afloat. He asked Jack, "How do you do that? Do you know how many of these things you could sell if they were incorporated into the hottest video games?"

Jack pushed the two buttons again and the view disappeared except for the window in the wall overlooking the sea. The restful room was back. Jack showed him how to change the settings on the remote control. "Just wait until you do that after nighttime. Laura and I love just lying in bed watching the stars, it is fantastic. We actually had a dolphin surface and it looked like it was going to swim right up to our bed. Of course it didn't but I wondered if it would."

Jack pulled out a drawer and gave Ethan the operation manual for the Viewport and then said, "I like the idea and market for one of these systems incorporated in a video game system. I'll have you work up a design and then have you talk to the viewport engineers. It'll probably give you more money than you can believe," He headed toward the door to the suite when he stopped and opened the top to a jewelry box on the dresser by the door. He walked back to Ethan and handed him a NovaStar medallion. He took Ethan's old COMSEC medallion. Jack got serious and told

Ethan about the capabilities of the defense system and warned him to always keep the medallion with him while he was resident in the Sea Base. "This one will get you into places you couldn't get to before." Jack then showed him the apartment's Mini-War Room annex where he could work from unless called to the real War Room.

Jack's mood lightened and he said, "Come on, let me show you the rest of the base that you haven't seen yet."

The level below the living room housed the exercise gym, laundry, storage areas, the Armory, the firing range, and additional rooms for food and supplies.

In a separate area on the living room level were the control room that defended the Sea Base, and the conference room that Ethan had been meeting Laura in for Bible and Torah training. Jack then took Ethan down to the lower level and through another tunnel. They found themselves in a huge, sunlit green house, arboretum, and garden. There were several birds flying around in the area. Jack then led his one-man tour down a hall that led to an Olympic-sized swimming pool with changing rooms and a sunning area. Ethan was already acquainted with the large exercise and training rooms. Then they toured the mechanical equipment area that controlled all of the life-support systems and finally wound back up at the living room.

Jack asked him, "What do you think?" Ethan shook his head. "It is all incredible and almost unbelievable that I am a part of it all."

Jack laughed, "Remember that all this is a reward we don't get to spend much time enjoying." Jack sat down on a functional couch and put down a tablet he had been carrying. He took out several sheets and showed them to Ethan. "Here is your profile and your job offer. You can see that as a part of the Core Team your salary will be one million dollars a year with bonuses that will quadruple your income each year. All of your medical needs, dental, hearing, sight, etc. is one-hundred percent covered by the team. We have counselors who can assist you as to investments or plans you might want to set up. Remember, we have approximately three years before the Lord gathers us to Him for the Wedding Feast of the Lamb."

Jack looked at Ethan for a few seconds. "Uh oh, I may have spoken out of turn. You didn't know the Lord when we were asked to stay for the first three and a half years so you weren't given the option to fight on for the Kingdom of Yahveh and to be raptured at the mid-point of the seventh week of Daniel." Jack sat back and thought about that.

Ethan said, "I did get a chance to meet the Angel Rose and she gave me the choice between Heaven and Hell. She actually downloaded a trailer for both of them for me. I suddenly realized that the Father and Yahshua give everyone a choice because they love every person. I want to be a part of a Kingdom like that. I chose Heaven and that's when I made my decision to ask Yahshua into my heart as my Lord and Savior. Does that count?"

Jack raised an eyebrow. "Could be, I'll include that question the next time I pray for wisdom. Most likely you have been added to our merry little band. Yahveh seems to know about these type of things in advance."

Jack stared at Ethan for a minute. "You do know that salary and the bonuses are above and beyond the fact that your living expenses are included in your employment. The only thing we demand is that you give one-hundred and fifty percent of your ability to accomplishing the tasks that the Father gives us to do. You will be in more combat than most soldiers in their Military career, and in danger constantly, and it will require you to grow in your faith and in your abilities to stay the course."

Ethan smiled, "I do understand it and I am looking forward to it. I feel that I am actually doing something for God. My earlier life wasn't anything but selfishness."

I appreciate everything the team provides and I do realize I will make more money than 99.99 percent of the people in the world and probably won't have the time to spend it. But, seriously, you have offered me a great chance to do something worthwhile for people that can't do it for themselves. Also, like I said before, I feel good about doing something for Yahshua after all that He did for me at Calvary." Ethan thought for a second, "I'm rambling on, aren't I?"

Ethan got up and shook Jack's hand. When he spoke it was from his heart. "You can count on me."

CHAPTER FORTY

Laura sat in the War Room at her console and added a twelfth position to the existing consoles. She could see anyone at any console because the large wall screen was located above the end of the horseshoe shaped desk that the consoles were located in. She got up and walked down to the new position which was the closest to the big screen. She sat in the new position she had just created for Ethan Reaper.

She didn't like the proximity to the screen and the acute angle he would have to see the screen at. She got up and placed a call to the Site Maintenance group. She explained her problem and they said they would send a technician over immediately. Seven minutes later there was a tap at the door. Laura opened the door and admitted a nice-looking man in tan pants and a utility shirt with lots of pockets. He smiled and said, "Hi, I'm Joe Slone from Site Development and Maintenance." He looked at the layout of the room and asked Laura to detail the problem and her desired results.

Laura took Slone down to the last seat on the console and had him sit in it. She brought up a blank standard form and then a video for him. "The problem is that the people on this end and the other end of the horseshoe are too close to the main screen and have a distorted view of the information displayed there. I need everyone to have a clear view of the information on that screen."

Joe Slone nodded his head. "I can see the problem. Is one of the requirements everyone be able to see all of the other people in here face to face?"

Laura thought about that. "In the beginning it was helpful. But now, I'm not sure it is that important. The function of this room is to allow everyone to interact together or individually or in small groups as needed. We can get camera views of all the other member's head and shoulders on the monitors at each position. Each position is a nexus for communications, electronic, video, etc., but there are times the overall problem is displayed on the large screen for everyone to comment on. So, no, I don't think the physical eyeballing of each other is that needed."

Joe nodded his head. "Then I recommend that you rearrange your seating into four tiers with four consoles on each tier side by side. That way everyone will get the same view of the big screen. I recommend that you change the screen to an ADI LED screen like a Jumbo-tron by a major manufacturer. That way you can provide much more information, much clearer, and allow for any future expansion of this room. You would have four more positions available immediately and you could include additional seating on the floor below the working stations in the event you had to include a few dozen more people."

Laura thought about that and told Joe to create sketches of the layout and an estimate as to how long and how much the renovation would take.

Joe wrote some notes and then left for his department.

Laura was pleased with the solution and went to find Jack and tell him and the Connelly's about it.

While Laura and Joe were discussing the War Room in the Sea Base another conversation was taking place by the Mossad at an office in Tel Aviv. An agreement was reached and Hiram Tzahal, the Director of the Mossad picked up his telephone and called the Prime Minister's office.

An hour later Jack's cell phone chirped. "Jack Malone, how can I help you, Director Tzahal?"

The Director chuckled quietly. "I think we need some help with spiritual matters, Mr. Malone. Could you and Mr. Connelly meet with me this evening?"

Jack sensed an ominous undertone to the invitation. "Certainly Director, where and when?"

"If you would be so kind as to attend to me at my office around 7:00 P.M. tonight I would appreciate it."

Jack replied, "We will be there, but, if it is all right with you I would like to bring David Zahavy with us because of his experience and knowledge in Institute matters. He could make it easier to determine our involvement."

Hiram Tzahal paused for a few seconds and then agreed to the addition of David. "We will see you three at 7:00."

After he hung up, Jack went to talk to Mark who was teaching weapons in the firing range classroom.

As he walked into the classroom Mark was showing four trainees how to rapidly breakdown an M-8 rifle and reassemble it while not looking at it. "You need to be able to field strip and reassemble this weapon in the dark without help." Mark looked at Megan Cole, Ethan Reaper, Carol Moffet, and a new replacement for the SOG named Hiram Levinson, and they all nodded to their instructor.

Mark indicated to Jack that they should step out of the training room. Mark looked back at the trainees and said, "All right, begin." Then he turned out the lights and shut the door. He looked at Jack with a facial expression that simply said, "What?"

Jack told him about the Mossad Director's request for a meeting in about three hours. Mark called up his schedule on his phone. "Yeah, I can do it."

Mark opened the door and turned on the lights to find all four trainees holding completely reassembled rifles. He said, "Assuming that you all tore the rifles down before reassembling them, you did well." He picked up a pair of NVGs and reached for the light switch. "Let's do it again."

Jack called David and explained the meeting request and asked him to attend as agreed to by the Director. David accepted quietly. As David disconnected the call he recognized the uniqueness of the meeting. He thought to himself, "Normally, Director Tzahal wouldn't deal with people outside the organization personally. This could be something major and important for both groups."

Laura found Jack and told him about the proposed renovations to the War Room. Jack agreed they needed to do something because the newer Core Team members were complaining about sore necks trying to watch the main screen. Jack then told her about his feelings of urgency and importance about the upcoming meeting.

As normal, Laura was praying in the Spirit while she listened to Jack describe the meeting that evening. She said, "I also feel that there is something monumental in the Heavenlies about this meeting. Let's pray, and then see if Carol can shed light on it."

CHAPTER FORTY-ONE

Jack, Mark, and David were shown into the Mossad's office right at 7:00 P.M. There were two other men in the office and the Director introduced them as Elon Lukin and Abram Cahn.

David immediately recognized Abram as the Director of the Kidon Assassins and Elon as one of his top field agents. The Kidon were part of the Collections Group, the largest department of the Mossad, which is tasked with many aspects of conducting espionage overseas. Employees in the Collections Department operate under a variety of covers, including diplomatic and unofficial. David nodded to both men who nodded back. David had been one of the Mossad's best in his position as Manager of Mossad field agents. There was an easy camaraderie and understanding between the three men.

Evaluating the three men of the Crossfire Team, Director Tzahal of the Mossad sighed. "Gentlemen, I have read the reports of your team's accomplishments over the last few years. Admittedly, I had many doubts at first. Then I began to see your stand for Yahveh. People I have known for years: people who are at the top of their professions in intelligence and defense of their countries have convinced me that what the reports say is primarily the truth. I still wasn't convinced until I had a talk this morning with Rabbi Chanan. He convinced me thoroughly. The event he went through at the Portal to the Undersea Base has deeply affected him and his understanding of the powers ranged against Israel. He is adamant about your team being the only ones that can defend our nation in the supernatural realm. He has nothing but the highest praise for you and your team."

"We have encountered a critical situation where we need your help. My charter normally does not allow me to involve anyone outside our organization into our operations except as contract workers who are not aware of our real nature or our plans. This situation is so far off normal I am at a loss to know how to attack it or defeat it."

The Director looked at the Kidon's two men present in the meeting. "I want to stress my confidence in the Kidon and their ability to handle the toughest cases given them. I have no doubts about their ability or their loyalty to Israel. Normally, they operate unseen and the results of their work are meticulous and free of any other group, including those in Collections"

"But, Director Cahn came to me with a problem that is more than they can handle this time. My direction from the PM is to solve this current dilemma quickly, quietly, and efficiently. When Abram came to me with his problems, I researched our assets, including Rabbi Chanan. Based on his recommendations to include your team, which as I said is a major deviation from our normal operation, I took it up the ladder to my boss."

The Mossad Director stared at Jack, "It seems that the PM also has nothing but high praise and confidence in you and your team. So, I need to know if you are willing to coordinate with the Kidon and work together to resolve this matter."

Jack had been praying silently as Director Tzahal talked. "Director Tzahal, I told the Prime Minister that we would be willing to help Israel in any way we could. I have been in prayer while you were discussing your dilemma and I believe that Father Yahveh wants us to help resolve the matter. As a team we are led by Yahveh to do His works. Apparently, your matter is one of the works He wants us to attack. So, yes, we are willing to work with the Kidon, whose personnel and operations we have great respect for, to resolve the supernatural problems they are running into."

The Director smiled, "Good, then I will turn this meeting over to Abram so that he can bring you up to date on this operation which we have named "Damocles."

Abram turned to the three Crossfire warriors and smiled. "To begin with, let me explain the history of the name "Damocles".

"Judge no one happy until his life is over" is a familiar theme in Greek and Roman philosophical writing. One variant of this is the Sword of Damocles, which is used to describe a sense of foreboding and might translate into English idiom as "walk a mile in my shoes before you judge my life." The story about Damocles' sword begins with Dionysius (II) who was a Fourth Century B.C. tyrant of Syracuse, a city in Magna Graecia, the Greek area of Southern Italy."

"To all appearances, Dionysius was very rich and comfortable, with all the luxuries money could buy, tasteful clothing and jewelry, and delectable food. He even had court flatterers to inflate his ego. One of these ingratiatory types was the court sycophant, Damocles. Damocles used to make comments to the King about his wealth and luxurious life. One day when Damocles complimented the tyrant on his abundance and power, Dionysius turned to Damocles and said, "If you think I'm so lucky, how would you like to try out my life?"

"Damocles readily agreed, and so Dionysius ordered everything to be prepared for Damocles to experience what life as Dionysius was like. Damocles was enjoying himself immensely... until he noticed a large, heavy, and very sharp sword hanging directly over his head. This sword was suspended from the ceiling by a single horse hair. This, the tyrant explained to Damocles, was what life as ruler was really like."

"Damocles, alarmed, quickly revised his idea of what made up a good life, and asked to be excused. He then eagerly returned to his poorer, but safer life"

Abram smiled again. "Damocles is an apt name for this operation because the man at the heart of the matter, has realized his play acting to impress his master, has now put him in an extremely dangerous situation. He is attempting to return to his less glamorous, but safer life. This would bring a death sentence from his master and therein lies the problem. If he finds a way to run away and shirk his duties they will hunt him down and kill him, slowly. If he can't run away, the power and duty he has had placed on him will kill him because he can't control it. Why do we care? Because this man is critical to preventing the death of thousands of Jewish people and a possible end to our nation's future. So, we can't have him dying. Let me elaborate."

"Bashshan Nazari is the only son of a very rich Saudi and the apple of his father's eye. He wasn't demonstrating the proper Arab manhood aggression so his father bought him a position as an Officer in the Iranian Army. The officers in the Iranian army didn't see him as a Line Officer so they dumped him into a small radical group aligned with the Military that worked on "special projects". He was assigned as the Second in Command behind a terrorist with the rank of Major. Because of other considerations we'll call the terrorist Major Abdulla. For the last three years Major Abdulla has been building a mysterious device that he assures his Commanders will kill thousands of Jews."

"Bashshan had little or no training in Military life or combat but he was a supremely good sycophant with a fairly good mind. He found a Sergeant who taught him how to create the proper reports on the efforts of Major Abdulla for his superiors. Bashshan quickly learned how to make the reports much clearer and concise. He also learned how to embellish them so that the progress of Abdulla's project met the required due dates."

The Kidon Director saw that the three new Israelis were clearly understanding and paying strict attention to his words. "Bashshan got the Sergeant assigned to his staff and used the Sergeant's advice in doing his daily duties. Unfortunately, Bashshan didn't even try to learn how and why things in the Military worked; he would just call the Sergeant to find out when and how to do things."

"Bashshan eventually figured out what the Major was creating and it literally scared the water out of him. He asked to be reassigned but he was a victim of his own success. Neither Major Abdulla nor the Military wanted to lose his ability to dissect and present complex issues so that they could be understood and acted on."

"Unable to get away from the focus of the effort being designed by and for the Major, to deliver to somewhere in Israel, and very scared of whatever the Major was developing, Bashshan turned to drinking. As you know, alcohol is forbidden for Muslims and Bashshan was risking his life as well as his job. We had one of our agents develop an underground "bar" relationship with him. We were surprised when he started talking about his project with his new friend."

"He had almost gotten to the good part of what the Major is creating when an event happened that changed everything. The Major had to attend a meeting three miles from his lab. He took the Sergeant as a driver. On the way there, an Iranian rebel group detonated an IED that destroyed their car and killed both of the men."

CHAPTER FORTY-TWO

Kidon Director Cahn continued, "Bashshan Nazari had suddenly lost his boss and the man that supplied him all of his Military ability at the same time. He didn't know what to do or how to do it. The Iranian Military leaders decided that they didn't want Major Abdulla's project to be lost. After the nuclear strike against their country, there weren't too many talented terrorist leaders who could continue the work and deliver the death blow to Israel. The wonderful reports from Bashshan had clarified everything that the Major was doing, so no one else had the full confidence and knowledge of the project, with the exception of Bashshan."

"The Military leaders promoted Bashshan to the rank of Major and told him that it was his duty to complete the Major's project. Humbly accepting the new rank and duty Bashshan had to be terrified on the inside. He has no clue as to how Major Abdallah was doing whatever he was doing on his project and now he doesn't have the Sergeant to tell him what to do. His promotion and assignment to lead the project to destroy Israel happened one week ago."

"So, now we come to why we need to involve your team in this operation. When Bashshan was moved into his new position, everything we had working, our contacts within the support group, our attempts to infiltrate the core group of Officers that know what is being planned, our observation teams, even our Kidon efforts have become blocked or exposed."

"It is like Iran is suddenly in on our operations. Our best operatives are being arrested, or killed outright. Two days ago we received a burst transmission from a hidden camera within the laboratory where the Major worked. We had managed to install it during a down time. The action it shows is exactly like some of the combat images of your team battling demons which don't show up on the videos." The Director took a large iPad tablet and turned it around so the Crossfire Team members could see it.

"Watch this," he said as he turned it on. Three men were searching the lab when one of them yelled and backed up quickly. All three men were terrorized and tried to defend themselves from something unseen. One by one they were killed by unseen hands and slashing weapons. The video ended with the death of the third man by beheading.

Jack had been praying during the video and felt led to join forces with the Kidon against the Iranian plot. "Who were the men that were killed?" He asked the Director.

The Director shook his head. "We weren't able to identify them except that they were Iranian and opposed to whatever operation the Military was running. Our intelligence people think that they were local opposition forces within the Nation of Iran."

"We haven't lost many of our people but all of our attempts to get involved in this operation, to determine the threat to Israel, is totally blunted. Even our Elint is blocked like never before. What do you make of all this?"

Jack knew that the Director was evaluating the Crossfire Team's competence and knowledge and seeing if they could really help them in this matter.

"Director Cahn, I can tell you this much. That battle, actually that slaughter, was done by demons that are most likely tasked with making sure that the Iranian operation succeeds. The blunting of your operatives and anything they try is typically a demon-controlled process, including transmission of electronic intelligence, or ELINT. I will have to have our people seek Yahveh to determine the path we need to take and how best to help your group."

Jack smiled at the man, "If this matter follows the normal course we will be able to assist your people in establishing what the threat is and removing that threat to Israel. I understand the need for rapid action so I assume that we will need to be back here in four to five hours with a plan of action."

Director Cahn stared at Jack for several seconds. "Why do you think that this will follow a "normal course"?"

Jack waved his hand to include everyone in the room. In Ancient Jewish History there is no word for "coincidence". We have found that with Yahveh there are no coincidences today, either. This select group of people would not be here if Yahveh didn't want us to be a part of this urgent matter. Since He did collect us here, then it follows that we need to be a part of it and He will command us to confront the demonic part of the problem for you."

The Director nodded his head. "Good. I'm very glad that you accepted my request for this meeting and I look forward to seeing you in a few hours."

After the Crossfire Team left for their base, Elon asked the Director, "Do you think they really are in such contact with God?"

Hiram Meir nodded to Elon, "Take a few minutes and talk to Rabbi Chanan. You will hear truth about this team. I know my faith in Yahveh has been increased greatly after I talked to him about them."

Mark commented to Jack and David as they rode back to the Portal, "Are they being straight with us, or, are they trying to advance some agenda that we don't see?"

David answered, "I worked for the Mossad for twenty-two years and I can assure you that both of your statements are true. I have also known Abram for over ten years and he is a shrewd man. If he talked to the PM and to Rabbi Chanan, then he is sincere in attempting to solicit our capabilities."

David put his hand on Mark's shoulder. "But, never forget the spy world they live in has many levels and Abram is active on all of them. I believe he is being up front with us on his request for a cooperative effort. But, I don't know what else he sees as an advantage to the Kidon that he will secure by our working together. I will tell you that, without a doubt, Abram's primary focus is protecting Israel at all costs and in action, not in politics."

Jack nodded, "That's the impression I got from the man. He never looked down or away when he made statements. As you both know, looking away is a sure sign of a person who isn't telling the truth when they speak."

Jack prayed for Heavenly protection to keep the demonic enemy from overhearing what he was going to do. He keyed his cell phone and got hold of Carol Moffet. "Hi Carol, I have a request for you and the Matrix." Jack explained in broad strokes what the problem was and what they needed. Carol agreed and hung up.

Mark smiled, "Going to see what the Heavens have to say about this, right?"

Jack nodded his head. "I've gotten a leading that we need to start gearing up for a major effort in this matter. Mark, why don't you convene a Core Team War Room council for when we return?"

CHAPTER FORTY-THREE

Jack stood in the door of the War Room and surveyed the assembly of personnel. He started at the left side of the big "U" nearest to the big screen. There was Sean Murphy, Megan Cole, Colonel Owens, (the leader of the SOG), David and Alexis Zahavy. Nearest to the door were Laura, Jack's position, Mark and Sarah Connelly. Continuing on down the far side of the "U" were Charlie Wu, Linda Wu, Carol Moffet, and Ethan Reaper. Jack thought, "Thirteen warriors dedicated to Yahveh's work."

He walked into the room and took his seat next to Laura. "All right, ladies and gentlemen. Here is the situation. Jack recounted the meeting with the Director of the Mossad and Abram Cahn, Director of the Kidon. When he was finished, he defined the things they needed to decide on. "But, before you start conferring and considering the options, you need to hear what Carol has to add." He nodded at the young woman with the experienced eyes.

Carol looked at the people around the table. "Jack asked me to go to the inter-dimensional spiritual Matrix. I spent several hours last night reviewing the lines, false leads, and action events between the Mossad, the Kidon, the Iranian efforts to destroy Israel, of which there are always several ongoing, and our team."

"I can tell you that there are far more spiritual demands and requests for inter-dimensional access than a simple plot to destroy Israel. This particular effort is only a small part of the on-going demonic effort to accomplish the destruction of the Jewish people. But, and I stress the word, but, this effort with Bashshan Nazari has suddenly become critical to the demonic efforts for the scattered remnants of the Iranian Government since the destruction of the leadership and their nuclear efforts."

Carol slowly looked around at the faces and said, "This "event" has the potential to be the most spiritually dangerous and most intense battle this team has ever been involved in, by a full magnitude."

"You will be going up against the second highest power in the evil kingdom. This project is under the direct supervision of Belial. Belial is a Prince of Hell. His domain is over the Northern Reaches of Hell. He commands eighty legions of demons and the sins under his command are lies and guilt. The reason he has such power is that his element is the Earth itself. Against Belial, your armor and swords will probably not defeat him, if you run into him. His power is almost the highest in the kingdom of the demons. The only one more powerful there is his master, Satan himself."

Jack smiled, "Carol, you know the Word of God. As it states in the Amplified Bible, Luke 10:19 *"Behold! I have given you authority and power to trample upon serpents and scorpions, and [physical and mental strength and ability] over all the power that the enemy [possesses]; and nothing shall in any way harm you."*

Jack shook his head, "While we have no power to combat spiritual enemies in our own strength, all power over the enemy comes from Yahshua and all glory is to Him. I believe that the second ranking power in hell won't be any more dangerous to us than what we have already met on the field of battle here on Earth. Yahveh is Supreme and His Son has all authority over everything. That will include Belial or even Satan, if we are doing battle per the Father's bidding, when we come against them."

Carol nodded, "I know, but the Matrix doesn't show us with a winning strategy if we come up against Belial."

Laura smiled, "Let's pray and see what the Father says about this."

As the entire core group prayed, a subtle change took place in the atmosphere of the room. Jack felt a surge of purity or righteousness and he opened his eyes to behold the angel Rose and behind her were dozens of more angels which began to sing softly a hymn of praise to Yahveh.

Jack felt his spirit join in that beautiful melody and soon he, along with everyone else there, was singing their heartfelt adoration to the Yahveh of the Universe. As the song ended all of the angels except Rose faded out of sight.

Rose floated in a circle as she looked at each one of the Core Team. Her eyes fell on Jack again and she spoke. "Jack, your people here are pure of heart and in love with Yahveh and Yahshua. I am so proud to be associated with the Crossfire Team. The Most High has heard your prayers concerning a conflict with the realm of darkness and He sent me to tell you this. *"My children, not so long ago Yahshua used your team and loyal, believing Russians to fight the demons. I did not tell you that I needed you to fight, and for some to die, to bring Qixalpaq out of the Second Heaven, as was foretold by the prophets. This time you have earned My trust and now you are to face a similar situation with the knowledge that some could die."*

"Belial is a demonic force that has one hundred or more times the strength of Qixalpaq who reported to two levels of demons under Belial. Your swords did not stop Qixalpaq and they will not stop Belial either. This battle will have to be fought by you in the physical so that, strictly on the spiritual plane rather than the physical plane, I can deal with Belial. He is far too strong for you to beat him sword to sword. He must be fought through My Son's power. I require Belial to stand forth against you in person. He must come against you so that I can limit his ability to pervert my commandments to kill hundreds of thousands of my believing children in a manner which he is not allowed. I need your force to stand against his demons and be seen defeating his demons so that through pride and vanity he will overstep his bounds to personally defeat you. Then and only then can I bind him for breaking his word to Me. If he sees you becoming victorious, he will enter the fray. But, he too made an oath to remain in the Second Heaven. I have agreed with Satan that I won't condemn Belial to the pit and I will not. But, I will restrict his operations sufficiently to prevent the massive damage he wants to do without my permission. But beware, Belial is very devious. Stay in prayer and fight the good fight. My angels will be with you as will I."

Rose faded from sight and Jack prayed his thanks to the Father in Heaven for His love and guidance. He then looked around the War Room. "I think we've got our marching orders."

"Last time we lost Mark, Sarah, Frank, and others. Laura and I were defeated and wounded such that we could not continue the battle. The Father had to keep us unsuspecting and innocent of His plan so that our actions would truly deceive Qixalpaq. Yahveh restored us all after the battle."

"This time He has included us in His plans and told us up front what has to be. If we die this time it might be permanent. I am proud of everyone here and will be full of sorrow if some of us don't make it back. But, to leave this life is to be with the Lord." The Core Team silently stood up and raised their fists into the air with a unified commitment to serve their Yahveh to the fullest extent of their ability, regardless of the danger. "To Yahveh be the glory."

Mark clapped his hands. "Great! Now all we need to know is when, where, and how we are going to battle Belial's forces."

CHAPTER FORTY-FOUR

Mark's answer wasn't long in coming. Carol pushed her chair back and sank to her knees on the floor of the War Room. The white diamonds at her forehead and throat blazed with the intensity of the Esteem of Yahveh.

Jack felt an unusual but very strong urge to personally pray in support of the young woman as she did her duty to the Father and the Team.

As Jack prayed he fell into a peaceful place and he started to blink. He suddenly found himself floating above the Matrix and he sensed Carol's spirit near his. He asked, "Is this what it's like?" It was a glorious feeling of awesome potential and trust, but it also gave one a feeling of tremendous responsibility.

Carol's voice resounded in Jack's mind. "Well, hello there! I have never had anyone accompany me here before. I'm honored and impressed that it is you. Of course, you do realize your mind has been expanded and elevated to be able to comprehend the existence and interaction of all the dimensions so that this place makes sense to you?"

Jack quietly laughed in his mind. "Yes, I do understand that ability is necessary to...to be here. What are you seeing in the Matrix concerning our future battles?"

Carol proceeded to point out the critical paths and points to Jack, but he could understand very little and interpret even less. Not only were there thousands of interweaving paths that were moving through time but everything was constantly changing in other ways. New tracks were being added and others disappearing. Jack now realized the awesome power of those Heavenly years of training that Carol had gone through. They were critically important to the understanding of what Jack could see in the spirit.

Jack felt a sudden danger and he looked around but didn't see anything that seemed dangerous. Carol suddenly gave a strangled "Guk" sound and Jack focused on her. She was having problems breathing and her face was turning red. Jack prayed for discernment and a demon was revealed choking Carol.

Jack willed himself to attack the demon and found himself approaching the demon in the spirit. Jack started praying to Yahshua for strength and as he approached he got the demon's attention. Jack intoned, "You foul essence, this woman has no part in you and you have no right to attack her. I call on the angels of the Most High God, Yahveh, to stop your attack and to send you to the pit to wait for judgment, never to return until you have been judged by Yahshua."

At the mention of the Lord's name, the demon let go of Carol and suddenly opened its mouth in a soundless scream of defiance. He was suddenly held in place by two very large angels and the three of them disappeared from sight. Jack asked, "Carol, are you all right?"

A thought was impressed on Jack's mind. Carol's voice sounded strained, but understandable. She coughed twice and then said, "I've never, ever had contact with a demonic spirit while I've been over the matrix. This is a new level of attack that Hugo never warned me about. I've got to find out what this is all about."

Quicker than thought, Jack found himself next to Carol, facing Hugo in a huge, quiet, neutral space. Hugo shook his head and frowned. He spoke in a deep bass register unlike his earlier, milder tones. "Stay here. I have to deal with something before we discuss these new things."

Hugo faded out of sight only to reappear seconds later. He looked tired and one side was covered in demon stain. "All right now, I believe we have time to talk."

Carol was distressed at Hugo's appearance yet she spoke up bravely. "Hugo, are you all right?" Hugo smiled, "Yes, my dear, I'm fine."

Carol shook her head, "I feel like I did when I first started this business. I don't understand what is happening. I've never had anyone accompany me when I am reading the Matrix, and I never had a demon try to strangle me, either. What is going on?"

Hugo smiled briefly. "There are many things going on, Carol. But, to the issue of new things you've experienced this time. These events have occurred because the Most High created and continues to support the Crossfire Team and eleven other teams like it. This has caused us to enter into an undefined area of the Most High's covenant with Satan. Satan feels irritation at the new factors and has decided to cross new barriers that have restricted him before now. He feels that Yahveh isn't playing fair as previously agreed to and is attempting to reassert his control over the Earth and parts of Heaven."

Carol thought for a few seconds and nodded. "I see, one of the devil's attempts is to remove my "spying" on him and his plans. Now, instead of complaining about it to God, he is taking direct action against me."

Hugo nodded, "That is true but it is not the whole story. When the Matrix was created, the devil didn't want anyone but himself and his demons along with Yahveh and His Angels to be able to read the future plans. Yahveh told him that He would define who could see the Matrix and named off all of the peoples, angels, etc., that also would have access to the Matrix. Up until now it was a working arrangement."

Carol smiled, "Yeah, up until me."

Hugo made a small frown, "Yes, up until you."

Jack spoke up. "Hugo, it is my belief that Yahveh sees all things; past, present, and future. If that is true, then how could He not see this coming and prevent the attack on Carol?"

Hugo took a deep breath. "Because, with eight billion people on the Earth today, He has to balance literally trillions of simultaneous, on-going events every second of your time. He knew this would come about, but, in His view, it was more important to let other things progress. As an example, Satan felt that his decision to attack Carol was a success, so he made many decisions which affected hundreds of other things. Once that happened it changed his relationship with other forces. When Yahveh took his ability to attack Carol away, it was too late for him to reverse all the things he had started, which will now affect other things that will deny him capabilities, because everything is as it was before this event occurred. Please notice also; Yahveh didn't leave Carol alone to face this new danger, he provided a defender for her, you."

Jack's mind whirled at the complexity of events that the Father juggled constantly. The demands, requirements, and complexities of multi-dimensional warfare and interactions were beyond mind boggling.

Three chairs appeared and everyone sat down. Hugo sighed, "It's been a very busy time lately and that is not going to improve for a while. But, I have time to bring you up to speed on the latest changes that are going to affect how you do things." The angel looked at the two humans. "To prevent any additional attacks on Carol I am going to assign three angels to protect her whenever she has to enter into the place of the Matrix. Because this unauthorized, and most likely illegal action by the demons in one of Yahveh's closely controlled activities, meaning the attack on Carol during her latest visit to the Matrix, the devil has been given an ultimatum. He has been told that he may only allow three demons into that particular space while Carol is there. Any more, and Yahveh will eliminate all access permanently and Satan will no longer be able to use that space. The angels will be more than sufficient to protect Carol."

"This action then eliminates the other "new" thing, which was the necessity for Jack to be at the Matrix to defend you."

Hugo smiled at Jack. "The Most High thanks you for being willing and faithful to defend Carol. She needs additional training in how to enter into her analysis of the Matrix and ignore the warfare going on around her."

Jack finished the blink he had started before he was sent to the Matrix.

CHAPTER FORTY-FIVE

Jack finished his eye blink and found himself back in the War Room at the Sea Base.

No one in the War Room noticed Jack's absence in the spirit because no time in the human dimension had elapsed while he was gone. Laura asked, "Jack, should we try to determine where this battle will take place?"

Jack shook his head. Then he looked over at Carol still kneeling on the floor with her diamonds glowing. "No, first we need to wait to hear from Carol when she returns from the Matrix. I believe that our Father will give us target information either directly or through Carol when it is time. Until then I want us to concentrate on continuing our battle with the RHONE. Since we can't find an informant within their ranks or insert an agent because of their demonic covering and control, I believe that we will be allowed to use Yahveh's angels to give us the information we need to find and engage their troops."

He looked at Mark. "Why don't we continue with the accelerated training in combat for all of us? I'll tackle advanced swordsmanship, you handle weapons and tactics, Laura can use whichever troops, Core Team or SOG she needs to seek the Lord in prayer to determine how we can be victorious through Yahshua's strength for the coming spiritual battle. I really want everyone to continue their physical training as much as possible to get us into the best possible shape we've ever been in. We are going to need it."

As everyone headed out to accomplish their duties, Carol's diamonds faded out and she got up and sat in her chair. She looked at Jack and Laura and smiled. "Hello again. I just spent a wonderful three days with Hugo on mental concentration and focus. Very interesting and helpful. I don't have any new information on the Matrix yet, but the battle is going to be pretty soon."

She looked at them and smiled again. "It's kinda like following a miles long garden hose and suddenly finding a bulge where the action is. Well, this bulge is getting larger than any I have ever seen. There is more spiritual power being poured into this nexus by both sides than normal. I am sure that we will be the arrow that busts the bubble. I just don't know how big that energy pack is going to be by then."

Carol looked tired suddenly. "I think I will take a nap to catch up on the three nights I've missed in this training." She looked at Laura, "You know, normally I don't come back tired but this time I just feel spent."

Jack smiled, "Well, you are getting older you know."

Carol looked at him in alarm. "Don't say that, ever. I'm just into my twenties and should have..." She stopped talking and thought about what she was saying. Then she shrugged her shoulders, "Three years or so."She shook her head. "Well, actually it really doesn't matter. Does it?"

Laura smiled, "Listen Sweetie, You've always known that when you leave this earth, you will be with the Lord. Nothing could be better than that. Missing a few decades here on Earth will actually be a blessing. I know that it may seem unfair because you probably won't have time to find your breshet, get married, and have a family. But, the reward you will receive will be so much better, you'll forget everything else. This life is a stage where you only have so much time to make your necessary choices before you stand before Yahshua. I assure you that all the things of the Earth will be as nothing compared to your future life with God."

Carol slowly nodded her head. "You're right, you're exactly right. I was so focused on what I'm doing, I forgot that. I don't have to prove to myself or anybody else that I'm a woman that loves Yahshua."

She got up and waved as she headed for the door.

Jack looked at Laura. "For a young woman, she is carrying a huge load on her shoulders. I know she is capable and has a ton of grit, but while she gives it all to the Lord she's still human. She needs much more contact, downtime, and support with us and other believers to bolster her spirit."

Laura looked after Carol and thought about that concept.

The entire group, Core Team and SOG went into a concentrated training routine to get their physical bodies in the best shape they had ever been in during their lives.

Laura trained along with the others and in spare time put together a small group to resolve the spiritual aspects of the coming battle. She included Sarah, Carol, David, and oddly enough, Ethan Reaper and Megan Cole. Those were the people she felt that Yahveh told her to include. Megan had been a Messianic Christian for years but Ethan just became a believer a few weeks ago. Laura thought, "Oh well, Yahveh knows better than me who should be on this group."

The first two meetings of the group were quick, basically to set up the team and define the goals. They also decided on a routine they should follow. Laura asked for each of them, as well as herself, to fast any outside distractions such as computers, television, cell phones, or casual chatter except when it was important to their Crossfire Team duties.

She knew she shouldn't ask them to fast food at this time of accelerated physical training and food didn't distract them from paying attention to God.

As they met for their third meeting they opened with a sincere prayer for the Father's guidance and then sang several songs as the Spirit led them to bring the anointing and presence of Yahveh into their meeting. After they worshiped Yahveh they had a few minutes of silent prayer to prepare each person. Laura was about to start the discussion when Yahveh dropped a word in her spirit. She smiled at the others, "We are going to have a guest speaker at the meeting today."

The atmosphere changed and the angels Caleb and Hugo appeared at the empty end of the table. Caleb was more than impressive in his youthful personain pure white with a gold-hilt sword. His voice was a deep bass which came out of him in an almost musical fashion. It was very satisfying to their spirits.

Caleb looked at each of them carefully, almost as if he was searching their souls. Then he nodded, "Warriors for God, you have asked for guidance in spiritually confronting Belial and the demonic forces he will have stand against you. This is a most intelligent request and the Most High has given this task to Hugo and myself. We consider it an honor to assist you and the rest of the Crossfire Team."

Hugo looked like, well, like Hugo always looked. He smiled at them through his mustache and beard. "With the exception of Ethan Reaper, I have met each of you during your sword training. I want you to know I am impressed with the pureness of love you all have for Yahveh and Yahshua. Ethan is on a fast track to his pureness of love in an extremely short time."

Hugo continued, "To overcome Belial's demons in combat on the spiritual plane you will have to meet several special requirements that are doable but will require an intensity of true focus and belief. So, to place you in an environment that is conducive to your training we will take you to a realm that will provide no distractions."

The team found themselves in a Heavenly setting but to Laura it felt different than the times before when they had been there, like during sword training.

Laura asked Hugo about it. "Hugo, what is the difference I'm sensing about being here?"

Hugo laughed, 'the difference is that you are "really" here, physically, not just in the spirit. You need to experience this as a physical human being."

Laura looked at the other team members and said, "Oh."

The consensus of the others was muted. As far as they knew, only Laura had been in heaven physically after being hurt during combat with demons and brought to the Master by an Archangel.

CHAPTER FORTY-SIX

Hugo had the team members stand up and form a line. He then walked down the line and as he passed each one his anointing affected that person.

When that happened to Megan Cole she felt energy pass through her mind and her body. It was powerful, not unpleasant, but it caused a shift in both her perspective of things around her and the sense of the balances within her.

Hugo then stepped back in front of the team members. He looked at each one and then nodded. Standing to Hugo's right, Caleb drew his glowing sword and held it upward. The visible energy of the Esteem of Yahveh grew in density and power as it gathered energy from Yahveh and then separate arcs of light sprang from the sword blade to each of the team members. Megan felt like she had been connected to an immense power source and every molecule in her body felt like it increased in energy a thousand times more than it had felt like before. She could sense her physical being growing in power.

The arcs of energy faded out and Caleb sheathed his sword and then he faded out of sight.

Hugo nodded his head slowly. "What the Most High has done through Caleb and myself was to cleanse and empower every single atom of your being and mind. This will be necessary in the coming battles. Each of you was physically and mentally in good shape as far as human beings go. But, that would not be sufficient for the coming combat. Now, every muscle, organ, sinew, cartilage, and brain cell in your body is pure, clean, and up to a Heavenly condition. You harbor no illnesses, no injury, not even degradation due to aging. Your physical being is ready for battle. Now we need to bring your attitude up to the same level."

Hugo smiled gently, "Some of you still have a remnant of a spirit of fear of the enemy in your sub-conscious. Remember what Yahveh's Word says in 2 Timothy 1:7 *"God has not given me a spirit of fear, but of power, and of love and of a sound mind. For the Spirit Yahveh gave us* does not make us timid, but gives us power, love and self-discipline. "

"When you feel that you don't have enough faith. Romans 12:3 tells you, *"God has given to me a measure of faith.* "For by the grace given me I say to every one of you: Do not think of yourself more highly than you ought, but rather think of yourself with sober judgment, in accordance with the faith Yahveh has distributed to each of you.*"

"If you feel that you are too weak to battle these demons, Psalms 27:1 *says, "The Lord is the strength of my life. Yahshua is my light and my salvation, whom shall I fear? Yahveh is the stronghold of my life of whom shall I be afraid?"*

"If you feel that Satan has got control over you, I John 4:4 tells you, *"Greater is He that is in me than he that is in the world. You, dear children, are from Yahveh and have overcome them, because the One who is in you is greater than the one who is in the world."*

"When you feel defeated, remember that Yahveh always gives you triumph in Yahshua as you've read in 2 Corinthians 2:14, *"But thanks be to God, who always leads us as captives in Christ's triumphal procession and uses us to spread the aroma of the knowledge of him everywhere."*

"When you feel injury, recall what you learned in Isaiah 53:5 *"By His stripes I am healed. But He was pierced for our transgressions, He was crushed for our iniquities; the punishment that brought us peace was on Him, and by His wounds we are healed."* Also, in Matthew 8:17 *"Yahshua Himself took my infirmities and bore my sicknesses. This was to fulfill what was spoken through the prophet Isaiah: He took up our infirmities and bore our diseases."*

"If you are bombarded by the demons telling you that you are in bondage, remember 2 Corinthians *3:17, "Where the Spirit of the Lord is, there is liberty. Now the Lord is the Spirit, and where the Spirit of the Lord is, there is freedom."*Or if they try to impress on you that you are condemned, repeat Romans 8:1, *"There is no condemnation to me, because I am in Christ Yahshua. Therefore, there is now no condemnation for those who are in Yahshua,"*

"In your mind you must keep the statement, *"Yahshua is my strength and His Word has power. Through Him I have the victory! These are the Scriptures that defeat the enemy."*

Hugo nodded at the assembled cast, "Never forget that "Yahshua" will grant that the enemies who rise up against you will be defeated before you. They will come at you from one direction but flee from you in seven"

The last Scripture you need in your arsenal is this. Always remember that Psalm 91 Verse 13 tells you *"You shalt tread upon the lion and the adder: The young lion and the dragon you shalt trample under foot."* This is the verse that gives you the power to defeat the enemy regardless of his strength because it is the word of Yahveh and Yahshua has already defeated every one of the enemy, and they know it." Yahshua gave you the control through Mathew 16:19. *"Whatever you bind here on Earth is bound in Heaven and whatever you loose here on Earth is loosed in Heaven."*

Hugo waved his right hand and everyone knew deep in their heart each of the applicable Scriptures.

Caleb reappeared and addressed the team members. "Now, each of those Scriptures has become a part of your spirits because you know that each and every one of them is true. Satan, Ba'al/Belial, and the other demons were defeated and the victory is already ours. Your belief in these scriptures as you face the enemy will allow you to have victory. Can they still kill the body? Yes, they can kill your body. Can they defeat your spirit? No, they cannot defeat your spirit, unless you sin and invite them in. Can they possess your soul or your spirit? No, regardless of your errors or mistakes Christ possesses your soul and spirit."

Hugo stepped forward, "I know you are all very smart and are probably asking yourself, "Why this review on basic tenets?". I'll tell you why. Because none of you were absolutely sure that these scriptures were true. That little bit of doubt would have given the enemy the edge to overcome you. At this point you are absolutely convinced that your life in Yahshua gives you complete ability to overcome the enemy."

Ethan Reaper asked, "Hugo, does that apply to Belial, too? Are we able to overcome him?"

Hugo did a human thing by tipping his head to the right a bit and smiling slightly. "Technically, yes, in reality, no. Yahshua overcame Satan and all his minions such as Belial. But, remember the power of Yahveh present in you is dependent on how closely your righteousness matches that of Christ. Yahshua was a sinless man. He never rebelled against the Most High; He never sinned in the entirety of the time he was on Earth. Unfortunately, humans cannot say that. The ones that do say they are sinless are liars. True, the blood of Christ absolves you from all your sins, but that is His righteousness that covers you. The reason that is important is because the righteousness of a person equates to a level of power in the Heavens."

Hugo shook his head, "As you face higher and higher levels of demonic personalities you need higher levels of righteousness to defeat them or in other terms, balance out their level of unrighteousness with your level of righteousness. That is why Laura could not stop Qixalpaq in Russia. His level of unrighteousness exceeded her level of righteousness."

"Remember we're talking about Laura's level of righteousness. Yahshua's level of righteousness is her covering, and will ultimately decide her fate when she passes from her Earthly life. But when she is in combat with evil on Earth, during her life time, it is her level of righteousness that determines her power to overcome her opponent's level of unrighteousness. That is why as an individual human who has had to exist on the Earth and live in sin with other people; their individual righteousness does not match up with the upper levels of the demon's unrighteousness. Yahveh loves you and when He sees you, He sees the righteousness of His Son Yahshua which covers you after you gave him control of your life and walk with him in obedience. He is your Savior. Hence, the saying, "As you are in Christ, you are as white as the driven snow".

Laura asked, "Hugo, won't the rest of the other members of the team have to go through this training before we will be ready to do battle with Belial's forces?"

Hugo grinned, "No, Laura, they have been going through it at the same time you have."

The Heavenly realm faded from view with Hugo waving goodbye.

Laura found herself in the conference room.

CHAPTER FORTY-SEVEN

Laura shook her head and sighed. "Well, we accomplished our directive and now everyone will be spiritually competitive during the battle. The attendees got up and quietly left the conference room to go back to their regular routines.

Laura thought over what Hugo had said about each person's level of righteousness and at times in her past, since she received Yahveh's anointing and her armor and sword, she realized that she now understood many things she had wondered about before. She left the conference room and looked for Jack and found him in the War Room. "What do you think of that?"

Jack shook his head and smiled. "I think I need to assign more tasks to you, especially if they involve spiritual aspects." He stopped and thought. "Oh, I already do that." He laughed and she joined him.

Jack's memories were awakened and he was reminded of his first demonic combat when he confronted what he then saw as a powerful demon in Colorado four years ago. It was as fresh in his mind as if it were happening right then.

------------------------******------------------------

The Colorado Bureau of Investigation undercover agent, Carol Tuccine, sat tied onto a straight backed chair. Ten or twelve ugly red welts dotted her body, especially her arms. Her face looked like she had tried to break through a door with it and there was blood on her legs.

Don Miland stood there with the box holding the Holy Treasure in his hands as he turned to see who was stupid enough to interrupt him. His eyes grew wide at the sight of three heavily armed men standing in the doorway. All three pistols were aimed directly at him. He dropped the box and put his hands into the air above his head.

Jack motioned him to back away from the moaning woman. He did as he was instructed. Mark kept his pistol aimed directly at the man's chest. Jack could see that

Mark's knuckles were white with the effort he was exerting not to fire the entire magazine into the man.

Jack and Jim Grady cut the woman's bonds loose and moved her to a couch. Jim saw a sink and got a wet rag and wiped the blood off of her to determine the extent of her injuries. Surprisingly, she was still alive and even functioning. She had lost two teeth and had a terrific shiner around her right eye. Several other bruises were starting to form on her face and abdomen and she had those nasty welts over her arms. For some unexplained reason, Don Miland had not resorted to stripping her and attacking her that way. But, at least she didn't seem to have any broken bones and the blood was mostly from her mouth and some superficial surface wounds.

She coughed and Jim helped her to a sitting position. Jack was mad enough to seriously hurt the crime boss. "What caused those welts?" he asked her.

She started to answer and had to try for the second time. She pointed at Joe, "Mr. Macho there wanted me to tell him who I worked for and I didn't want to. So he used an ice cube to deaden the skin and then put a hot cigarette against the skin. That way you get a really deep burn before you feel anything."

Jack turned and walked over towards Joe like the angel of death. But Mark stopped him with the comment, "We need some information from him, first." Jack gritted his teeth and backed off. Looking around he spotted the box that held the crucifixion nail and went over to it. Picking it up, he opened it and made sure it was intact, which it seemed to be.

Jack was turning to tell Mark to take Don Miland upstairs when there was a malevolent scream of rage from the next room.

The fact that the scream was inherently evil and that it shook the entire room wasn't lost on any of the men. Mark and Jim grabbed Carol and made a run for the door. Joe, realizing that he was in more trouble than he could imagine, made a run at Jack in an attempt to retrieve the box.

Sensing Joe's move, Jack turned, drew his pistol and shot Joe in the upper thigh of his right leg. The Hydro-shock hollow-point bullet imparted so much power that it spun Joe backward, around in a circle and dumped him on the floor. His whole right leg was numb and he couldn't move it.

Time seemed to stand still suddenly. The wall between the room they were in and the one behind it seemed to melt and collapse at the same time. Jack's soul felt a fear that he had never known, much worse than when he was being baptized. A Stygian blackness existed behind the wall and began to flood into the room. As the three men and the woman turned to run, the door slammed shut before them and they were trapped. The darkness pulsed with evil and a sick hunger.

Jack realized he was facing a power far beyond his capabilities to understand, let alone handle. In a few seconds both he and his friends would be consumed and damned forever. Jack tried to hide the box behind him, but a shadow swept forward and knocked the box out of his hands and to the floor. Jack felt like his skin was slimy and imagined that he could feel every hair on his body writhing around like worms. He was filled with a feeling of total failure. The though raced through his mind that this is what he deserved and he wasn't worth anything. A horrible malaise came over him and he wanted to hide. He was ugly, miserable, and Yahveh had walked off and didn't want him at all.

Then the memory of the peace he had felt when he had touched the spike in the hotel room strengthened him. "That wasn't right!" Jack was still a brand new Christian but one thing he was absolutely sure of was that the love of Yahveh never wavers. Once you accepted Jesus you were saved by putting on Christ, Yahveh never left you, ever! He fought through all the pity and guilt he was feeling and concentrated on Jesus. The ultimate peace he had felt when he had touched the spike came back. Not completely, but enough that he was sure that it was man that walked away from God, not the other way around.

Jack turned to the only hope he had. Instead of continuing to quake in absolute terror like his body and soul demanded that he do, he prayed. He prayed out loud to the Son of Yahveh to save them. As he remembered it later, this was an extremely earnest prayer. He had been in the presence of the Lord God Almighty and he was eyeball to eyeball with a principality of darkness and this was as real as it could get.

With the sensation that a building had been slammed to the earth, sound stopped. There was complete silence in the room. Not just quiet with little background noises but an absolute total lack of sound. A light whiter than white flooded the room with a visible power. The flood of white light enveloped Jack, Mark, Jim, Carol, and the box and pushed the malignant blackness away from them. Jack smelled a beautiful fragrance of flowers and the peace of the Holy Spirit filled them all. The terror he had felt melted away as if it had never been there.

------------------------******------------------------

Jack shook his head at the memory. The last four years had very definitely widened his knowledge and experience in dealing with the demonic. But, he knew that Yahveh had given him that growth so that he could stand against the enemy and do Yahveh's works here on Earth, even if this could possibly be his last battle.

CHAPTER FORTY-EIGHT

After his afternoon workout at the gym, Jack felt a familiar urge and after showering and dressing he headed for the War Room. He didn't make it all the way. Almost everyone in the team was standing or sitting in the large living room adjacent to the War Room. Jack saw Mark talking to Sarah and Laura and he veered over to them. "Hi! What's going on?"

Laura smiled a tentative smile and shrugged. "I don't know. All of us felt led to be here. Not only the Core Team but the SOG personnel, also. I see you got the message, too."

Jack nodded and was about to reply when there was a sudden push-pull of energy in the room and the angel Caleb appeared. Caleb was in his youthful and very strong persona and he impressed every one of the warriors as he rotated and considered everyone there. Caleb spotted Jack and the others and directed his attention to them. "Warriors of the Crossfire Team, the time has come for you to counter the demons of Belial. The Most High has asked you to stand for the Kingdom of Yahveh and to do your best."

"The battle will be on the Plains of Megiddo, near Mount Tabor and South of Nazareth. Be there by noontime. To Yahveh and Yahshua is the power and the glory!" Caleb faded from sight.

Mark spoke up, "Full body armor, M-8s and helmets. We will give you the order of battle when we are there. May Yahveh be with you and sustain you all."

Su Li raised her voice over the hub-bub of many people speaking. "Be at the airfield in twenty minutes. We'll travel by helicopter to the valley."

Jack caught Charlie as he started for the armory. "We want you to bring the large containers of ammo, grenades, and LAWs just in case there are illegal demons there." Charlie nodded and took off at a jog.

Laura came up to Jack, "We will be victorious." She hugged him.

He returned the hug and he said, "Or, some of us will die and still be victorious." He put his arm around her and they headed to the armory to get their gear. He looked at her and asked, "Am I pleased that Yahveh did not tell me to bring the Crucifixion Nail with me?"

Laura thought about that and laughed, "Trust the Father".

The two Chinook Helicopters lifted off of the tarmac and vectored into the flight tunnel to travel to the surface of the ocean. Once more in free air they turned to the left and headed for the Valley of Jezreel, South of Nazareth.

Su Li was about to ask either Jack or Mark where to land when she saw a bright light blinking near a large open area of ground roughly two miles ahead of them. She talked to the other helicopter. "Mike, follow me."

The two helicopters set down near the bright light which vanished while they were landing. The troops disembarked and formed up in squads.

Jack checked the time and found it was twenty minutes before noon. He looked over the whole Valley of Jezreel and felt at home there. The wind was softly blowing from the South and the sun was shining clearly. The temperature was hot but not uncomfortable and the aroma of the land was sweet.

Mark gave the very minimal orders of battle to everyone there. "We will fight from groups of four. That will give us twelve groups. Two tiers. First tier will shoot everything that comes at us until the enemy is twenty yards away. Then drop your weapons and start praying. Engage the enemy with your words and your swords. If necessary, fight back-to-back in four square if possible, to prevent attacks from your rear. Fight until you can fight no longer. The victory is ours and Yahveh is with us."

Ethan Reaper walked up to Jack. "I get it that we are the point of the spear here and that the Father has commanded us to fight this battle. What I don't understand is why the fifty or so of us have to stand against probably huge odds but can't utilize the Force Generators or the forces of the IDF?"

Jack smiled at the young man. "Ethan, the IDF could only shoot these things. If they are here legally then bullets don't count, but our swords will. The major reason we have to stand against the odds is not only because Yahveh told us to do it, but, because the enemy is after us, not the whole Israeli population. The Crossfire Team *is* Satan's objective. They would not come to this battle if we would not contend with them. If we used the Force Generators, they wouldn't battle with us very long before they broke off and we couldn't bring Belial out of the second heaven. We are anointed to stop demons that enter our dimension. We are the target, and we are the solution to stop them."

Ethan nodded his head. He looked around and in his particular humor he asked Jack. "Okay then. Any idea where a group this big can go for a beer and a meal when this is over?"

Jack shook his head and grinned. "After it is over, we'll let you pick."

The battle-com network came to life with Mark's voice. "Okay people, form up in your battle squads, the enemy is emerging to our North."

Jack grabbed Laura and quickly kissed her on the lips. "I love you so much. Win, lose or draw this looks to be the defining battle for the Crossfire Team. So let's win it."

Jack's team included Laura, David, and Alexis and they formed up in their square and Laura knelt down so that Alexis could fire over her at the enemy. There was a cloud of dust coming toward them out of the North, spread about two hundred feet wide and she could make out individual demons.

Mark timed out the approach of the first rank of demons and when they were approximately 35 yards away he spoke into his combat microphone. "Weapons Free, Fire at will!"

CHAPTER FORTY-NINE

Over forty-five assault rifles fired almost as one and many of the enemy were wounded and began to vaporize. The optical sights on the M-8s allowed for exceptional accuracy at that range. Most of the rifles continued to fire in a calculated sequence and many more of the demonic shapes were knocked out of the battle. Charlie Wu and five other warriors begin to fire rifle grenades and destroy several demons with each strike.

The leading demons veered and jinked to spoil the aim of the humans but were losing too many of their army to the accuracy of the warriors. The demons attempted to scare the soldiers by impressing fear onto them, but to no avail. They used every trick they knew to deceive and frighten the small group facing them but were unsuccessful in finding chinks in their spiritual armor. The destruction of the demons actually brought the advance to a halt fifty feet away from the front ranks of the team.

Many demons tried to turn back or retreat but were cut down by not only the warriors but by their fellow demons for trying to escape.

Jack was waiting for the real challenge and he saw it start as many of the demons behind the front lines kept advancing, ignoring the bullets and blasts of the grenades. Each of these had a club, a sword, or claws and teeth as they charged toward and against the front tier of the warriors.

As the hideous creatures closed with the team, rifles were forgotten and golden and silver armor along with the swords of Yahveh's Esteem flashed as bright as the noonday sun as the team members stood to battle against the legal demons. In less than five minutes the battle had become a whirling, smashing, and deadly hand-to-hand combat to the death for all involved.

Eight of the team, led by Charlie Wu, continued a rifle and grenade assault against newer demons and had considerable success eliminating dozens of the illegally present creatures.

By now the odds against the team were around four to one with the demons holding the upper edge in sheer volume. Charlie was finally able to see the rift that the demons were coming out of behind their lines. He quickly grabbed a LAW (light anti-tank weapon) and fired it at the rift. His aim was true and the missile exploded inside the rift and slammed it shut.

Charlie was elated and then just as quickly disappointed as another rift was opened close to where the first one had been. Sighing he picked up a new LAW and aimed it at the new rift. As the missile approached the rift a large black sword batted it to the side where it exploded with no effect to the rift.

The temporary closure of the first rift had given the team a chance to reduce the numbers of demons present and they fought all the harder to do just that. The battle had shifted to a one-sided slaughter as the team reduced the demons much more efficiently than expected.

Jack's hopes rose only to be dashed when demon archers started sending four-foot long black arrows at the team members. Swords and armor deflected the majority of the arrows but not all of them. Two of the team went down while deflecting the arrows to the surge of demons which overwhelmed the distracted warriors and brought them to the ground.

The battle changed to a melee with more demons being skewered by demon arrows than warriors and small battles broke out in areas by themselves. Jack saw Mark slashing his way through demons to get to the team members that had been swarmed and were down on the ground.

The demons saw the tide of the battle turning for them because of their superior numbers of legal demons.

Suddenly there was a loud cry of Holy Anger and the demons were screaming and yelling as they were suddenly facing three times the number of human warriors in armor than before. The new warriors tore into the demons from left and right and quickly terminated dozens of demons before they could turn and fight back.

Jack recognized several of the new warriors as other members of different teams from around the world. The ones he saw that he knew had fought together with them before.

Re-energized, the Crossfire team surged through the distracted demons and capitalized on their sudden equality in numbers. Jack saw Laura go into high speed and he matched her as they tore through the legal demons in front of them.

This time the tide of battle had definitely swung to their side and they voiced their power in Holy anger as they decimated the enemy on the field. Jack noted that there weren't any more demons coming out of the new rift to replace their losses. That concerned him and he spoke into his combat microphone to Mark. "Why aren't they bringing in more demons?"

There was no response from Mark. Jack didn't have time to check on his friend because he was still deep in demons of his own and he concentrated on eliminating every one he could. Jack prayed in his battle prayer for Mark's protection. He also spoke the word of Yahveh concerning his power to trample on Serpents, but it didn't seem to affect the attacking demons.

As he sliced a demon in half he saw a larger demon behind the first one and two other demons ran to the side to let the bigger demon get to Jack.

Jack continued to pray a fervent prayer for power and protection from Yahveh as he did an overhead slash to the front of the huge demon. The demon smashed Jack's sword to his right and it raised its large black sword to slash Jack from helmet to heel before Jack could parry the blow.

As the big sword came crashing down on him he saw Laura step in from his left and swing her blade upward in a savage blow. The huge black sword sundered into fragments when it struck the bright blade and Laura converted the direction of her blade into a cross body slash that opened the huge demon up from its right shoulder to its waist on its left side. The big demon started to collapse and leak copious amounts of black smoke as it fell.

Reverting to his training, Jack continued to bring his blade from his right to his left around Laura's body. A smaller demon was attempting to cut Laura's legs out from under her when Jack's blade beheaded it.

Laura spun to her left and went back-to-back with Jack in high guard position. Jack was in mid guard when the large demon finally crashed to the ground and dissipated completely. There were no more demons facing them within blade distance. Jack took a deep breath and said, "Thanks honey, you saved my life, again."

Laura looked at the battles around them and said, "It ain't over yet."

CHAPTER FIFTY

Jack stepped to his right and looked over the battle field and was gratified by the sight of the warriors cleaning up the last demons. He saw that there were ten or eleven people lying on the ground and mostly not moving. That touched his soul and he prayed for Yahveh's mercy on all of them. He couldn't determine if Mark was one of them or not.

Laura had been watching the rift and tapped Jack on the arm so he would also look in that direction. There was activity as some of the demonic forces were issuing out of the rift. Also, Jack had continued to pray in his head and neither Laura's or his armor or sword had disappeared. Jack squared his body up to confront whatever was approaching them. He noticed a half dozen armored warriors moving up and standing with him and he turned his head and nodded to them. They nodded back and prepared for battle.

Someone bumped him from behind and he glanced back to see why. He smiled as he recognized Mark standing behind him. Looking at Mark's helmet he could see the remains of his combat microphone dangling from one wire. Jack asked, "Did a sword get that close or did you chew it off from frustration?"

Mark chuckled a low chuckle. "Sword".

Jack noticed that Sarah came up to the front next to Laura. She looked really ready to start fighting again. Jack could tell from the amount of demon stain on her armor she had been battling up close and personal.

Laura tipped her head to Jack's side. "It looks like they've decided to bring in the heavyweights for round two."

Four major demons were striding across the ground towards the warriors. They all had capes or something of color which probably denoted them as higher than the normal demons. Jack estimated they were at least eight feet high and very stout. They carried large black swords with silver grips. Definitely a higher class of demon. Jack began to earnestly pray for the Father's help against these monsters.

While he didn't see angels arriving to help he noticed that the feeling of Holy anger was growing with every step the enemy made toward them. When the anger rose to an almost uncontrollable force. Jack couldn't wait any longer and charged the second demon from his left. He noticed as he ran toward the demon that there were warriors running with him but his focus was on the demon and destruction was in his mind and his heart.

Jack noticed as he approached the enemy that his perspective was changing. Either the new demons weren't as big as he had thought them to be or else he was getting bigger. As they clashed, Jack felt the power within him ratchet up to somewhere between the energy needed to drive a battleship in combat up to something even greater, like that of a Saturn five launch vehicle somewhere near five million pounds of thrust.

As they met, the demon tried to cut Jack in half with a mighty swing of his huge sword from Jack's left across to the right. Jack simply raised his shield and blocked the big blade as he ran the demon through with his glowing blade. No, that wasn't quite right. With his flaming blade that was radiating the energy of Yahveh and rivaled the sun in brilliance.

As he ran the demon through Jack's charge slammed him into the demon at full speed. Jack was amazed as the demon was crumpled and knocked backward off of Jack's sword. Actually, the demon was blasted backward a long distance. The crushed demon was venting gray smoke and dissipating quickly but the collision hadn't even fazed Jack. He thanked Yahveh as he looked around for more giant demons to run over.

The exhilaration at so easily destroying the giant demon was wonderful but couldn't overcome the Holy anger filling Jack at the moment. He noticed that none of the other large demons had survived the battle with the warriors. He looked at Mark and saw the wrath of Yahveh on his friend's face. It wasn't pretty at all.

Jack turned to face the rift as the other warriors lined up alongside.

It was obvious that there were normal demons racing to get back into the rift and get away from the armor bearers.

Suddenly things changed. The bright sky darkened and the wind grew cold, the ground shuttered as a single demon exited the rift. This was a different demon from any they had met before. He exuded evil and total control. The demon spoke a word and all of the smaller and regular demons running for protection were consumed in flames and died where they were. This demon looked at the warriors with contempt and every step it took toward them made the ground shake.

Jack recognized the inherent superior power radiating out of this creature and made a calculated guess. He spoke quietly but everyone around him nodded as he said, "Belial".

As the second highest demonic force in the Universe headed their way it displayed an eight-foot long ebony blade in its right hand and a gloating, confident sneer as it would kill each of these minions of Yahveh one after another and greatly enjoy the carnage.

Jack didn't even wonder about the battle to come. He raised his sword and stepped forward to contend with the dark lord. Failure wasn't even a concept that entered Jack's mind which was still full of Holy anger against all enemies of Yahveh. Win, lose, or draw he was going to contend with this monster with all of his might, strength, but, above all, his faith.

As Belial raised his blade to smite Jack a sudden peace came over Jack and removed all the anger in him. Jack lowered his blade and smiled at the supremely confident creature of evil.

Jack's change of attitude didn't affect Belial in the slightest. He would destroy this minor pest and remain in total control. He swung his blade from above Jack with a powerful blow.

CHAPTER FIFTY-ONE

Strangely, as Belial used every muscle he had to power down his strike against the puny human, his mighty blade kept going down slower and slower until it stopped moving just above the silver armor.

Being led by God, Jack casually swung his blade up and tapped the larger sword hovering above him. Belial's great blade sundered into a thousand pieces and fell to the ground.

Without conscious effort, Jack spoke to the larger demon. The words weren't his but they came from Yahshua and they came out of Jack with great power and conviction.

"Belial, you have defied Yahveh yet again and now you have also broken your agreement not to leave the Second Heaven. Although you deserve destruction, Yahveh is merciful even to such as yourself. Half of your power is taken from you and all of your plans are reduced in scope and effect by half. You no longer have the power to defy Yahveh in the small amount of time on this Earth. Your time is short and your destiny is the Lake of Fire. You will suffer great anguish and ridicule for the rest of eternity along with your master, Satan. Now! Bow in submission and return to your lair."

The huge black demon dropped to his right knee and said, "I obey Master" and faded from view. Jack was staggered by the evil hatred he saw in Belial's eyes as he knelt before God.

The rift slammed shut with finality and disappeared. The darkness fled from the sunlight. Everyone's armor and swords disappeared. Jack didn't feel tired at all. He was jubilant and full of thankfulness. He turned to the other warriors there and as a group they all knelt and offered their thanks and love to a Yahveh they knew loved them.

As some of them got up, Jack rose and shook hands with several of the people he didn't know. Then all over the battlefield people disappeared. Jack stood there breathing the air and thanking the Father over and over again.

He found Laura, Sarah, and Mark still praying their worship and thanks.

As they stood up Jack put his right arm around Laura's waist and his left around Mark's waist while Mark gathered in Sarah with his left arm. They walked or gleefully limped back toward the remainder of the team and the SOG in such peace it was beyond incredible. Even the parts of their bodies that didn't want to work didn't bother them.

Their joy was diminished as they came to others and saw eight bodies covered in Military ponchos on the ground.

Jack sighed and asked, "Who did we lose?"

Charlie had his left arm in a sling and a clipboard in his right hand. He offered the clipboard to Jack.

Jack saw that the Core Team had almost survived intact. They had lost Colonel Owens and seven of the SOG members. He shook his head and knelt down again to pray for the fallen. The rest of the team and the SOG joined him.

Somewhat later Mark collapsed suddenly and Laura and Sarah knelt down beside him. Jack joined them and asked Mark what had happened.

Mark sighed a big sigh. "Well, according to three witnesses, I was helping one of our guys who had been smashed to the ground when their group was overrun and the lights went out. Apparently two of the larger demons had grabbed one of their smaller members and they swung him around and into my back hard enough to cause me to pass out. According to Sean Murphy, my body crushed a smaller demon and killed it because they couldn't find it after they picked me up. The demon that hit me was killed by Megan Cole who then chased the other two until she cut them down. After I woke up I thanked everyone for letting me sleep through the last few minutes of the first wave battle."

Jack gave Mark a hand but as Mark tried to stand up a wave of pain passed across his face and Jack let him back down quickly. Mark grimaced from the pain and looked at Jack. "You're in charge buddy; I'm down for the count. My back is messed up badly. Sorry."

Jack looked at Laura and then they knelt down and laid hands on Mark's back. Laura petitioned Yahveh for Heaven to heal Mark's back. Mark wasn't showing any improvement and Jack had a thought. He started to pray the breaking off of curses, assignments, and any and all enemy action against Mark. People crowded around and laid hands on anybody that had a hand on Mark. Jack felt the power and the anointing of the Holy Spirit and prayed with fervor and power. He felt the anointing break the curse that had been placed on Mark and then the pressure to pray diminished.

Jack looked at his best friend in the world and smiled at him. "You had a piece of the demon that hit you stuck to you and that was the reason your injuries were so painful. How do you feel now?"

Mark moved and checked for pain. He took Jack's hand and rose to his feet. "I feel a lot better, thanks for praying that way. It never crossed my mind that the squishee of my collision could curse me like that."

Jack used his combat microphone and called Su Li and told her to bring the two helicopters near to where they were so nobody had to walk. He was surprised when Alexis answered him. "Su Li is feeling a little too damaged to fly right now. So, Mike White and I will be doing the driving for the next few days." She stopped talking for a few seconds while she listened to somebody's voice. Then she returned to the conversation. "Su Li says to tell you, "hours, hours not days"."

As they flew back to their base Jack tried to remember all the events and the emotions of the battle. He looked at Mark and said, "When you are up to it, we need to talk, Okay?"

CHAPTER FIFTY TWO

The team returned to the Undersea Base in the evening. They gave the bodies of the eight warriors that were slain over to the Israelis for autopsy and preparation for burial. They then scheduled a farewell service for the fallen in three days after notification of the next of kin.

Everyone filled out their "after-action" reports to the best of their ability and turned all their equipment into the armory for cleaning and restoration as needed.

There was a solemn air to the return that had as much to do with the sadness for the fallen and their families as it did with the injuries and wear and tear to the surviving team members. The hurts and pain didn't really take hold until the next morning. Mark was still limping and as he looked at the other troops in their various pains he commented to David. "This place looks like a hospital recovery room for the walking wounded."

Laura smiled and looked over at Sarah who was using her arms to let herself down into a soft chair. "Mark is right about the condition of everyone here. Yesterday they gave their all and then some. If we hadn't been training and conditioning so hard I think the death toll would have been a lot higher."

Sarah looked around at the other invalids and shook her head. "To tell you the truth I am sure we were being especially protected by the Father in the battle yesterday. Statistically there is no way that we fought our way through that all-out demonic assault with only sixteen percent killed in action. And why did eight of the SOG die and none of the Core Team? I'm not complaining, I just don't understand."

Laura had been praying about that, part of the night before. "Sarah, I don't have any definite answers but I think that Yahveh blesses all of us who labor for Him. I heard from some of the other SOG troops that Colonel Owens, who technically was part of the Core Team, and the two four-man groups they were in were especially targeted because they were in the rear tier and out of sight for the rest of us who were fighting to the front of the assembly. The demons wanted to take out every one on the rear tier without alerting those in the front tier until they could attack us from the rear as well as the front."

Sarah saw Ethan Reaper with bandages on his head, face, arms and apparently, from the way he was gingerly walking, his back end. She asked him if he could survive the trip over to where she and Laura were sitting. He nodded and slowly made it over to them and stood there.

Laura asked him to sit down and talk to them for a minute. Ethan sort of smiled on one side of his face and shook his head slightly. "No thank you Laura, I'd rather stand if you don't mind."

Sarah grinned, "Something get you in the rear?"

Ethan frowned for a few seconds and then realized he was supposed to say something. "Unh, not really. But, I have to say that while that armor is over the top fantastic for diverting black swords and bullets, there is absolutely NO padding when you get knocked to the ground. It's like landing on concrete in your underwear." He stopped to think for a few seconds. "Not that that has ever happened to me." He looked to see if they were buying his story.

Laura asked, "Ethan, you were on the back tier of four man teams, right?" He nodded. "Can you tell us why we lost eight warriors in the right end of the second tier and nobody else?"

Ethan looked at Laura with a lost look. "Because there was one demon who knew Military tactics. He had a dozen other demons that apparently followed his orders. I was one group away from them and while we were in constant combat the ones attacking us were undisciplined and generally not very smart either. I could only look occasionally but I think I saw what Mark is teaching in Military Tactics being used against us. I'm going to call the smart demon "Napoleon" because of his use of tactics."

"Napoleon sent six of his troops to engage the front of the four-man team of group ten, the farthest out group in the second tier. While the first six were carefully skirmishing with the four warriors, Napoleon sent the other six in a sneak attack at their back. This is how they eliminated Colonel Owens and three of the troops. There was almost total surprise when our guys couldn't turn to defend their backs. If you think about it that was a small version of what they planned to do the whole front tier when they had killed off the rear tier."

"Napoleon then did the same thing to the second group of four in tier two, group nine, and it worked again. Please remember this special group of demons was not attacking in a one-on-one attack. The teams were already engaged with dozens of other demons who simply attacked willy-nilly with no coordination whatsoever. The reason I saw these tactics is because I play so many computer games and that is a frequently used tactic. At least I used to play a lot of computer games when I had the time. You overload the frontal attack drawing all attention in that direction and then you use a small number of troops to attack from the rear, where they are not expected, and decimate the defenders."

"Anyway, Napoleon was leaving the dead group 9 and heading for our group. I sort of disrupted his operation and that was when Charlie shut the first Portal and the pressure dropped off a bit. Once his plot was discovered Napoleon sent all of his remaining troops to attack us head on. He did that to give him time to fall back and escape. When the second Portal opened I saw the big weasel slip back inside the rift."

He looked sad, "It took them less than four minutes to destroy each of the other two groups. I kept calling Mark on the combat net but he didn't answer. So I did what I could but I so wish I could have done something before we lost those eight guys."

Laura put her hand on his hand and smiled. "Ethan, it sounds like you at least saved your group by seeing and disrupting Napoleon's operation. You did what you could. I know it is hard to see your fellow warriors die but take heart that Yahshua was watching and he knows you did what you could. Sadly, those aren't the only friends you may lose before we're called to be with Yahveh."

Ethan made an attempt at smiling and turned and slowly left for wherever he was going in the first place.

Sarah watched him go and told Laura, "You notice Ethan said that he *"sort of disrupted Napoleon's operation"?*

Laura nodded her head.

Sarah smiled, "I read the after-action reports this morning before everyone else got up. I also saw several of the video's the COMSEC center made of the battle. Ethan was battling with and took out two demons facing his group, group 8, and then charged the six demons that were angling to get behind his group. He was able to take down two of them before two more warriors from one of the other teams, the one from Italy, I think, joined him and dispatched the other four. Think about it, this guy was a computer nerd three months ago. He charges six demons single-handed, and kills two of them by himself. The thing that amazes me is that this brash young man who didn't care about anyone else three months ago was willing to put his own life on the line to protect the other people in his group and then is humble enough about what he did to downplay his part in it." Sarah looked at the walking pile of bandages disappearing down the hall toward the Armory and nodded her head. "This one is a keeper."

Laura agreed with her.

Alexis walked up and sat down with them. "I finally sedated David for his injuries and he's sleeping deeply now. How are you two faring?"

Sarah smiled, "I've had worse bangs and bruises and lived to tell about it. You don't look like you got hurt at all. How did you do that?"

Alexis laughed quietly so as to not disturb the other wounded warriors that were within ear shot. "I teamed with David and Megan Cole who were awesome in action. I seemed to get the smaller demons or ones that weren't really dedicated or something. I got a lot of jabs and slashes but I didn't get slammed or knocked down even once."

Laura was smiling, "Yeah, sure. I saw you dancing with the demons that were looking a little exasperated trying to hit or corner you somehow. You need to show Mark that two-step you did."

Sarah grinned, "I read the "after-action" reports and watched you on the videos. You were far more adroit at making your demonic opponents miss you than most of us. I want to practice that low speed-high speed combo you used to set them up and knock them down. I think everyone could benefit from that strategy."

Alexis shook her head, "Possibly, but I saw you bull-dozing three or four demons and chopping them down like trees. I don't think I could do that either."

Sarah smiled, "I'm maybe a little more sensitive to the Holy anger than you guys. It just didn't allow me to use finesse."

Laura laughed, "And we're all paying for that testosterone fueled-violence this morning, too."

Laura asked, "How do the demons overcome the armor to kill our warriors?"

Sarah frowned. "They don't overcome the armor of God. They overcome the warrior by immobilizing the person and battering them senseless. Then their armor disappears because they stop praying.

Laura said, "Oh."

CHAPTER FIFTY-THREE

Four days later Jack and Laura got Mark, Sarah, David, and Alexis together in a conference room to discuss some things that had happened in the battle.

Jack had compiled the entire story from the videos and from the "after-action" reports from the troops. He shook his head to show his feelings about the efforts of everyone on the team. "Again, I can't possibly sort out the hundreds of acts of valor exhibited by every one that fought in the Jezreel Valley battle. There are so many highlights that it would literally take twice as long as the battle did to just mention them."

He looked around at the little group and remembered their exploits during the combat. "Mark, I am still amazed that you are alive after what happened to you when you were smacked down by that flying demon. You neglected to mention that when you were hit, that knocked the demon you were fighting off of Spec 4 Louis Tolliver, who was on his back on the ground at that time. That demon slashed you in the face with its sword just as you got propelled over the Spec 4 by the flung demon. That is why you couldn't answer back on the battle-com because the sword actually struck so close to your face it amputated your combat microphone."

He looked at the others there. "I can show you a lot of selfless actions by the three of you that probably turned the tide of battle in our favor. One especially near to my heart was Laura's blocking a blade that would have created two half-Jacks. Thank you all for your fighting skills and your commitment to do the will of Yahveh. I am going to have Charlie make up a video compilation of all the bravery every single person showed in this battle. I'll have Charlie Photoshop in the demons based on our reports and his imagination.

He turned to Laura and smiled. He spoke into the air, "Charlie, you also contributed more than you know to that battle. There was your bravery and, I must say it, your ability in Martial Arts. I've quite honestly never seen anyone jump over a whole herd of demons waving swords to do a flying kick to the head of that big demon which you then eliminated before landing on the ground. That was excellent and I'm sure you'll take all the honors at the next tournament for Karate, especially if they allow demons to participate."

Everyone, even Charlie, laughed at that comment. Jack continued, "But, your prototype "diamond in the rough", Ethan Reaper deserves a special commendation among all the humble heroes in that battle for his selfless actions. Let's see if we can't come up with something special for him."

Charlie concurred having been notified by Sarah and Laura and having reviewed his actions concerning the operation of the demon "Napoleon"

Jack threw the paperwork on the conference room table. "I don't think I will ever forget the empowerment Father Yahveh gave us when we went up against those four large demons. By the time I got to mine I had to be ten feet tall and as solid as if I had a Force Generator working for me. Amazing, literally amazing."

Mark was feeling a lot better after several days of rest and was back to thinking like normal. "Okay, enough of the reminiscences. I think we need to find out why there was one unique demon with tactical smarts when they haven't seem to have been able to come up with them for thousands of years. Any suggestions?"

David dryly said, "Well, we could do like the people in the TV dramas do and raid Napoleon's home in hell, kick in his door, and interrogate him until he tells us the secret of his knowledge."

That got some hearty laughs. Jack shook his head again and realized he was shaking his head far too often lately. "No. That won't work. Any reasonable suggestions?"

Laura was back to thinking like herself, too. "I think we need to pray and ask Heaven why this particular demon is so smart. Somehow that bothers me at a deep level. Why just that one?"

Agreeing to get together that evening to pray about "Napoleon", the group broke up and went separate ways.

Jack and Laura walked out into the empty living room and sat on a couch. Laura snuggled up on Jack's shoulder. She asked, "After facing Belial what is left for us?"

Jack made a snorting sound. "According to Carol our dance card is filling up fast. You know, new levels, new devils."

The Crossfire Team will return in

"*The Gates of Hell Crossfire*."

If this story has awakened you or moved you to seek the love of Christ and His power for your life, whether you've never accepted Jesus as your savior or you've fallen away, repeat the following prayer and begin a most wonderful journey into eternal life with Him today.

Father Yahveh in heaven, As You said in Your Holy Word, (Romans 10:9) that if we confess the Lord our Yahveh and believe in our hearts that Yahveh raised Jesus from the dead, we shall be saved.

(The prayer on the next page is a sample prayer when asking Jesus into your heart as your Savior. You can also pray this in your own words.)

Salvation Prayer

Dear Yahveh in heaven, I come to you in the name of Jesus. I confess to You that I am a sinner, and I am sorry for my sins and the life that I have lived; I need your forgiveness. I believe that your only begotten Son Jesus Christ shed His precious blood on the cross at Calvary and died for my sins, and I am now willing to turn from my sin.

Right now I confess Jesus as the Lord of my life and my soul. With all my heart, I truly believe that your Holy Spirit raised Jesus from the dead. Today I accept Jesus Christ as my personal Savior and according to Your Word, right now I am saved.

I thank you Jesus, for your unlimited grace which has saved me from my sins. I thank you Jesus that your grace that never leads to license, but rather it always leads to repentance. Therefore Lord Jesus, transform my life so that I may bring glory and honor to you alone and not to myself.

I Thank you Lord Jesus, for dying for me at Calvary and giving me eternal life.

Amen.

If you just said this prayer and you meant it with all your heart, believe that you are now saved and have been born again.

You may ask, "Now that I am saved, what do I do next?" First of all you need to get into a spirit-filled, bible-based church that teaches the Scriptures, and you need to study Yahveh's Word.

Once you have found a church home, you will want to become water-baptized. By accepting Christ you are baptized in the spirit, but it is through water-baptism that you publically announce your obedience to the Lord Jesus. Water baptism is a symbol of your salvation from the dead. You were dead but now you live, for Jesus Christ has redeemed you for a price! The price was His atoning death on the cross. May Yahveh Bless You!

www.ingramcontent.com/pod-product-compliance
Lightning Source LLC
Chambersburg PA
CBHW061132200626
46817CB00016B/1219